THIRD BLOW

A Novel of Suspense

J. T. Bishop

Eudoran Press, LLC

Dallas, Texas

Copyright © 2020 by J. T. Bishop

J. T. Bishop/Eudoran Press LLC
6009 Parker Rd. Suite 149 #205
Plano, TX 75093
www.jtbishopauthor.com

Publisher's Note: This is a work of fiction. Names, characters, places, and incidents are a product of the author's imagination. Locales and public names are sometimes used for atmospheric purposes. Any resemblance to actual people, living or dead, or to businesses, companies, events, institutions, or locales is completely coincidental.

Book Layout © 2014 BookDesignTemplates.com
Edited by G. Enstam and P. Creeden
Cover by ebookorprint

Third Blow/ J. T. Bishop. -- 1st ed.
ISBN 978-1-7325531-4-9

To Gwen...
Your knowledge, wisdom, and insight made this book exceptional and has been a guiding light to me for as long as we've known each other. I am blessed to be your friend.

Other Books by J. T. Bishop

The Red-Line Trilogy

Red-Line: The Shift (Available for free at jtbishopauthor.com)
Red-Line: Mirrors
Red-Line: Trust Destiny

Red-Line: The Fletcher Family Saga

Curse Breaker
High Child
Spark
Forged Lines

Detectives Daniels and Remalla Series

First Cut
Second Slice
Third Blow
Fourth Strike – Now available for pre-order

Jace awoke with a start, blinking his eyes, trying to focus. Pictures of space and the planets drifted and changed on his monitor and a puddle of drool had collected on the files beneath him. Rubbing his face, he looked around his office and checked the time. Four a.m. He'd fallen asleep at his desk.

The couch against the wall beckoned. He kept a blanket and pillow for nights like these when he didn't want to go home. Home was too quiet and he would only return here tomorrow. His friends had left the bar around midnight, his girlfriend, Devyn, included.

He spied a water bottle and took a sip, his fingers shaking. The dream still lingered and he took a deep breath, trying to shake it off. He had never been one to have nightmares, but for the last two months, he'd been dreaming the same dream.

He remembered most of it. Two women and a man. The women were running toward Jace, trying to find him. Jace could see them, but couldn't reach them, no matter how hard he tried. He knew they needed help. A man chased them; his face cloaked but his eyes gleaming. And he smiled. It was more of a leer than a smile, as if the man knew Jace's torment. The women got closer and Jace was close to reaching them, but the man always got to them first. Screaming, the women fell to the ground, writhing in agony, grasping for help, while the man grinned, and Jace would wake up, breathless and sweating.

He had no idea what it meant. God knows he'd been to enough shrinks in his life that he could probably be one himself, but it didn't make sense. In the dream, he knew the women. They were important to him, but when he woke, he had no idea who they were or their connection to him.

He took another swig of the water, his heart rate slowing. The dream tonight had changed. The women were running, but this time, Devyn was with them. She'd run to him and he'd grabbed her. But her face twisted into a grimace, and she'd said *I'm sorry* and she'd been yanked from his grasp, and the man had been there, rising up in Jace's face and he'd spoken. *I did it for you.*

Jace exhaled and rubbed his face. The dream faded, but he still heard the man's voice in his head.

Pushing back from the desk, he put his hands on his knees and debated calling Devyn, but she would kill him if he woke her from her sleep, especially when she had to get up in two hours.

Deciding to shake it off, he stood to get the blanket and pillow, when his cell phone rang. He picked it up from the desk, and eyed the caller id. It was Justin, his best friend. He'd been in the bar earlier playing cards.

Wondering why his friend was calling him at four a.m, he answered, trying not to think the worst, but also feeling an uncomfortable twist in his gut. "Justin? What's up, brother? You okay?"

There was quiet at first, but then he heard heavy breathing. For a minute, he thought Justin was playing with him when he heard Justin whisper. "Jace."

That twist in his gut became a sharp spike. "Justin, what's wrong?"

Justin gulped in air and he sounded terrified. "Jace?" His voice was high pitched, as if he was on the verge of tears.

"Justin?" Jace's heart rate tripled. "Tell me what's wrong."

"I...I...I'm sorry." He could barely get the words out.

Jace grabbed his jacket and keys, planning to go to Justin's apartment. "Justin, I'm heading over. Stay put."

"Please," said Justin, but distant, like he'd turned from the phone. Was he speaking to someone else?

"Is someone else there? Justin?" Jace left the bar without even locking the door behind him.

Justin's voice returned. "I'm...so sorry. I didn't mean..." A sob escaped. "...to hurt you."

"Justin, what are you talking about?"

Jace threw on his jacket, keeping the phone to his ear, and got on his motorcycle parked in front of the bar. "I'm coming. Whatever it is, we'll figure it out."

Justin sobbed again. "Please, I did what...no..." His voice sounded distant again. "No." It was almost a wail.

"Justin?" Jace heard a gasp and a gurgle and then the phone went quiet. Jace's heart stopped and he froze. "Justin? Buddy? Hold on."

He heard a thud and then a muffled noise, like the phone had been dragged across something. Jace waited and was about to start up the bike when another voice spoke. It was deeper than Justin's and more guttural, and it whispered. "I did it for you." Then the line went dead.

CHAPTER TWO

Eight Hours Earlier

"Three aces. Read 'em and weep." Jace put the cards down with a grin, and chewed on the end of his cigar.

Simon cursed at him, throwing his own cards on the table. "That's three in a row, asshole."

"When you got it, you got it." Jace chuckled as he gathered the money into a pile.

Simon ran his hands through his hair. "You keep doing this; you're going to put me in the poorhouse, mate."

Henry came over with a beer and sat. "I haven't left this game yet with any money. You'd think I'd learn." He leaned close and spoke to Jace. "Who's the new bartender?"

Jace glanced toward the bar, seeing Danni wiping down the counter. A customer sat on a barstool with his head down and a drink in front of him. He was the only customer in the bar, other than the men playing cards.

"That's Danni. Hired her last month," said Jace.

"She's cute," said Henry. "What's her story?"

Simon reshuffled the cards. "Out of your league, Henry. You need to stick to your party girls."

Henry frowned. "Out of my league? She works in a bar."

"What's wrong with working in a bar?" asked Jace.

"Nothing," said Henry. He raised his hands. "No offense."

"It's seedy, mate. When's the last time you turned a profit on this place?" asked Simon.

"Seedy fits my personality," answered Jace. "And who needs a profit when I can keep taking money from you guys." He patted the bills in front of him.

"You didn't tell me her story," said Henry, glancing toward the bar.

Jace took a swig of his beer. "She's a tarot reader. Works here part time."

Henry looked at Simon. "A what reader?"

"It's like a fortune teller," said Simon. He reshuffled again. "Only with cards."

"Does she read palms?" asked Henry.

"Probably. I didn't ask when I interviewed her. She's got her card on the bar. She has a website," said Jace. "Deal 'em up, Simon. I need more money."

"She seeing someone?" asked Henry.

The door opened, and a man entered. He was tall and wore a dark suit with his tie loosened.

Jace sighed. "Hell if I know. Why don't you go ask her?" He smiled. "There's that son-of-a -bitch. Where the hell you been, Justin? I'm taking money off these fools and I'm getting bored."

Justin walked up to the table and pulled his tie off. "Work sucked today. But I'm here now. Time to take that money in front of you and put it in front of me." He slid his jacket off and threw it in a nearby chair, turned his shirtsleeves up and sat.

"Hey, Danni," yelled Jace through his chewed cigar.

Danni looked up from straightening the bottles. "Yeah?"

"We need another round. I'm about to take these suckers' life savings." Jace finished the remains of his drink with the cigar still in his mouth. "And I need sustenance."

"Coming up," said Danni.

"We'll see about that. Deal, Simon," said Justin.

Henry stood. "Deal me out of this one. I'm going to see if she needs help."

Simon chuckled. "Good luck, mate. Something tells me you're going to need it."

Justin glanced toward the bar as Henry walked toward it. "He likes Danni, huh?"

"Yup," said Jace.

"Did you tell him she's turned down everyone who's tried, including me?" asked Justin.

Simon dealt the cards. "I thought you were dating Liz."

"We broke up," said Justin.

Jace picked up his cards. "He has no idea. Why crush his hope? Law of averages says she'll say yes eventually."

"We'll see about that," said Justin. "She told me it wasn't the right time. She's staying single for now until the cards indicate otherwise. No offense. Can you believe that? Strangest rejection ever."

"What about you, mate?" asked Simon, studying his hand. "You tried?" he asked Jace.

"I'm dating Devyn," said Jace. He threw a chip in the pile.

"Thought you two broke up," said Simon.

Jace raised a brow. "We got back together. Last week."

Simon added a chip. "You two break up and get together every month."

"I know," said Justin. "They're like musical chairs. First, they're on, then they're off. You never know where they'll be when the music ends."

"It's called love, brother," said Jace, putting his cigar in the ashtray on the table. "That's what makes it fun. She's a firecracker. She keeps me on my toes." He checked his watch. "She's supposed to come by tonight. Should be here soon."

"God help us," said Justin. "Last time she came to one of our games, we all got so drunk, we broke your chandelier."

"Chandelier? Since when did you have a chandelier?" asked Simon.

"Exactly," said Jace. Danni walked up holding two beers.

"Here we go," he said, taking a beer from her and she gave the other to Simon. Henry carried the other two.

"Danni's a pretty name," said Henry. "Were you named after someone?" He gave one of his beers to Justin, who chuckled.

Danni made the slightest sigh, which Jace heard. He could almost feel her impatience.

"Actually, Danni's not my real name. Thanks for the help." She turned to head back to the bar.

"Really?" asked Henry, stopping her. "What's your real name?"

Jace, curious, listened too. "Yeah. What is your real name?"

She shook her head. "It doesn't matter. I shouldn't have said anything."

"Well, now you've got us all curious," said Jace.

Danni ran a hand through her shoulder length dark brown hair. "It's not important."

"I'll give you a twenty-dollar tip if you tell us," said Justin.

She narrowed her eyes. "Based on what I know you four will be drinking tonight, you'll be giving me more than a twenty-dollar tip."

"She's right about that," said Jace. He took a gulp of his drink.

"Fifty dollars, then, from each of us," added Henry.

Jace choked on his drink.

"Excuse me?" asked Simon.

"C'mon. Don't you want to know?" asked Henry. He watched her with soft eyes. "I know I do."

"Oh, God. Your crush is going to cost us fifty bucks each?" asked Justin. "Shit."

"I'm in," said Jace, wiping foam from his lips. "I'm curious, too. Plus, I'll make the money back anyway from you chumps."

"We'll see about that. I'm feeling lucky tonight, *chump*," said Justin.

Jace laughed. "Spill it. Your real name for two hundred bucks. What say you?"

Danni looked between the men. "You won't use it? I hate the name, so if you use it, I reserve the right to spit in your beer."

"Deal," said Henry.

Justin widened his eyes and Jace shrugged.

"Fine," said Danni. "It's Daisy."

"Daisy?" asked Jace. "Really?"

"I love that name," said Henry.

"Oh, Christ," said Justin. "Who said he could come?"

"We needed a fourth player," said Simon.

"Are we done?" asked Danni. "I need to get back. Prep the bar for the damage you're going to do tonight."

"Don't bother," said Jace. "No prep needed. Daisy."

Danni stiffened and glowered. She eyed his beer.

Jace grabbed for his glass. "I get one free pass. I'm your boss."

Danni set her jaw. "You're lucky I got the King of Cups today. Otherwise, I'd christen it."

Jace winked at her. "Guess I'm lucky with the cards tonight. Hear that boys? Get ready to empty your pocketbooks."

Danni turned to leave.

"Maybe we could get a drink sometime?" asked Henry.

Danni put her hand on his wrist. "I'm sorry, Henry, but no. The lovers' card is just not in the deck for me right now. But I wish you well."

"But, wait—" Henry turned as Danni started to leave, when the door opened and a woman stepped in. She wore a short red mini dress, with a low-cut top, and her ample blonde hair and breasts were teased to their highest positions. Seeing the group, she yelled out. "Let's get this party started."

Jace stood. "There's my baby. Get your ass over here, sweetheart."

Devyn ran over and threw herself into Jace's arms, planting a kiss on his lips. "I missed you, babe," she said.

Jace caught Danni rolling her eyes as she turned and walked away. "What's it been?" he asked. "Twenty-four hours?"

Devyn pouted. "The longest twenty-four hours ever."

Jace pulled her close and kissed her again.

"Are we gonna play cards, or are you two going to have sex right here while we wait?" asked Justin.

Devyn smiled and slid down Jace's body until she stood. Her skirt rode up and she pulled it down. "You're just jealous, Justin. When's the last time you got laid, huh?" She grinned.

"Go easy on him, baby. He just broke up," said Jace. "He's in need of a good woman like you."

Devyn's face fell. "I'm sorry. I wish I could help, but you know Jace has spoken for me, right babe?" She leaned against him.

"You know it. You're all mine." He hugged her and she wrapped her arms around his neck. "What would I do without you?" he asked.

"Maybe play cards?" asked Simon.

**

Three hours later, Danni rubbed her nose. Cigar smoke and raucous laughter from the four poker players filled the small bar area, but so far, no major damage had been done.

The man at the bar with his head down studied his phone, but would look up when he was ready for another drink. He'd only moved twice to use the bathroom. Danni kept an eye on him, assessing his sobriety.

"You good?" she asked him. "Want some water?"

"No, thank you," he answered.

She nodded.

"Full house," yelled Jace from the table, slapping his cards down.

The men cursed and Devyn shrieked.

"That's my baby." She sat in his lap and kissed him. Danni could see Jace grab her ass and squeeze it. Devyn rubbed his chest. "God, it turns me on when you win."

"I'm always on when you're around, babe," said Jace. He ran his hand up her thigh and Devyn squealed.

Danni shook her head.

The man at the bar snorted. "Disgusting, isn't it?"

Danni frowned. "What?" It was hard to see his face because he wore a hoodie over his head and the only time he looked up from his phone was when he ordered.

"That kind of behavior. The two of them should be in a hotel room. It's embarrassing."

Danni studied him. Despite the hoodie, tufts of unruly sandy blonde hair stuck out from the edge. "They are a bit loud."

"Loud? He might as well take her right there on the table. I don't know how his friends can put up with that crap. I'd kick his ass and show her the door. One wrong move in that dress, and her tits are going to fall out, which I'm thinking he's hoping for." He continued to study his phone.

Danni watched Devyn and Jace. Devyn sat in his lap as Justin shuffled and dealt, while her hand stroked the back of Jace's neck. Although Danni didn't like it either, the man was talking about her boss, and a surprising defensive bubble rose up from her belly. "If you don't like it, maybe you should find another bar."

He smiled. "Did I hit a nerve? I know you don't like her either. It's written all over your face."

Danni picked up a tequila bottle and wiped it down, feeling exposed. Was she that obvious? "What I think doesn't matter. I just work here."

The man glanced over at the poker table. "He owns the place, right?"

"How do you know that?"

"I've been in a few times, before you got here. I saw him with the previous bartender. He can be a bit intimidating."

Danni observed her boss, chewing on his cigar and swigging his umpteenth beer. The man could drink his friends under the table. No matter how many beers he consumed, though, Danni had never seen him drunk. His size likely had something to do with it. He stood easily at six foot four and had the physique of Thor, although Danni had no idea when he went to the gym. Sleeve tattoos ran up and down both arms, and she assumed covered his back and chest, although she couldn't be sure. He drove a Harley Davidson, and his long, wavy brown hair looked perpetually windblown. His face was rarely clean shaven, and he usually sported the five o'clock shadow. Female patrons frequently ogled him longingly, wishing their husbands and boyfriends could be him. Jace Marlon was the consummate bad boy. Desired by women, and hated by most men, save his best friends. "I've seen him yell at the maintenance guy. Thought the guy was gonna pee his pants."

"He ever yell at you?"

Danni observed the customer who'd barely spoken for the last two hours, wondering why he'd become so chatty. She figured the alcohol had loosened him up. "He got pissed once, when I dropped a bottle of bourbon."

"Did you pee your pants?"

"No. I told him to chill. The bottle was almost empty. I don't scare easily."

The man put his phone away. "Lucky for you."

Another squeal from Devyn caught their attention and they glanced over. Jace was saying something in her ear and she squeezed his thigh.

The man groaned. "I think that's it for me. I'm going to call it a night."

"I'll close you out."

"No need." He pulled out a hundred-dollar bill and threw it on the counter. "Thanks for the service."

"Let me get your change."

He held up his hand. "Keep it." He glanced at the poker table. "Something tells me you may need it." He looked back toward her and Danni got a good look at his face. The strands of long wavy blonde hair poking out from his hoodie framed his blue eyes and his narrow, but chiseled face. Something about his appearance made her pause.

"Do I know you?" she asked.

"No, you don't." He patted the bar. "Good night." He paused. "Daisy."

Danni opened her mouth to comment when Justin stood. "Well, that's enough for me. I don't have any money left."

Henry threw down his cards. "Same here. This fool keeps winning."

Jace grinned through his chewed cigar. "Told you, losers. That the cards were in my favor. Right, Danni?"

Danni watched the stranger leave.

"What does Danni know about it?" asked Devyn. "She's just a bartender."

Danni sighed. She'd met Devyn a week after starting work at the bar, and it was clear the woman did not like her.

"She does those tarot cards, baby," said Jace. "And mine were all awesome today, right Dan?"

"I didn't pull any cards for you today," said Danni. She wiped the bar where the stranger had sat and put his glass in the sink.

Jace took out his cigar. "But you know if you had, they'd have been the best ones."

"Those silly things?" asked Devyn. Devyn glanced over at her. "You don't really take those seriously do you?"

Simon stood also. "I think I'm calling it a night, too, mates. My lovely Sheila will be wondering where I am." He slid on his jacket.

Jace gathered his money into a pile in front of him. "It's been fun, fellas. Thanks for the donation to the Jace Marlon Betterment Fund. Lots of tacos and beer for me."

Justin rolled his eyes. "Don't forget your biggest contributor. And your best friend. Save a beer and taco for me."

Jace put his cigar in the ashtray. "Just say the word my friend. I can't have you starving and thirsty. Got to keep you strong and fit, so you can go out and make more money for me to take from you." He laughed good naturedly and Devyn slid off his lap as he stood.

Danni threw the rag into the sink. "Don't forget. You guys owe me two hundred bucks."

Devyn frowned "Two hundred dollars?"

Simon groaned. "Thanks a lot, Henry."

Henry stood, pushing his chair in. "Come on. She worked hard tonight."

Justin shook his head. "Give it up, man."

Jace dug through his money. "Don't worry about it, gents. Let me put you out of your misery. I'll cover your asses." He pulled out the two hundred dollars. "I can't have my buddies suffer without their lunch money."

"You're loving this, aren't you?" asked Justin. "I can't wait to hear what you expect in return."

Jace folded the money and brought it to Danni, who put it in her pocket. "I love winning...and knowing you owe me."

"You're going to want me to fix that chandelier, aren't you?" asked Justin.

Jace laughed. "You were the one swinging on it."

Devyn leaned against Jace. "Two hundred. For what?"

Jace eyed Danni. "Henry made a deal with her, and we went along with it." He winked at Danni. Danni appreciated that he kept her real name to himself.

"We were all swinging on the chandelier," said Justin.

"But it broke when you did it," said Jace, smacking his friend in the arm.

"Just my luck," said Justin.

The men talked, and Devyn walked over to the bar. Seeing her, Danni acted busy but Devyn spoke from behind her.

"You have your cards with you?" she asked.

Danni turned to face her. "My cards?"

"Yes. Your cards. Do you have them?"

"Yes. In my purse."

Devyn smiled. "Do a reading for me."

Danni hesitated. "This is probably not a good time or place."

"Why not? Do they work or not? Or are you just scared to read me?"

Danni wiped the bar, trying to think of a way out.

Devyn snickered. "Just like I thought. You probably have no idea what you're doing. You'll read cards for Jace but not for me? Interesting." She whispered. "You're not his type, you know."

Danni eyed the woman in front of her. Tarot was not something to be read in anger, but this woman was pushing her buttons. "Fine. I'll get them."

"Great. Maybe get me a tequila shot while you're at it."

Danni went to her purse behind the counter and pulled out a purple cloth bag. She opened it and pulled out her deck. It was the traditional Rider Waite deck and the one she used the most. Walking back toward Devyn, she stopped and grabbed a glass and filled it with water.

"I didn't ask for water," said Devyn, leaning over the bar. Her heavy breasts looked like they were about to spill out onto the counter.

Danni brought the water over. "It's better if you stick with water for the reading."

Devyn eyed the glass with distaste. "Boy. You do take this seriously, don't you?" She pushed the glass aside.

Danni held out the cards in front of Devyn. "Shuffle and think about the question you want to ask."

"What you doin', babe?" Jace came up behind Devyn and nuzzled her neck.

"See you, Danni," said Henry and Simon. They headed for the door.

"Good night," said Danni.

Justin walked up. "Really? You're getting a reading?"

Devyn nodded. "Let's see what she's got." She shuffled the cards.

"I'm gonna head out, man," said Justin. "I got to get up early tomorrow." He shook hands with Jace.

Jace stepped back from Devyn. "Okay, brother." He grasped hands with Justin and pulled him in for a hug. "We ridin' this weekend?"

"If you can break away from your lady, I'm up for it."

"I think I can manage a few hours. Let's head up to the hills. Get away for a bit."

"You two riding those damn bikes?" asked Devyn. She finished shuffling and put the cards down.

Jace raised a brow. "C'mon, baby. I love havin' you behind me on the hog, all close and personal."

"That thing ruins my hair. I look like I've been styled at the zoo instead of the salon."

"You always look good to me," said Jace, kissing her cheek.

"I'll give you a call tomorrow, bro," said Justin. "Devyn. Good luck with the cards." He waved and headed for the door.

"Nothin' to do with luck," said Devyn. "I want to know my future," she said to Danni. "Tell me what's going to happen this year."

"In regards to something specific?" asked Danni.

Jace said goodbye to Justin and came back to the counter. "Ask about us, baby. Let's find out what the cards have to say."

Devyn glanced at him and Danni sensed some hesitation, but then Devyn agreed. "Okay, let's ask about us."

"I'll use the three-card spread. It will give some insight to the past, present and future."

"Cool," said Jace.

Danni took the cards and cut them. Then spread them out in an array in front of them. "Pick a card."

Devyn studied them, then pulled one and put it face up. It was the Two of Pentacles.

"What's that mean?" asked Devyn. "Why does he have a funny hat?"

A man with tall hat on his head held a pentacle in each hand.

"Don't worry about the hat. He's like a juggler, balancing two objects. In a relationship reading, that represents a couple, or two people. So, the two of you."

"That's right babe." Jace came up behind Devyn and put his arms around her.

"Pull another card," said Danni.

Devyn debated, then pulled from the deck and put it on the counter. It was the Seven of Swords. Danni held her breath. That card typically meant deception. Someone wasn't telling the truth.

"That guy is carrying a lot of swords," said Jace. "What's that card mean?"

Danni wondered what to say. "This one can mean overcoming trials and tribulations, which it seems you two have had. It could also mean deception, or not being completely honest." She figured if Devyn wanted to play the cards, she ought to the know the truth.

"We have definitely had our trials, right babe?"

Devyn had gone quiet. "Deception, huh?" She glanced back at Jace. "You telling me everything, hon?"

He turned serious. "I'll admit. I didn't tell you tonight how gorgeous you are. Does that count?"

She smiled, and Danni sighed. "Pull one more."

Devyn studied the cards, then picked. It was the Ten of Swords. Danni's heart sank.

"What the hell is that?" asked Devyn.

"Guy's stabbed to death," added Jace. His face fell. "That can't be good."

Danni wondered how to phrase it, but the card left little to the imagination. "Uh, well…no. It's not great." She struggled with what to say. "It's a card of endings."

"Endings?" Devyn asked. "What do you mean?"

Danni eyed the card. "It means hope is lost. A warning to move on and end your struggle. Betrayal and false friends. Be aware."

"That's ridiculous. Are you saying we're doomed?" asked Devyn.

"It's just a stupid card, baby," said Jace. "It doesn't mean anything."

Devyn glared. "Is that what it really means? Or are you just saying that?"

Danni pointed. "It's a man with swords in his back. You think it's a card of sunshine and butterflies?"

"Draw another card," said Jace. "Ask for more clarification. I've seen you do that before."

"Another card? You're sure?" asked Danni.

Devyn didn't think twice and pulled a card from the pile. Danni sighed. It was the three of cups.

"Now we're looking better. Those three ladies look happy. They're drinking, partying. That's our card, babe. Everything's looking rosy, right?" asked Jace.

"Sure," said Danni. "It is a card of merriment, having fun."

Devyn relaxed. "Finally, a decent card." She took Jace's hand.

Danni continued. "But, to be clear, in a relationship reading, it can also mean there's a third person involved."

"A third person?" asked Devyn, her smile fading.

"Well, we know that's not true. Just proves these cards are just a game. Those ladies are enjoying themselves. That's how I see it. Maybe it means we can have that threesome. I'm ready when you are, babe." He pulled her close.

Danni could see Devyn's face, and she sensed Devyn knew the cards weren't talking about the threesome Jace was suggesting. Danni swiped the cards up and began to straighten them.

"You're having fun, aren't you? At my expense," said Devyn.

"You wanted a reading. I gave you a reading," said Danni.

"C'mon babe. You can't take the cards seriously. It's just a bunch of goofy pictures," said Jace.

"I think she's saying whatever she wants." Devyn cocked her head. "Are you trying to break us up?"

Danni tried not to roll her eyes. "I read the cards you pulled. There's no motive on my part. You can take what you want from it."

Devyn stared. "I can't believe you waste your time on this stuff." Her phone beeped. "What a sad life."

Jace rubbed her back. "Like I said, it's just a game." He scowled at Danni, who scowled back.

Devyn checked her phone. "Damn it. I have to go in tomorrow. Shit."

"What?" asked Jace. "I thought you had the day off."

"It's Marta. Her kid's sick. She's asking me to cover for her."

"So tell her no."

"Normally, I would, but she covered for me when I called in sick to hang out with you, remember? I owe her."

"Babe, we were going to sleep in. I was gonna make you breakfast in bed." He slid his arms around her. "Plus a few other things I was gonna make happen." He nibbled her ear.

Danni put the cards back in their pouch and in her purse. "I'm going to clock out." She'd had enough of Jace and Devyn's PDA.

Devyn pouted. "I'm sorry, babe. We're going to have to postpone. I have to be up in six hours. I go home with you, and I won't sleep at all. We'll do it tomorrow."

Jace let out a deep sigh. "Oh, man. You really know how to make a man suffer."

"I'll make it up to you. I promise." She slid her hand down his chest. Danni turned away to avoid seeing more.

"I'll drive you."

"The hell you will. I'm not getting on that motorcycle. I'll call a service." She pulled back and typed on her phone.

"Are you serious?" asked Jace.

"Do I look like I'm joking?" She eyed Danni. "Why don't you hang out with her? She can pull more stupid cards for you."

"I want you baby, not the cards."

Danni grabbed her jacket from the hook and slid it on. "I'm going home anyway. It's late."

"There's a car nearby. He can be here in ten minutes. You can wait with me," said Devyn.

"I'm headed out. You need anything before I leave?" asked Danni.

"No. I'll make sure Devyn gets home, and I'll close up." He spoke to Devyn. "Since you have to leave, I might as well catch up on some paperwork."

"Paperwork? It's late. You'll just end up sleeping on that bumpy couch in your office, if you sleep at all. You need to go home and rest up. You're going to need it for tomorrow." Devyn ran her hands up his arms.

"You didn't mind the couch the other day." Jace grinned.

Devyn giggled. "We weren't sleeping."

Danni did roll her eyes then. She walked to the end of the bar and toward the door. "Good night."

They didn't look her way, and sighing, she left.

CHAPTER THREE

Danni opened the door to her small apartment, and threw her purse on the clothes-covered sofa. Hearing a meow, she saw her black and white cat dart into the room. "Hey, Seymore." She squatted and petted the cat's ears. Purring, Seymore rubbed against her legs. Yawning, she stood and went to the refrigerator and pulled out a beer. She took a foil-wrapped taco from her jacket pocket and put it in the fridge. She'd stopped at an all-night taco truck on her way home and had enjoyed of couple of Taco del Fuegos. They were greasy, fried, cheese-laden and delicious. She rarely ate them, but after tonight's encounter with Devyn, she felt like indulging. She'd ordered two, but only ate one, deciding to save the other for lunch the next day. Seymore meowed at her feet and she took out some milk, poured it in a bowl and put it on the ground. Seymore wasted no time drinking from the bowl.

As the cat drank, she sat at her circular dining table and opened her laptop. The screen whirred to life. She typed her password and opened her email. She had three that were unread.

The first one was from her dad. Sighing, she opened it and read the first few lines.

Hi, Dais.

It's your old man. You won't return my calls, so I thought I'd try to reach you this way. Please don't shut me out. I know we've had our...

She sighed and stopped reading, deleted the email, and moved on to the next one. The microwave dinged as she read. It was a request for a tarot reading from a new customer on her website, a woman nicknamed *Lovelorn52*. A relationship question. By far the most common request. She read through the email quickly and determined it would be better to do the reading in the morning when she would be fresh, and had not been drinking alcohol. It was always better to read the cards when clear-headed. She marked it as un-read and went to the next email. Another new tarot reading request. From someone nicknamed *BrotherlyLove*. Only this one was different. Not the usual *does he or she love me* or *should I pursue him or her*? This one was a request for a full reading to answer a specific question. She read through the email.

Hello,

I heard about you and your website recently and want you to do a reading for me. I will be direct because I don't wish to waste your time. I am angry. I've done things that I believe were necessary and I know had to be done. I can see what others cannot. I can do what others won't. Because of who I am and where I come from, I know I must follow this path. My abilities allow me to do things most do not understand. I will use whatever means necessary to finish what I have started. What are my odds of success?

Danni looked up from the email. Was this guy serious? Or was this a joke? A chill moved through her. Rubbing her head, she kept reading.

I heard you were good. Your prices are reasonable, which I can appreciate, but you should consider charging more. It's important to value your services, like I value mine.

I look forward to hearing what your reading reveals.

And you should consider using your real name. I personally like Daisy.

Danni sat up straight. Her heart thumped. What was this? This person knew her name?

She pushed back from the seat, staring at the screen, rereading the email. Her finger hovered over the keys, and she almost deleted it, but something stopped her. Deleting it wouldn't make it go away. This person knew her personally, but how? Was it someone from her past? The only person who ever used her real name was her father. Maybe an old boyfriend, but it would have been from years ago, and that made no sense. The only people who knew her real name...

She went still. Shit. The bar, that night, she'd told Jace and his friends. They knew her name. Devyn came to mind. Could it be her? Had Jace told Devyn her name was Daisy?

Logically, it was possible one of them was messing with her. They knew she practiced tarot and she wondered if they were joking around and having a good laugh, probably sitting around the computer right now, waiting for her response.

Danni closed the screen. That was it. She'd go in tomorrow and tell Jace to stop being stupid. She wasn't playing along.

Convinced it had to be a joke, she stood and pulled off her shirt, ready for a hot shower and bed. She took a long pull from her beer, needing it after that strange request.

Taking a last look at the computer, a strange feeling crept up her body, almost like an electric current moving through her. The thought occurred to her that maybe this wasn't a joke. That whoever it was, was serious, and expected an answer from her.

She gulped back another swig of beer and put the bottle on the table. Shrugging off the email and the weird feeling, she headed into the bathroom for her shower.

CHAPTER FOUR

Jace sat atop his bike, a cold spike of dread running up his spine. The streets were empty and quiet at that hour of the morning, and he could almost hear his heart thump. "Justin," yelled Jace into the phone. "Justin?"

He heard nothing. The line had been disconnected. Jace started up his bike at the same time as dialing 911. The bike roared to life, and he took off down the street, grateful that traffic was light. He told the woman who'd answered 911 about the phone call from Justin and to send the police. He gave them Justin's address; thankful he could re-member it. He had a mind for detail and numbers. The woman wanted him to stay on the line, but since he was on his bike, he hung up, telling the woman he would meet the police at Justin's. Zipping through traffic lights and taking tight corners, he made it to Justin's in six minutes. Sirens wailed in the distance as he jumped off his bike, and ran into the lobby of Justin's building. The elevator doors were closed and he hit the button. One opened and he jumped on, hitting the button for Justin's floor.

"C'mon. C'mon," he spoke to himself. He'd tried Justin again after calling the cops, but there had been no answer.

The elevator slowed and stopped and Jace ran off, taking a right. He flew down the hall, reaching Justin's door, and banged on it. "Justin? Are you there? It's Jace." He banged again.

There was no answer. Jace tried the knob and it was unlocked. He opened the door and took a step inside. "Justin?" The sirens below grew in volume.

Taking another step, he stopped. The tiny kitchen to his left was empty, but the den in front of him was in disarray. Jace could see the broken wooden coffee table, and an overturned chair. He moved closer but stopped when he saw the blood.

It dotted the carpet and got heavier as Jace moved into the room. Then he saw a pair of legs. Jace stepped around the counter and his friend lay on the carpet, wearing a partially opened robe, and nothing underneath. His eyes were open, his face was frozen in a grimace and his throat was slashed. Blood soaked the carpet.

Jace stood in mute horror. His body went ice cold, his ears rang and everything went quiet. He blinked and tried to keep breathing. Everything in him wanted to go to his friend and hold him, but he knew Justin could not be helped. His best friend was dead. Pain and agony welled up inside him, and he wanted to scream. Where were the cops? What was taking them so long? Who would do this and why?

"No." It was all he could say.

His heart raced so fast that he almost went to his knees when he heard a sound from the bedroom. Everything went white when it occurred to him that the killer could still be there. Enraged, Jace stomped across the floor, not caring what he might face. If he found the killer, Jace would attack first, and think later. The man who took his friend's life would die, even if he had to sacrifice himself to do it.

After entering the bedroom, he stopped cold when he didn't see a killer, but another body instead. A woman, in a near see-through bathrobe, wearing lingerie. She lay face down and her blonde hair spilled out onto the floor. Blood poured from her belly and he could see her hands clasped at her midsection. She moaned, and Jace recognized the noise he'd heard. He rushed to her side, carefully pulling her back, seeing the damage done to her, and seeing her face.

He sucked in a breath and his stomach lurched. He recognized her. The heavy makeup, wild hair, and pouty lips. It was Devyn. His girlfriend was dying in his dead friend's apartment. His mind couldn't make sense of it. What was she doing here?

Instinctively, he knew, but he couldn't admit it. But it wasn't time to worry about Justin and Devyn's cheating. Blood poured out of her and her hands were drenched in it. Pulling himself together, he carefully laid her back on the ground. She moaned again, but was barely conscious. Seeing a blanket on the bed, he yanked it off.

"Hold on, baby. Help's coming." He balled up the blanket and pushed it against her wounds, trying to move her hands away. "I got to slow the bleeding. Let me help."

She gasped in pain, and grasped onto his wrist as he held pressure against her belly. "I know it hurts. Hang in there, Babe. Please don't die."

Her eye lids fluttered, but her eyes remained shut. Jace had no idea if she knew he was there or not.

Shouts of "Police" came from the front and Jace yelled. "In here."

An officer who looked to be in his twenties ran into the room, gun drawn. "Hands up," he yelled. "Don't move." His cheeks were red, his hands shook and he breathed heavily.

Jace roared. "Do I look like the one who did this? She's dying. She needs help. Get an ambulance."

Another officer ran in. He was older, with a slight paunch to his midsection, but just as red in the face. "Stand down, Ronson. Check the rest of the room and call an ambulance." He ran to Devyn's side. "What happened?"

Jace tried to think. "I found her like this. That's my best friend in the other room. He called me." He couldn't think of what else to say. Emotions rose up and his chest constricted. "God. He's dead. Justin's dead."

"Who is she?" asked the officer.

"This...this...is Devyn. I found her like this. I think she's been stabbed." The constriction tightened and it became hard to speak.

"Okay. Keep holding pressure. Ambulance is on its way."

His radio squawked to life and he answered. Ronson checked the bathroom, and spoke on his radio, requesting medical assistance. He looked green and Jace wondered if he was about to puke.

Another groan from Devyn and a squeeze from her hand made him look down. He held his breath when he saw her eyes were open.

"Devyn?" he asked.

She tried to speak, but only moaned.

"Don't talk. Stay still."

She whispered anyway, and he had to lean in to hear. "I'm sorry," she said.

The constriction in his chest became too much to bear and a tear escaped and ran down his cheek. "Shhh. Be still."

She pulled on his wrist, and he felt the blood soak through the blanket onto his hands. Fear rushed through him.

She started to speak again but her labored breathing made it difficult.

"Please, don't talk," he said.

But she kept trying. "He said...he said..." It was almost too quiet to make out, but Jace wondered if she as trying to tell him what happened. Did she know the killer?

He leaned close. "What is it, babe?" His voice shook.

Her eyes closed and Jace thought she'd lost consciousness, but they reopened and she spoke, her voice stronger. "He said he did it for you." She stared at him for a brief moment before her eyes closed again and she went limp.

CHAPTER FIVE

Jace wandered the hospital corridor, still trying to comprehend the insanity of the last few hours. Running his hands through his hair, he still saw the blood in his nails, and his fingers shook.

The paramedics had arrived not long after the police, and they'd pushed Jace aside and taken over. They'd rushed Devyn into an ambulance and Jace had followed. The police wanted to talk to him, but he'd told them they could find him in the emergency room.

Now, hours later, Devyn was in surgery. The doctors had stabilized her and wheeled her away, and Jace had found the waiting area. He'd sat for a while, just thinking. The card game seemed years ago. He recalled the laughter and fun, drinking with his friends, Devyn sitting on his lap, her hands sliding down—

He stood, unable to sit any longer. Trying not to think, he walked out into the corridor and paced. Moving back and forth, he tried to keep Justin's death grimace out of his mind, but he couldn't do it. The blood, the stare, the partially open robe, Devyn in her lingerie. Tears threatened but he swallowed them back.

"Shit," he said out loud into the hall, slapping his hand against the wall. A nurse at her station turned and a lady in a wheelchair scowled. "Sorry," he said, "I'm sorry," and he kept pacing.

The elevator dinged and the doors opened. Two men got off and turned toward him. They wore jackets with collared shirts, and would have looked like any other bored relative waiting on news of a family member if it weren't for their badges cuffed to their waist band. Jace didn't acknowledge them until they walked up.

"Jason Marlon?" one of them asked.

He stopped. "Yeah. That's me."

The first one gestured. "I'm Detective Mellenbuhl and this is Detective Garcia. We'd like to talk to you about what happened this morning."

Jace released a held breath. "I'm a little preoccupied, gentlemen. Can this wait? My friend is in surgery, and I don't know if she's gonna make it."

Garcia spoke. "We understand this is a difficult time, but this is a murder investigation, and the faster we can get started, the sooner we can catch who did this."

The woman in the wheelchair stopped and listened. She looked up at Jace with a raised brow.

"Perhaps we can go to a quiet area to talk?" asked Mellenbuhl, frowning at the woman, who frowned back.

Jace shook his head. "Sure. What the hell. I've got nothing better to do." He waved a hand toward the waiting room he'd been sitting in earlier.

He followed them in and the door closed behind them. One woman sat in the corner, wearing a floral dress and chunky jewelry. Jace could see her silver roots as she bowed her head over her knitting. They moved to the opposite corner and spoke quietly.

Jace crossed his arms. "Like I told the officers at the scene, I don't know anything. I found them after Justin called me. I rushed over and—" His throat closed.

"I know this is hard, Mr. Marlon, but you understand why we have to ask. Can you tell us again exactly what happened?" asked Mellenbuhl.

Jace composed himself, and eager to get this over with, he told them the events of the morning. The phone call, what Justin said, him rushing over and finding them, what Devyn told him before she lost consciousness.

Mellenbuhl and Garcia made eye contact and Garcia scribbled in a notebook he'd pulled out of his pocket. "And how did you know the female victim?" he asked.

Jace closed his eyes. "We were dating." He opened his eyes in time to see one of the detectives raise a brow. "Yeah. I know what it looks like."

Garcia nodded. "Did you know this was going on?"

Anger bubbled up. "Absolutely. I knew all along that my best friend was screwing my lady. What kind of stupid question is that?"

Mellenbuhl kept a flat face. "Mr. Marlon. It's a logical question and one we have to ask. You have to admit, you finding your best friend's body while he's messing around with your girlfriend could be construed as possible involvement."

The anger bubbled over and his voice raised. "Then why don't you do your damn jobs and find out the truth, instead of wasting my time here while my girlfriend could be dying. Do you honestly think I'd call the cops if I did this?" He rubbed his face in frustration. "Jesus, what do my tax dollars pay for? Two clowns in suits who ask stupid questions while a murderer runs free? Hell. Put me in a Batman suit and I could do better."

Mellenbuhl narrowed his eyes. "Sir, I think you need to—"

"Excuse me, dear," said a quiet voice.

Jace turned to see the woman with her knitting standing beside Garcia. "Could you help me?" she asked. "I seemed to have lost my phone." She put her knitting in a bag and gestured toward the room. "I know I had it. I was just sitting over there, and I went to call my husband, and I couldn't find it."

"Ma'am," said Garcia. "We're conducting an—"

The woman ignored him. "I'm frantic. My poor mother is having hip surgery and I need to talk to my family. I don't know what to do."

She held the sides of her head and tears welled up in her eyes. "Oh, my poor mother."

Mellenbuhl sighed. "You said you lost your phone? Did you try calling it?"

"Yes. I did, but it's not ringing, but I'm just so upset, I'm not thinking straight. Can you please help me look? I was sitting over there, but for a while I was out by the nurse's station." She held her chest. "Oh, my. I'm feeling a little winded."

"Have a seat, ma'am," said Garcia. "Stay calm. We'll look."

"Thank you, dear. I appreciate it. You're so kind." She fanned herself with her fingers and glanced up at Jace. "Will you sit with me, dear?"

The two officers paused, but then when Jace sat beside her, they walked away. Garcia went out into the hall and Mellenbuhl checked the opposite corner of the room.

Jace felt a hand on his arm, and he looked at the woman. His tangled emotions had prevented him from paying much attention to her plight, but then it occurred to him he was not the only one worried about their loved one. Her eyes were bright and shiny, and she wore no makeup, but there was something about her that made him feel better. Warmth spread up his arm at her touch. She leaned in. "You know, dear, it's better you keep your wits about you in this situation. No need to make enemies. You need these gentlemen right now."

Jace squinted. "Excuse me?"

She patted his arm. "I know you're upset, and rightly so. But be careful."

Jace studied her. Those bright blue eyes held a depth to them he hadn't expected. The warmth in his arm spread to his chest. "Who are you?"

She smiled. "Just someone who's looking out for you. You've had a frightful night. And you shouldn't be here alone. Is there anyone you can call?"

Jace tried to wrap his mind around this woman. "Do you know me?"

She patted his arm again. "Not really. But I wish I did." She patted her neckline and pulled a necklace out from under her shirt. It had a black cord and a round green stone. "This is Moldavite. It's a powerful, high vibration stone. I want you to wear it. It will help protect you from the negativity and lighten you up a bit." She pulled the cord over her neck and handed it to him.

Jace held the necklace. "I can't take this. I don't know you."

She pushed it toward him. "We don't have time now, dear. Just trust me. We'll talk more later." Her demeanor shifted as Mellenbuhl returned.

"I'm sorry, ma'am. I don't see a phone anywhere."

Garcia stepped back into the room, shaking his head. "No phone."

"Perhaps we can call it?" asked Mellenbuhl.

Jace stared as the woman turned frail again. "Oh, I suppose. But I tried that already. I suppose we could try it again."

Jace studied the green stone in his hand as the woman offered her number to the detectives. Heat bloomed in his palm and raced up his arm, much like the woman's touch. Mellenbuhl dialed and the woman looked over and winked at him.

"It's ringing," said Mellenbuhl.

A loud chime of bells tinkled and the men turned toward the sound as the woman lifted her knitting bag, and started digging through it. "Oh, silly me. It's in here." She pulled out a cell phone. "I can't believe I did that."

Mellenbuhl and Garcia's faces fell. "It's okay, ma'am. We're glad you found it," said Garcia.

"Would you help me up, dear?" she asked Jace. "My knees these days aren't what they used to be."

Jace somehow knew her knees were just fine, but he took her arm and helped her up. She took hold of his elbow and spoke into his ear. "Remember what I said. Take the help where you can get it."

Standing, she smiled. "I should go check on my mother." She eyed the stone in Jace's hand. "That's a nice necklace. You should wear it."

Garcia and Mellenbuhl stared at the rock and then at the woman. "Ma'am, did you—"

The waiting room door opened, and an older woman in scrubs walked in. Her hair was up in a bun and she wore glasses. She looked over at the men. "Are you here for Devyn Palmer?"

Jace stepped forward. "I am. How is she?"

She held out a hand and Jace shook it. "I'm Dr. Chambers. I did surgery on Miss Palmer. She did great. Came through with flying colors.'

"Really?" asked Jace. "She's going to be okay?"

"As long as she can stay away from infection for the next forty-eight hours, I'd say yes. Her prognosis is good. In fact, I've never seen anything like it."

Jace stilled. "What do you mean. She was in bad shape."

The doctor nodded. "Exactly. To be honest, when I first saw her, I doubted if we'd be able to save her. Her injuries were life threatening, but when I opened her up, I was shocked."

The detectives moved closer to hear and even the strange woman lingered by the door.

"Shocked? By what?" asked Jace.

"Considering the blood loss, and location of the wounds, I expected far worse damage, but amazingly the injuries were less severe than I anticipated. It was almost as if..." She shook her head.

"What?"

"It's hard to explain, but it was almost as if she was partially healed. It was the damnedest thing." The doctor put her hands on her hips. "I don't know what happened, but your friend had someone looking out for her."

Jace stood there with his mouth open. From the corner of his eye, he saw the woman who'd given him the stone smile with a faraway look, and then leave the room.

"When can I see her?" he asked.

"Not for a while yet. She'll be in recovery, and then I'd like to keep her in ICU overnight just as a precaution. Once she wakes, and we get her settled, we'll let you know, but it will probably be this afternoon before she can have visitors, so you might get some rest and get something to eat."

The heaviness in Jace's chest lifted, and he rubbed his eyes. "Thank you, doctor. I appreciate it."

"You're welcome." She pointed to his necklace. "That's a nice piece. Is that Moldavite?"

He eyed the stone. "Yes. A friend gave it to me." He rubbed the rock between his fingers and slid the cord over his neck. The warmth hit his chest and the tension in his back and shoulders faded. He thought of the strange woman. "How's the lady who's having hip surgery? Is she okay?"

The doctor frowned. "Who?"

Garcia pointed. "The woman who was just here. Said her mother was having hip surgery."

The doctor shook her head. "No. No hip surgeries today. Besides, those wouldn't be done in this wing of the hospital. Your friend must have been confused." She waved and turned to leave. "Go get some rest."

CHAPTER SIX

Detective Aaron Remalla poured more coffee into his mug, his long, dark hair pulled back behind his neck. "You want some? It's a fresh pot."

His partner, Detective Gordon Daniels, sat at his desk and drank from his water bottle. "That's your fifth cup. How are you just standing there? You should be running in place and juggling baseballs."

"Fifth cup is child's play. I'm just getting started." He returned the pot and sat at his desk.

His partner eyed him. "Didn't sleep?"

Rem rested his head in his hand. "Slept fine, except for the five-hour *Alien* marathon.

"Alien? Since when do you watch documentaries? You still thinking about that thing you saw in the sky?"

Rem rolled his eyes. "*Alien*, the movie, bonehead. You know, with Sigourney Weaver? Ripley? Ring any bells?"

Daniels put his water down. "None."

"You really need to get out more." He sighed. "I should have watched a documentary though. Probably would have helped me sleep." He rubbed his face. "And that thing in the sky was weird. It moved at odd angles."

"Probably a drone."

"Not at that speed."

"God knows what the military has at their disposal. Could have been anything." Daniels studied him. "How inebriated were you at the time?"

Rem shrugged. "I may have had a few beers, but I know what I saw."

Daniels chuckled. "That won't fly in a court of law."

"Yeah, well, thankfully, I'm just talking to you."

"Thankfully." Daniels sat back. "So, why aren't you sleeping?"

Rem closed a file folder and threw it in his desk. "This case sucks."

Daniels hit a few keys on his laptop and closed it. "This case is no different than any other sicko case we've had. Two guys robbing liquor and drug stores and assaulting the owners. Just another day on the job."

"Until yesterday when they actually killed someone." He recalled having to tell the wife that her husband had died at the scene. Her wails still echoed in his ears.

"It wasn't a good day. But we've had them before."

"I know. I guess it just catches up with you, you know?"

Daniels nodded. "I know. Want to catch a few beers on the way home tonight?"

Rem tapped on the table with a pencil. "Nah. You go home to Marjorie and J.P. You've been here more than there since this case started."

"Marjorie won't mind. She gets it when we have to take a little time to process what we do."

"I guess that's one way of putting it."

Captain Frank Lozano walked into the squad room, wearing a blue suit and yellow tie, and carrying a file. His stoic face told Rem he had a lot on his mind. "How's it goin', Cap?"

He stopped by their desks. "Daniels. Remalla. How's that robbery case? Any leads?"

Daniels swiveled in his chair. "We're hoping the video at the latest store may have the perp's face. They've pulled the footage. We're going to check it today."

"That's great. I hope we get lucky." He sighed and rubbed his sweaty face with his shirt cuff.

"You okay? You look a little stressed, Cap," said Rem. He opened a drawer and pulled out a chocolate bar. "I've got some candy if you're interested." He waved the bar.

"Put that away. You know my blood sugar can't take it."

Rem ripped open the wrapper. "Then I guess I'll have to eat it all by myself."

"New case, Cap?" asked Daniels. "I heard about the murder this morning over on the west side. Is that ours?"

Lozano huffed. "I put Mel and Garcia on it. It was ugly. Guy got his throat slashed. And a woman was stabbed. They think she'll pull through though."

"That's something, at least," said Rem. "Any initial suspects?" He popped a piece of chocolate in his mouth.

"Guy who found the vic was the best friend. His girlfriend was the one who was stabbed in the best friend's bedroom."

Daniels winced. "Ouch. Doesn't look good. His best friend and girl-friend?"

"That's motive," said Rem.

"Mel and Garcia are talking to him in interrogation one. He came in on his own. No attorney. We'll see what he has to say." He pointed at Rem. "He owns a bar, apparently. Called Brando's. You heard of it?"

Rem pushed a strand of his long hair back behind his ear. "This may come as a surprise, but I don't know every dive bar in the city."

"Unless they serve tacos," said Daniels.

Rem shrugged. "Well, you got a point there. Do they serve tacos?"

"Not that I know of."

"Well, then, I can't help you." Rem cracked his knuckles and sat back, popping another piece of chocolate in his mouth.

Lozano frowned. "You know how you can help me?" He headed toward his office.

"What's that, Cap," said Rem through a mouthful of chocolate.

"Get that hair cut." He opened the door to his office.

"Sure thing, Cap. First thing." Rem waved. "But first we got to review that footage. Right, Daniels?"

Daniel sat straight. "Yup. Footage. We're on it."

Lozano grunted, shook his head, and walked into his office.

Daniels stood. "You know, one of these days, you're going to have to actually cut it."

Rem ate the last bite of his candy bar. "We'll see about that." He spied the empty wrapper. "Sorry. Did you want some?"

"I'm good." Daniels opened his drawer. "You want some dried kale?"

"I'd rather eat dirt."

"Probably be better for you than that candy bar. You could use the fiber."

Rem stood and pushed his chair in. "I'll eat fiber when I get my hair cut. How's that?"

"I don't even want to know what your insides look like," said Daniels.

"One hundred percent pure muscle, partner. I'm a walking wunderkind."

Daniels raised a brow. "Wunderkind? Somebody's been reading their dictionary."

"When you got it, you got it. Muscles and brains, all rolled into one."

Daniels headed for the doors. "There's definitely something rolled up in there, but I'm willing to bet it's a Taco del Fuego."

Rem followed him. "Probably that too."

A woman walked into the squad room, looking lost.

Daniels stopped as he reached the doors. "Can we help you?"

She appeared to be in her mid-twenties, with shoulder length dark brown hair, and pretty almond eyes. She pulled her purse up over her shoulder and wrung her hands. "They told me to come up here. I'm came to see my boss. He called me to come pick him up."

Rem could tell from her movements she was nervous. "What's your name?"

"Danni. Danni Eldridge." She put a hand to her head. "Uhm…I work at Jace's…my bosses' bar. I heard about what happened. My God. Is Justin really dead?" She waved her hands. "I'm sorry. I'm rambling."

Daniels put a hand on Rem's shoulder. "What did you say his name was?"

Her brown eyes widened. "Jace? Jace Marlon? Oh, I'm sorry. I'm so flustered. His actual name is Jason." She touched her head again and her fingers trembled. "I'm sorry. I just…I just saw him…Justin…last night."

Rem eyed his partner, and knew exactly what he was thinking. "Did you say Jace?"

She nodded. "Yes. I work in his bar. I'm a bartender."

"At Brando's?" asked Rem.

"Yes. Do you know it?"

"No, I don't. Do you serve food?"

"No."

"Well, there you go," said Rem.

"Have a seat, Miss Eldridge." Daniels guided her to a chair and she sat.

"They…they…were all playing cards."

"Who was?" asked Rem.

"Jace, Justin, and Simon and…oh, God…what's his name…Henry. Then Devyn came in. Jace's girlfriend. They were all laughing and having fun. Then we went home, and now I hear this. Justin is dead and Devyn almost died too. Oh, God." She leaned over. "What is happening?"

Rem swallowed and tipped his head at Daniels.

"Would you give us a second?" asked Daniels. "I think your friend is being questioned. We'll find out what's going on."

She nodded. "Thanks."

Rem followed Daniels out the doors and into the hallway. "Did she say Jace?" said Rem.

"Sure did." Daniels stared off. "Maybe it's a coincidence?"

Rem gestured toward the doors. "It's been four months since the murder at Secret Lake. We tried to find some connection to the name Jace that weirdo Rutger mentioned, and couldn't. Rutger fell off the face of the earth despite our attempts to find him. We're finally getting back into our routines, and now this?"

"Like I said. Maybe it's a coincidence. Lots of people are named Jason and go by Jace."

Rem scratched his head, feeling the scar from the stitches he'd received after chasing Rutger through the woods at Secret Lake. "What do your ribs say?"

Daniels instinctively gripped his side. "Don't remind me."

Rem stood there, thinking.

"What do you want to do?" asked Daniels.

Rem looked down the hall. "Cap said they're in interrogation one?"

Daniels paused, his eyes narrowing.

Rem spoke softly. "Care to listen in?"

Daniels shook his head. "You are all muscle and brains, aren't you?"

"I would never lie about that." Rem smacked him on the shoulder. "Let's go."

**

They walked down the hallway and stopped outside interrogation one. Another door stood adjacent to it and they opened it and went inside, closing it behind them. A large piece of one-way glass allowed them a view of the room where Mel and Garcia were interviewing a big guy with wild hair and tattoos on his arms.

"Jeez, that man looks like he stepped out of a comic book of villains," said Rem.

"I bet nobody stole his lunch money," said Daniels. He hit the button on the wall that turned on the speaker. The voices from the interrogation traveled into the room.

Mel was speaking. He'd taken his jacket off; his tie was loose and he sat at the table. "I know you're frustrated, but you have to understand how this looks. We just need to be sure we have the story straight, Mr. Marlon."

The big guy groaned and held his head. "How many times do you want me to tell you the same thing?" He threw out a hand. "I didn't do this. Check the tapes. Surely there was a camera between my bar and Justin's front door that caught me on my way to Justin's or arriving at his apartment. Or the 911 call. I know that woman heard my motorcycle."

"We're working on that, Mr. Marlon," said Garcia, leaning against the wall. "But for right now, let's review it again. You said your friend called you early this morning at your bar?" His tan jacket was on, but he slid it off and threw it over a chair.

The man sighed. "Everybody keeps calling me Mr. Marlon. It makes me sound way more important than I am. Just call me Jace."

"Okay, Jace," said Garcia.

"Check that box," said Daniels.

"Yup," said Rem. "Damn, I wish I'd brought my coffee. It's gonna get cold."

"You can heat it when we get back."

"Tell us about the call," said Mel.

Jace shook his head. "I was working. I own a bar. We'd been up late playing cards. Everyone went home, so I stayed to get some paperwork done. Fell asleep at my desk."

"Who's everyone?" asked Garcia.

Jace clasped his hands together. "Me, Justin, Simon and Henry. Devyn came over, oh, and Danni was at the bar."

"Danni?" asked Garcia.

"Yeah. I just hired her as a bartender a couple months back."

Garcia nodded. "Devyn play cards?"

"No."

"Who won?" asked Mel.

"Me."

"How much?"

"I don't know. About a grand."

Garcia whistled. "You had a good night. Anybody mad you took their money?"

Jace shook his head. "Nah. We're all buddies. They'll take it back at the next game." His face fell and he swallowed. Daniels suspected that Jace was questioning if there would be a next game.

"What was Devyn doing?" asked Mel.

"She watched. Talked smack to the guys when I won. Sat in my lap." He stared at the table.

"Henry and Simon? Who are they?" asked Garcia.

"Just friends. Known them a while. Henry is an engineer, working on some building downtown. Simon is a manager at some financial firm. He does my taxes. I met them through Justin. They're good guys."

Garcia slid a pad of paper over with a pencil. "I need their full names and contact info. We'll need to talk to them. Add the bartender, too."

"Sure," said Jace.

"He's cooperative," said Rem.

"So far," added Daniels.

"Tell us about Justin," said Mel. "How do you know him?"

Jace finished writing and put the pencil down. "Danni is on her way here. You can talk to her yourself."

"Okay. About Justin?" asked Mel.

A Styrofoam cup sat beside Jace and he picked up and tapped it on the table. "We go...went...back a ways." He brought the cup to his mouth and drained the contents. "Known him since high school. We were both foster kids."

"Foster kids?"

"Yeah. Justin until he was fourteen. Me until...well...forever." He studied the cup. "When we met, we hit it off with our backgrounds. Started hangin' out."

"You guys get into trouble?" asked Garcia.

"Some. We smoked weed. Took his mother's car off-roading. Stole beer and toilet-papered a few houses. Kid's stuff." He held the cup. "I bought my first motorcycle with him." Staring off, he crumpled the cup in his hand. "Shit."

"What happened after high school?" asked Mel.

"I hit the road. Got on my bike and didn't look back. Justin went to community college. Eventually got a degree. We stayed in touch. When I was in town, I stayed with him. We took a few trips together. Dated crazy women, and went to crazy parties."

"When did you get the bar?"

"Couple years ago. I'd saved up enough money doing odd jobs, and I wanted to settle in one place. The bar sounded like the next best thing."

"How long were you dating Devyn?" asked Garcia, pacing behind Mel.

"On and off, eight months. We met at the bar."

"Justin meet her at the bar, too?" asked Garcia.

Jace sighed and ran his hands through his hair. "Is this going to take much longer? I'd like to go back to the hospital."

"It takes as long as it takes," said Mel.

Jace set his jaw, but continued. "Yes. Justin met Devyn at the bar."

"They hit it off?"

"What kind of question is that?" asked Jace.

"An obvious one," said Mel.

Jace's face hardened. "They were friendly. They got along. Why wouldn't they?"

"Was Justin dating anyone?" asked Mel.

Jace released a pained sigh. "A chick named Liz, but not very long. They just broke up."

"Why'd they break up?" asked Mel.

"I don't know."

"Justin didn't tell you?" asked Garcia.

Jace groaned. "He told me they weren't dating anymore. What else is there to say? It wasn't like they were engaged."

Mel and Garcia went quiet for a second. "You know her full name?"

Jace shook his head. "I don't know. Liz Monroe, I think?

"Add it to the sheet of paper. We'll need to talk to her too."

Jace scribbled on the sheet.

"You ever mess around with Liz?" asked Garcia. "Is that why they broke up?"

Jace looked up with an expression that easily reflected what he thought of this situation. "You motherfucker."

"Whoa, there we go," said Rem.

"I think he's pissed," said Daniels.

Garcia didn't back down. "He's sleeping with your girl, so maybe you were sleeping with his? Or was it the other way around?"

Jace smacked his hand on the table. "I never slept with Liz. I wouldn't that to Justin."

"But he did it to you," said Mel.

Jace groaned and sat back in his seat. "I suspect Devyn may have instigated that, and he...he...well...he caved." He rubbed his hands on his thighs. "Son-of-a-bitch, he caved."

"You said you and Devyn were on and off. Did you know she was seeing other guys?" asked Mel.

"I don't know, but I didn't ask."

"Were you seeing other women?" asked Mel.

"No. I wasn't."

"No one-night stands?" asked Garcia.

Jace scowled. "Jesus, you really are a prick, aren't you?"

"Just trying to solve the murder of your friend," said Garcia.

"By asking if I've had one-night stands?"

"Just wondering if Devyn had reason to be jealous, and if that's why she slept with your friend."

"And what? My one-night stand killed them? Is that your theory? God, please don't tell me you two are the A-team, because the B-team must really suck."

Rem chuckled. "Don't hate me, but I like this guy."

"He does have a certain charisma," said Daniels, "but then so did Ted Bundy."

"Good point," added Rem.

"You'd be surprised what we see out there, Mr. Marlon...Jace," said Mel. "We have to ask the questions you don't like because the touchy-feely ones rarely solve crimes. Your best friend and girlfriend were screwing around on you. You say you get a phone call and find them together. Based on the nature of this crime, and the way they were attacked, this was personal. The killer is pissed. So, it's likely he, or she, knows you and them. Which means, no matter how much you hate this, we have to ask these questions. If you were sleeping with someone who got more attached than you realize, then maybe that person went after Devyn, and took Justin down, too. You see our point, here? It's not our job to coddle you. And until we prove otherwise, at this moment, you're the prime suspect, which means we don't play nice. And you know why? Because we're the damn A-team."

Rem crossed his arms. "I think he got Mel a little riled up."

"I'm amazed," said Daniels. "Mel's a cool cucumber."

Jace stared for a second at Mel. "I didn't kill my best friend, or stab Devyn. Ask whatever the hell you want. That won't change."

"One-night stands?" asked Garcia. "Or anyone else we should know about?"

Jace squeezed the remains of his cup. "I've slept with one woman since meeting Devyn, about five months ago. Devyn and I had a fight. I got drunk at the bar. This lady came on to me, we ended up in my office after hours. She ended up throwing up on me and my desk. Not exactly romantic."

"What's her name?" asked Garcia.

"I have no idea. I couldn't have told you my name that night. I haven't seen her since, so I doubt she's your killer."

Mel nodded.

"Let's go back to last night," said Garcia. "The card game ends. What happens after that?"

Jace moaned like a man who'd been stabbed. "Henry and Simon said goodbye. Justin and I talked about taking a ride up into the hills before he left. Nothing special."

"Where was Devyn?" asked Mel.

"She...," he paused and snickered. "She was getting her cards read."

"Her cards?" asked Garcia.

"Danni, my bartender, she's a tarot reader. Devyn wanted a reading, so Danni pulled some cards for her."

"That's a new one," said Daniels.

"Tarot," said Rem. "Huh."

Mel looked at Garcia. "What did the cards say?" asked Mel.

Jace stared off and he rubbed his eyes. "Hell."

"What?" asked Garcia. "You remember something?"

Jace put his arm down. "The cards. She asked about our relationship. They suggested that a third person was involved." He looked away. "It wasn't a great reading."

"Interesting," said Rem.

"Interesting," said Mel.

"You said this Danni person is coming up here?" asked Garcia.

"She's probably here by now, considering how long this ridiculous conversation is taking," said Jace.

"You think Danni knew about Devyn and Justin?" asked Mel.

"I doubt it, but you'd have to ask her," said Jace.

Daniels spoke to Rem. "She strike you as a killer?"

Rem shrugged. "Danni? No. But then again, what do I know? I can barely function without a potful of coffee coursing through my veins."

"True," said Daniels.

Mel and Garcia shared a silent look that conveyed they were wondering how far to push on the Danni questions. It was a communication all close partnerships seemed to share. Garcia turned back to Jace. "You and Danni have a thing going?"

Jace bellowed. "Oh, for God's sake. No. Just because I have tattoos, grow my hair out and drive a motorcycle, doesn't mean I sleep with everything that moves."

"I know why I like this guy," said Rem. "He reminds me of me."

Daniels regarded his partner. "The only thing you two have in common is your hair."

"He's my alternate me," said Rem.

"Alternate you?"

"Me, in an alternate universe."

Daniels opened his mouth to speak, but Mel interrupted. Daniels shook his head instead.

"What did Devyn think of the card reading?" asked Mel.

"Thought it was stupid. So did I. Told her it was just a game. I don't think Devyn likes Danni, and this didn't help."

"Why doesn't she like Danni?"

Jace stared up at the ceiling and groaned out a sigh. "Shit. I think I may have told Devyn once I thought Danni was cute." He closed his eyes and Daniels could sense Jace knew the next question. He almost chuckled.

"So, you do like Danni?" asked Garcia.

Jace opened his eyes and looked back, his expression flat. "Yes. I thought she was attractive, so obviously I wanted her, even though I was seeing someone else, therefore I must have slept with her because God knows I'm a man who has no self-control, and can't make responsible decisions worth shit." He held out his hands. "You might as well slap the cuffs on me now, Officer."

Garcia stared back, saying nothing.

"Devyn was jealous of Danni? That's why she didn't like her?" asked Mel.

Jace put his hands down. "Devyn had her insecurities, just like everyone else."

"What did Danni think of Devyn?" asked Mel.

"I think the attraction was mutual. It's hard to like someone who doesn't like you," said Jace.

"What happened after the reading?" asked Garcia.

Jace paused. "The guys had left; Danni got her cards and was leaving." He hesitated. "Devyn got a text to cover for a coworker. Said she had to go home. Had to get up in the morning."

"A text? From a coworker?" asked Garcia.

"Did I stutter?" asked Jace.

Garcia frowned. "I'm guessing you were expecting her to stay with you?"

Jace tapped on the table. "Yeah. But she left."

"And went to Justin's?" Garcia raised a brow. "You thinking that text wasn't from a coworker?"

Jace stopped tapping and clenched his hands together.

Garcia continued. "That stinks. Your best friend texts your girl the minute he steps out of the bar, and she goes running. Maybe you're not as hot as shit as you think," said Garcia.

"He's pushing his buttons," said Daniels.

"Uh-huh," said Rem.

Jace and Garcia held eye contact and Jace shifted in his seat. "Sounds like you might have personal experience with that, detective. Wouldn't surprise me at all. Maybe you're not as hot as shit as you think," said Jace. They kept staring, neither backing down, before Jace looked at Mel. "Maybe you can ask me something that actually might solve this case." He cocked his head toward Garcia. "Because Pink Panther over here is struggling."

Rem crossed his arms. "Garcia looks like he wishes he could shoot lasers out of his eyes."

"He'd use 'em," said Daniels.

Mel ignored the comment and narrowed his eyes. "So, Devyn leaves the bar, telling you she has to work the next morning, and presumably, she heads to Justin's."

"Presumably, that's a good word," said Jace. "You've got her phone. I'm sure you can check to see who the text is from. Maybe Pink Panther can handle that."

Mel sat up. "Pink Panther over there has kicked more ass than you've grabbed, so watch your tone."

"This conversation can go as easy or hard as you want it, and right now, it's getting hard," said Garcia. "Which makes we wonder if you've got something to hide."

"He's got them both riled up," said Rem.

Daniels put a hand on the wall. "Marlon's keeping his cool though. No outbursts of anger."

Jace set his jaw, and Daniels expected another smart-ass comment, but Jace sat back and crossed his arms. "You gentlemen have any other questions?"

Garcia relaxed. "What happened after everyone left?"

"Like I said. I went to my office to work. Fell asleep at my desk. Got a phone call early this morning." He stopped and looked away. "I answered it. It was Justin." His voice turned gruff.

"And what did he say?"

Jace dropped his arms and rested his elbows on the desk. He stared at his fingers. "He spoke low. It was almost hard to hear him. He sounded scared. His voice quivered." He paused. "He said he was sorry. I didn't know what he was talking about. Then he said it again. Said he didn't mean to hurt me. He...he..." Jace sighed deeply and cleared his throat. "He sounded terrified. I told him I was coming over." He took a moment and laced his fingers together. "He got distant for a second, like he was talking to someone else, I think he said 'please,' then he came back on the line."

"You think he was talking to another person?" asked Mel.

Jace nodded, taking a breath. "That's what it sounded like. When he came back on, he started to say something like...like...'I did what you want' or something like that. But he didn't finish." He tightened the grip on his fingers. "And then there was a noise..." He struggled to continue.

"What noise?" asked Mel.

"A wet noise, like a gurgle, and...he was gone." Jace bit his lip and rubbed his face. "Shit, he was gone."

"He hung up?" asked Garcia.

"No," Jace looked up, his face furrowed, as if he'd remembered something, and he pointed. "That motherfucker that killed him came on the line. He spoke to me." Jace's face turned red. "That son-of-a-bitch."

"What did he say?" asked Mel.

"He said 'I did it for you.' Jesus. He said 'I did it for you.'"

Daniels went still and looked at Rem, who glanced back, his eyes wide.

"Holy shit," said Rem.

Daniel's mind whirled. "Holy shit is right." He narrowed his eyes, thinking. "You thinking what I'm thinking?

Rem paused, looking back at the men in the interrogation room. "Damn straight I am." He put his hands on his hips. "That asshole Rutger's back."

CHAPTER SEVEN

Danni bounced her knee in nervous anxiety. The detectives had not returned, and she still waited for Jace. She checked her phone for the millionth time. Only a few minutes had passed since the last time she'd checked it.

Crossing her arms, she replayed the previous night in her mind, and still couldn't believe it. Justin was dead and Devyn in the hospital. What had happened? Why was Jace here? Did he know who did it?

Needing something to occupy her mind, she tried a game on her phone but couldn't focus, then she flipped through some social media, but had the same problem. Accessing her email, she scanned it. That morning, she'd completed the reading and sent the results to *Lovelorn52*. They'd been favorable, and she'd told *Lovelorn* to stay ready, and that a relationship seemed likely this year.

BrotherlyLove's email sat in her read box, and she'd almost reopened it, when she'd received the call from Jace, and had rushed to the station.

Looking at her email now, she saw a new unread email from *BrotherlyLove*, sent an hour ago, which was about the time she'd arrived. Frowning, she opened it.

Hi, Daisy. Sorry...Danni.

I'd hoped to hear something from you by now. Your website states prompt replies within 24 hours. I truly hope you will be able to complete my reading within a reasonable time frame.

Of course, life gets in the way, especially when the unexpected happens, but I do hope to get my results from you soon. Best not to keep an angry man waiting.

Expect to hear from you soon.

Danni re-read the email, her heart picking up speed. *Who was this guy?*

If it was one of the men from the bar last night, would they still be messing with her after all this? And if it wasn't one of them, who else could it be?

Her mind replayed the previous evening, and she tried to think.

"Danni Eldridge?"

Looking up, she saw the two detectives she'd spoken to earlier. "Yes?" She stood and put her phone in her pocket.

The blonde one approached her. With his light hair gelled back, his leather jacket and muscled physique, he reminded her of a football player she'd once dated in college. A defensive lineman who'd liked to dress well, and liked the ladies even more, regardless of who he was dating. "I don't think we introduced ourselves before. "I'm Detective Daniels, and this is my partner, Detective Remalla."

She shook hands with both. Remalla reminded her of her ex's roommate. Just as handsome, but who rarely did laundry, ate pizza and ice cream for breakfast, slept till noon, and had women falling all over him. Sort of like her boss. "Detectives. Did you see Jace? Is he back there?"

"Yes, he is," said Daniels. "He's being questioned. Do you have a second? We have a few questions of our own." He gestured toward the hall.

"Me?" Danni shook her head. "I don't know how I can help you."

"You may have more insight than you realize," said Remalla. "It won't take long."

Danni glanced down the hall, wondering what to do, but then she thought of Justin and Devyn. "Okay. If it can help, then sure."

"Thank you," said Daniels.

She followed Remalla who guided her toward a small room not far from where she'd been sitting. There was a table with two chairs, and she sat in one of them.

"Can I get you some water?" asked Daniels.

"No, thanks. I'm fine."

"Actually. I'm going to get my coffee," said Remalla. "Would you like some coffee?"

"Yes, actually." She rubbed her eyes. "Coffee would be great."

"Cream? Sugar?" asked Remalla.

"Black with a little cream, please."

"Be right back."

He left the room, and Daniels took the seat across from her. "Long morning?"

She nodded. "You could say that. Is Jace okay? Is he in trouble?"

Daniels paused. "He found the bodies, or body. We just need to find out what he knows."

"You think he killed Justin? Because he would never do that. He would never kill anyone, and certainly not his best friend."

"There's a lot to figure out before we accuse anyone of anything. This will take time, but whoever did it, we'll find him."

She stretched her neck and arched. "I pulled the Five of Cups today. Now I know why."

Daniels squinted. "The Five of Cups?"

"Yes. It's about loss and emotional upheaval. I'd say it was accurate."

The door opened and Remalla returned, carrying two cups of coffee. He handed one to Danni and held the other.

"Thank you," said Danni, sipping the hot brew.

Remalla eyed the hallway and closed the door.

"Miss Eldridge," said Daniels. "How long have you known your boss, Jace Marlon?"

"Danni, please. Not long. He hired me a few months ago to bartend. I work there in the evenings."

"How well do you know him?" asked Daniels. Remalla leaned against the wall, listening and drinking his coffee.

"Uhm...well...fairly well. I see him almost every day, but we don't hang out after work or anything. He's a nice guy, though. A good boss, but has a bit of a temper." She held out a hand. "Not in a bad way. Not in an *I'm going to kill you* kind of way."

"He's raised his voice at you?" asked Remalla.

"He got mad once, when I dropped a bottle of liquor, but that's it. No big deal. He has a loud bark, but he doesn't bite, because the bark is all he needs. He looks pretty intimidating."

"True, that," said Remalla. "But he doesn't scare you?"

Danni almost chuckled. "I've faced worse. No, he doesn't."

"What do you now about his background? Does he have family?" asked Daniels.

Danni thought about it. "Not that he's ever mentioned. Justin is...was...the only family he has. Hell."

"Take your time," said Daniels.

She took a breath. "He's never mentioned siblings or parents. I asked once and he shrugged it off. Said he'd been on his own since he was eighteen and he wasn't looking back."

"What about his friendship with Justin? Do you know much about that?" asked Daniels.

"Not really. They go back a ways. To high school, I think. They both have motorcycles. Those big loud ones. Like to take rides on the weekends. They were sort of opposites. Justin was more practical, Jace...well...not so much. More of a free spirit. I think they balanced each other well."

"And Devyn? What did you think of her?" asked Remalla.

Danni couldn't squelch the grimace.

"Not a fan?" asked Daniels.

"Sorry. She's just…" She searched for the words. "A bit more verbose."

Remalla smiled. "She wasn't an introvert, I take it?"

"No, not at all. I don't think she'd know what the word means." She shook her head. "I shouldn't speak ill of her. I know she's lying in a hospital room right now."

"But?" asked Daniels.

"But…Devyn's flashy. Talk's a lot and but doesn't wear a lot. Has to be the center of attention and lays claim on the man she wants."

"That bothers you?" asked Remalla, sipping his coffee.

"It's annoying as hell. I mean, she can act and dress however she wants. That's her right. But she hung all over Jace, and made it very clear she didn't like me."

"You jealous?" asked Remalla.

She chuckled. "Is that what I made it sound like? No. Not jealous." She paused and sipped her own coffee. "I think I just always had a feeling about her. That she wasn't doing right by Jace. Her displays of affection were way over the top, like she was trying too hard. But Jace loved that about her, so you know, I'm sure that didn't help. He likes flashy ladies. Or at least it seems that way."

"You ever see him with anyone else?" asked Daniels. "Besides Devyn?"

"No. Not really. He can be a flirt when he gets drunk. He knows the ladies like him, and he can use that to his advantage, but no one serious. But again, I haven't known him that long."

Daniels nodded and Remalla studied his coffee.

"Tell us about the card game last night," said Daniels. "What happened?"

Danni gripped her cup and tensed, but she went through the events of the card game, telling them about who was there, how Jace won, and Devyn showed up and her PDA with Jace, the unpleasant tarot reading, Devyn's text, and when everyone left.

"You do tarot readings?" asked Remalla.

"Yes. I have a website. I do readings during the day."

"How long have you been doing that?" asked Remalla.

"A couple of years. I've got a decent a client base. But it keeps me at home. I took the bartending job just to get out of the house. Meet some people."

"Your reading about Jace and Devyn. Would you say it was accurate?" asked Remalla.

"If Devyn was sleeping with Justin, then yes, it was accurate." She tucked her hair back and sighed.

"You ever do any other readings for them?" asked Daniels.

"Not for them. Devyn always snickered at the mention of it. I've pulled a few cards for Jace though, just for fun, mainly. I think he's curious, but doesn't want to come out and say it."

"Anything unusual come up in the cards?" asked Remalla.

"Unusual? What do you mean?"

Remalla eyed his partner. "No secrets? Is he hiding anything?"

She looked between the two of them. "The cards don't exactly work like that. They're not a crystal ball."

Daniels nodded and shifted in his seat.

"Anything weird happen last night?" asked Remalla. "Anything out of the ordinary?"

"Weird?" she asked.

"Yeah." Remalla pushed off the wall and stood by the table. "Like a strange comment, or an uncomfortable moment…"

"…or a weird person," said Daniels. "Anything like that?"

Danni went still, immediately recalling the man at the bar with the hoodie. How could she have forgotten?

"Miss Eldridge?" asked Daniels, leaning in. "Did you remember something?"

She put her cup down. "Maybe. There was a—"

The door opened, and a man stood there, tall and lanky, with a wrinkled jacket and a badge on his belt. His face dripped with displeasure. "What the hell are you two doing?" he asked.

"Mel, we're in the middle of something here," said Remalla.

His voice rose. "Yeah. It's called our case."

Daniels swiveled. "We're talking right now. Can we table this?"

"How about we table it right into the Captain's office?" He held the door wide.

Remalla groaned. "Listen…"

Another detective stuck his head in. "Ma'am, will you give us a second?"

"Sure," said Danni.

Daniels and Remalla eyed her, offered an apology, and then left the room, closing the door behind them.

CHAPTER EIGHT

Mel stuck out a finger. "You two need to butt out of this. You got your own case, so go work that one."

Rem shot back. "Come on, Mel. We just had a few questions. Nobody's taking your case."

Daniels leaned against the wall in Lozano's office. The Captain sat at his desk, listening to his men argue.

"I think maybe you hear about a juicy murder case and want them all to yourself." Garcia sat in a chair and leaned in. "There are other cops out there capable of solving crimes."

Daniels pushed up. "What the hell does that mean, Garcia? What are you accusing us of?"

"Oh, I don't know. Maybe your heads got big after the Makeup Artist. You liked the attention. And maybe like the favoritism."

Rem shouted. "Favoritism?"

Daniels yelled. "Attention?"

All four of them spoke at once, each trying to be heard over the other.

The Captain stood slowly. "That's enough." No one listened. He spoke louder. "I said that's enough." His voice boomed over them and they all went quiet, but they stood rigid, their bodies taut.

"Garcia. Mel. Go finish your questioning. Keep me posted on your progress."

Garcia and Mel stood for a second, and then nodded, heading for the door.

"And Garcia."

Garcia stopped and turned. Lozano pointed. "If you've got an issue with favoritism, I suggest you tell it to my face, not throw it in somebody else's."

Garcia's face colored, but he nodded. "Sure thing, Cap."

"You two," he acknowledged Daniels and Remalla. "Have a seat."

Remalla approached the desk. "Cap, listen—"

"I said have a seat, Remalla."

Garcia offered a slight grin and closed the door behind him. Daniels and Remalla sat, and so did Lozano.

Lozano put his elbows on his desk. "Tell me what's going on, and don't give me that whole, *we're just trying to help* routine. What are you two up to?"

His two detectives eyed each other. "She...Danni...was just sitting there, waiting, Cap," said Remalla. "I don't know. I guess we just thought we should talk to her."

Lozano narrowed his eyes. He turned his attention to Daniels. "Are you going to try to blow smoke up my ass, too, because your partner sucks at it."

Daniels fidgeted in his seat and Remalla rolled his eyes. "Well," said Daniels. "It's sort of a long story."

"Try me," said Lozano.

Daniels looked at Rem who shrugged. Daniels sighed. "Okay. It goes back to the Makeup Artist case."

"Which you cracked," said Lozano. He paused. "You caught the guy."

"Yes and no," said Rem. He hesitated. "We think we may have a second murderer, unrelated to the Artist."

Lozano took that in. "Excuse me? How come I'm just now hearing about this?"

"Because it's thin, but it keeps getting thicker, which is why we wanted to talk to Danni," said Daniels.

Lozano picked up a pen and twirled it through his fingers. "Explain."

Rem took a breath and scratched his head. "Okay. You remember Rick Henderson?"

"Yes. He was one of the Makeup Artist's victims," said Lozano.

"That's what we thought, but basically, we have reason to believe Officer Henderson was not killed by the Artist, but by someone else. At the scene of his murder, *I did it for you* was written on the wall. Remember?" asked Rem.

"Yes, but that doesn't mean the Artist didn't kill him."

"No, it doesn't. But then we went to Secret Lake. When Madison Vickers was accused of killing her husband."

"But you found the murderer," said Lozano.

"We did," said Rem. "But Madison had a strange man following her around."

"Is that the guy who caused your injuries?" asked Lozano, fiddling with the pen.

"He is," said Daniels.

Lozano studied his men. "I still don't understand how he got the drop on you two."

They shifted in their seats. "Believe me, we don't understand it either," said Daniels, rubbing his ribs. "My ego still hurts."

"Anyway," said Rem. "He…the guy following her…used the same phrase. With Madison, and with us. He said *I did it for her.*"

Lozano tapped the pen. "And you think that somehow that connects him to the Artist?"

Daniels sat forward. "Not to the Artist. To the victim. Henderson. We think it has something to do with Henderson's connection to Jill."

"Jill Jacobs?" asked the Captain.

"Yeah," said Remalla.

"You still seeing her?" asked Lozano.

"I am," said Remalla.

Lozano thought about it. "So Madison Vickers had someone following her after her husband was murdered who used the same phrase that was used at Henderson's crime scene."

"Right," said Daniels.

"And you think Henderson and Vickers were killed by this mystery guy, and not by who we originally thought?" asked Lozano.

"Correct," said Rem.

Lozano nodded. "And what's the connection to this case?"

Rem raised a brow at Daniels, who continued. "When we were investigating the Vickers' murder, this mystery guy, he mentioned a name."

"You spoke to him?" asked Lozano. He glowered. "When? I don't remember reading that in the report." He tried to recall the details of the case. "I thought you chased him through the woods and he got away." He leaned in and held up two fingers. "It happened twice as I recall."

"We're not proud, but that's accurate," said Rem. "But he may have said a few things before he took off the second time."

"What, did you sit and have a cup of tea with him?" asked Lozano.

Daniels cleared his throat. "No. Not tea."

"It was raining," added Rem.

"Well, I hope you had your raincoat, Remalla," said Lozano.

"I wish I had. We got soaked." He looked at Daniels who shook his head at him.

"We did," said Remalla.

"I'm sorry you got your pretty, long hair wet while you talked with a perp who could be a murderer," said Lozano. He dropped his pen. "What the hell are you two not telling me? Why wasn't this little conversation in the report?"

Daniels rubbed his neck. "That really doesn't matter, Captain. What matters is what he told us. He said *I did it for her*. And then he talked about his family, and he mentioned a name. Jace."

Lozano did not miss how Daniels had avoided his question. He debated pressing harder, but reluctantly decided to table it for now. "Jace? Who's Jace?"

"Exactly, Cap. That's what we wanted to know," said Remalla. "When we got back from the lake, we tried to find someone named Jace who might have some connection to all this, but had no success."

"I'm not surprised," said Lozano. "Like a needle in a haystack."

"Until this morning," said Daniels. "When we met Danni Eldridge. Garcia and Mel were talking to her boss. The bar owner who found the victims this morning. His name is Jace Marlon."

"*Jace*, Captain," said Remalla.

"I'm not deaf, Remalla," said Lozano.

"So, we listened in on the interrogation," said Daniels. "Between Mel, Garcia, and this Jace Marlon. And guess what? Marlon got a phone call from his friend before he was murdered. A man came on the line and said *I did it for you* before the line went dead. Now that's either a hell of a coincidence or Rutger's back."

"Rutger?" asked Lozano.

"It's what we call him, the mystery man. He looks like a young Rutger Hauer. You know, from Blade Runner?" said Rem.

"Blade Runner? With Harrison Ford?" asked Lozano.

Rem shot out a hand. "See? Even the Cap knows it."

Daniels ignored him. "That's why we talked to Danni. This Jace has a friend named Justin – who's sleeping with Jace's girlfriend – who gets attacked, then is forced to call Jace and say he's sorry before he's murdered. We think Rutger killed the friend for Jace, just like he killed Vickers for Madison and Henderson for Jill." He ran a hand through his hair. "I know it's crazy but I think we're on to something."

Lozano grunted and leaned back in his seat. His two detectives stared and waited. They were his best men, and to be honest, Garcia was right. He did tend to favor them, but he'd be keeping that to himself. "Listen," he said, sitting back up. "I see what you're saying, and why you're saying it, but I can't go on a single phrase to justify sending you two on this goose chase. I need more. And we still haven't cleared Marlon yet. For all we know, he lied about the call and he's the killer. And Jace? That could be a total coincidence. If his name were Bill, you'd be watching that convenience store video footage right now."

"Captain—" said Remalla.

"I'm not saying you don't have something here, but I can't take Garcia and Mel off this and put you two on it based on that alone. Let them finish their questioning. If Marlon's cleared, then maybe we can start looking for this Rutger. But for right now, I need you to follow up on the robbery and murder from last night. There's a widow out there who needs answers, and you sitting here looking for a mystery man isn't going to get them for her."

Daniels sighed and Remalla nodded. Appearing defeated, they stood. "Okay, Cap," said Daniels.

Lozano picked up his pen again. "I'm guessing you two have been looking into this for a while now?"

Daniels pursed his lips.

"Maybe," said Rem.

"Does Jacobs know about this theory of yours?" asked Lozano.

Remalla stilled. "I wanted to tell her…"

"That means no," said Lozano. "What's holding you back?"

Remalla shifted on his feet. "Like you said, Cap, we still don't have a lot to go on. I hate to tell her but have nothing else to offer. It's gonna take the wind out of her sails, and I'd like to be able to offer more than a mystery man who looks like Rutger Hauer."

"We need to figure out what the connection is between Jacobs, Vickers and now Marlon," said Daniels.

"You see my point then," said Lozano. He stood. "Maybe once you have that, we might have a case, but until then, I need more than a phrase and a mystery man in the woods who resembles an actor."

His men shared a glance and walked to the door. "We hear you, Cap," said Remalla.

Lozano squinted. It wasn't like his men to agree so easily. "Stay off this case until we have more to go on, you got that?"

Daniels held out his hands. "Of course."

Remalla put a finger to his forehead and then aimed it back at Lozano. "You got it." He held up two fingers. "Scout's honor."

"It's three fingers," said Daniels.

"Whatever. Thanks, Cap." Remalla opened the door and left and Daniels followed, closing the door behind him.

Lozano eyed the door, watching his men walk away. He wondered how long it would take before they stuck their noses back into this case. His guess was maybe twenty-four hours. Forty-eight if he was lucky.

CHAPTER NINE

Danni held her coffee, staring into the dark brew. The detectives had just left and she sat in the quiet room, recalling the man at the bar, sitting there for hours, drinking but not drunk, listening to the men playing cards. He'd tipped her a hundred bucks, and what had he said? *Something tells me you might need it.* Why had he said that?

Sweat popped out on her skin, and her skin flushed, although she shivered. Her fingers shook, and she pushed the coffee away, suddenly feeling nauseous. The walls seemed to grow in size and the room became smaller.

She lowered her head, trying to take normal breaths, but her heart thudded. "No," she said to herself, breaking into a sweat. "No."

She pushed back from her seat and dropped her head between her knees, trying to offset what she knew would come next, the dizziness. She closed her eyes as the walls bulged out at her. "Shit," she whispered. This hadn't happened in years. A panic attack. Her heart hammered against her ribs, and her breathing escalated, despite her attempts to slow it down. Gripping the edges of the desk, she told herself to relax, but the intensity of the attack took hold and she knew she was close to hyperventilating. When she peeked out from behind her closed lids, the ceiling and walls loomed. She wanted, needed to breathe, but her lungs felt compressed. She couldn't get enough air. Her head swam and her vision swirled. She had to get out of this room and breathe some oxygen because there wasn't any left in this small enclosure. She was suffocating.

Standing, she bumped against the table, knocking over the coffee and spilling the remains of her drink on the table. Putting her hand on the wall, she took a second to get her balance before rushing out the door. She ran into the hallway, desperate to get outside. Sunlight on her face and air in her lungs would help. If she didn't, she was going to pass out in the hallway. Trying to pull it together, she saw the stairway where she'd entered the squad room and flew down it, careful to hold the rails, but moving as quickly as she could. She paid no attention to anyone she passed and thought she heard her name called, but she couldn't stop. Bumping into someone on their way up, she offered a whispered *I'm sorry* before hurtling herself through the lobby area and out into the sunshine. Doubling over, she grabbed a hand rail and held on, taking deep breaths. The sun warmed her back and she blinked as her vision cleared. Seeing the steps that led to the front door, she sat on one of them, her head down, trying to gather herself.

God. This hadn't happened since…when? God, she couldn't be sure. Maybe two years? They'd started in high school after her father disappeared and they'd happened frequently whenever she'd been stressed or fatigued. She'd seen a shrink, and he'd taught her how to cope and helped her learn some tricks to prevent it. They'd eventually stopped, and she'd almost forgotten about them, until now. Jesus, this had come out of nowhere. Or had it? Considering the events of the last twenty-four hours, she supposed she shouldn't be surprised. All of the strange occurrences had likely triggered it.

She sat for a few minutes as the light-headedness passed and her breathing slowed. People walked to and from the building without offering a second glance. Maybe police stations didn't think much of a woman having a meltdown in front of their building.

Thinking of her phone, she patted her pocket and felt it. She would have to tell Jace where she was, because she couldn't go back inside. She wondered if he even had his phone or had they taken it from him when they'd brought him in? Could she get a message to him and did she need to explain her sudden disappearance to the detectives? They would wonder where she went.

Sitting on the step, she wondered what to do next when she heard her name called.

"Danni," said a male voice.

Looking behind her, she saw Jace step out of the building. He wore his dark brown leather jacket over a snug-fitting t-shirt, his beat-up jeans, and his black motorcycle boots. His long hair blew in the wind. A woman walking into the building did a double take when she passed him.

He came over and sat beside her. "You okay? I saw you run out of the building."

She took a long deep breath, feeling confident the worst of it was over. "It's okay. I'm okay. Just…had a moment. I had to get out of the building."

"Yeah. These places do that to you."

"Are you done? Did they finish questioning you?"

"I doubt it. But I saw you run out. I called after you but you didn't stop. When they came back, I told them I was done answering their questions. I know they don't have enough to hold me. There's no blood on me other than Devyn's, and I know Justin's lobby had a camera, and I didn't touch anything at the scene. They'll figure it out soon enough. I told them if they wanted me to stay, they'd have to arrest me. They weren't happy, but they gave me the 'don't go far and be available' speech. Assholes."

She held her head. Thankfully, the dots in her vision were dissipating. "They're just doing their job. You want them to find the killer, don't you?"

"They aren't going to find him questioning me."

"But what if you know something? Something that might help lead them to the murderer."

"Right now, they're more interested in whether I'm the murderer, and I'm not. Although..." His face turned as hard as the concrete beneath her. "I think I talked to him." He clenched his hands into fists. "That guy better pray I never find him, because if I do..."

Danni put her hand on his wrist. "I'm sorry about Justin...and Devyn. I heard she's going to be okay."

He put his elbows on his knees and stared at the ground. "The doctors think so," he said quietly.

"That's good news, at least."

He picked up a twig and scraped it across the pavement, but it snapped when he used too much force. "She was in his apartment, Danni. She and Justin...shit...they were sleeping together...behind my back." He held his head. "He was my best friend." She heard him draw a ragged breath. "If he were alive, I'd kill him. But somebody beat me to it."

Danni didn't know what to say. An image of her mother, sitting on the couch, her head bent as she cried, came to mind. Danni hadn't known what to say then, either. All she could do was offer comfort, and she'd sat next to her and leaned in, shoulder to shoulder, head to head, while her mother sobbed.

She offered the same now, leaning close, her shoulder against his. He didn't move away and they sat there for a few minutes, letting the silence between them drown out the activity around them. After a few minutes, she spoke. "You want me to take you back to your motorcycle? Is it at the hospital?"

He straightened and tossed the twig away. "I guess. I'm debating whether to see Devyn. Part of me wants to, another part of me never wants to see her again."

Danni considered something. "She may know who the killer is. She might have seen his face. The detectives will want to talk to her when she wakes up."

Jace sighed. "I know. The cops stationed someone at her door to keep an eye on her and let them know when she wakes."

"If that's true, they're not going to want you to go near her, at least not until they talk to her first."

He rubbed his head. "I suppose."

"When's the last time you slept?"

"I got a few hours at my desk last night."

"You want to go home?"

"No. I don't. I can't handle quiet right now." He glanced over at her, and his brown, almost black eyes, studied her. "You want to go for a ride? Get some fresh air?"

Danni swallowed. That penetrating gaze pierced her and she understood now why women couldn't keep their hands off him. The way he looked at her made her feel like she was the only person on the sidewalk.

"Jace, listen. I talked to the detectives too. They were asking about you and what happened last night."

His face fell. "And what did you say?"

"I told them everything. That's all I could say, but then I remembered something, but I didn't get a chance to tell them because they left the room."

"What did you remember?"

"There was a man sitting at the bar last night. Did you see him? He'd been nursing a few drinks for most of the evening. He'd been there almost the whole time. He saw the card game; he saw you and Devyn and the guys."

His eyes darkened. "You think he had something to do with this?"

"He said something weird to me when he left. He tipped me a hundred bucks because he suspected I would need it. Why would he say that?"

Jace looked away.

"Not only that, but he didn't like you and Devyn, and your public displays of affection."

He looked back, glowering. "Come on," he stood and held out a hand.

She took his hand and stood; glad she could do it without swaying. "Where are we going? Shouldn't we tell the cops?"

"Screw them. We're going to the bar. We're gonna find that guy."

**

An hour later, after swinging by the hospital to pick up his bike and then stopping at a fast food place to get some breakfast tacos and some coffee, they were at Brando's, sitting in Jace's office as he pulled up the video surveillance footage from the previous night and sipped his hot brew.

"I didn't know you had video in the bar," said Danni.

"I just got it not too long ago. I caught the bartender before you stealing, which is why I kicked his ass to the curb. It's not much of a system. I got the cheap version. It's just one camera on the inside over the entrance, but I can see the register and anyone leaving. I figured that's all I needed." He shoved the last bite of his taco in his mouth and flipped through the screenshots, waiting for the footage to catch up with his clicking. "Damn internet. It's too slow."

"You get a discount on that, too?" she asked.

She'd pulled up a chair and sat next to him, and she sipped her own coffee. Her messy hair was pulled back and loose strands stuck out of the bun, her snug t-shirt had a piece of egg on it, and her wrinkled jeans had a ripped hem. Considering his frantic phone call to her that morning, he suspected she'd hastily dressed and bypassed a shower. The only makeup she appeared to wear was her lipstick, and Jace made an effort not to stare at her lips. Sitting there with him, she looked between him and the screen, and he thought she looked incredibly sexy.

"What?" she asked. "It's a fair question."

"Maybe when I start entertaining celebrities and turning people away at the door, I'll upgrade."

"You know, if you spruced this place up a bit, you might bring in more customers."

"I like it the way it is. It's got character. It fits my personality."

"You just don't want to spend the money."

"That, too."

The video finally loaded and the picture came into focus on the screen. He immediately sucked in a breath, not prepared for reliving the card game. Justin sat at the table, holding cards, along with Henry and Sam. Devyn was holding a drink, sitting next to him. Her hands were not visible, but he recalled where they were. He held his head. "Shit."

"You okay?"

He focused, trying to pull it together. "Yeah. Give me a second." Without thinking, he searched for the stone around his neck the strange woman in the hospital had given him, and held it. It had an unexpected calming effect.

"Take your time." She pointed at the screen. "There he is."

Jace looked up. The card game continued to one side of the screen, and on the other, he saw the bar and Danni standing behind it, just beside the register. At the counter sat a man wearing a hoodie, his head down, holding a phone. A drink was in front of him. The grainy image made it difficult to get a good look at him.

"That's him?"

"Yes. He was there for a while, and rarely looked up."

"What time did he leave?"

"Let me think. Not long before you guys finished playing."

Jace clicked the mouse, fast forwarding the footage, trying to ignore the card game. But he couldn't help but think of Justin and Devyn, sitting there, acting as if they barely knew each other, but planning to fu...

"Stop." Danni pointed. "There."

Jace blinked, and refocused. The man had stood. Jace hit pause and backed it up a few frames. The cursor circled, waiting for the video to catch up.

"Did he ever tell you a name?" he asked.

"No. And he paid in cash. So, no credit card."

"Do you recall him being in there before? Was he familiar?"

She sat back, thinking, and picked the egg off her shirt. "Maybe if I'd seen him in the last few days, but beyond that, I couldn't tell you who'd been here. What about you?"

The cursor twirled and Jace thought back, trying to recall the man sitting at his bar the previous evening. "Hell. Madonna could have been there, and I wouldn't remember."

"You would if she'd sat in your lap."

He offered her a sideways glance.

"Sorry. I didn't mean anything by that."

He looked back at the screen as the image appeared. "Yes, you did. But it's okay. I can handle the truth."

They leaned in as the video ran, and watched as the man in the hoodie stood, pulling something from his pocket.

"That's where he paid me," said Danni.

The man dropped the money, said something, and turned, heading toward the door.

"Look up, you bastard," said Jace, wishing now he'd bought a better surveillance system. The image was black and white and although the man was moving toward the exit, he'd have to get up close and personal for them to get a good look at him. but Jace would settle for any picture of his face that might help in identifying him.

The man neared the door, eyes down, holding his phone. But just as he was about to leave, he looked up, smiled directly at the camera, and waved.

Jace's blood ran cold.

CHAPTER TEN

"How's your head?" asked Daniels. He took a swig of his beer.

Rem rubbed his eyes. "It's better, considering we sat through hours of video looking for customers who might match the description of our perps. How's yours?"

Daniels stretched his neck. "It's still attached. But nothing a home cooked meal and a beer can't cure."

"Marjorie outdid herself. Great spaghetti, and she makes a mean meatball."

"That she does," said Daniels. "You caught her on a good day. Usually we pick something up. We're normally too tired to cook."

"It's got to be hard working full-time and raising a six-month-old, especially with the hours we keep."

"Yeah. It's been fun. Thankfully, J.P. is sleeping better through the night. That helps."

"Kid's sleeping better than I am." Rem picked up his beer, sat back on the couch, and drank from it.

Daniels started to ask a question when Marjorie walked in. He stood. "Leave the dishes. I'll get 'em before I head up."

She patted him on the chest. "They're all yours, chief." She smiled at Rem. "Sorry not to be social, but I'm going to turn in. It's been a long day."

Rem stood. "Thanks for dinner. It was delicious. We could have ordered pizza, though."

"You two eat enough crap. We all needed a good meal. Besides, I like to cook, especially when I have two strong men to hang out with J.P."

"He go down okay?" asked Daniels.

"Like a baby," said Marjorie with a wink. "I think his Uncle Rem tuckered him out."

"Just wait until he can throw a football," said Rem.

"Or eat a taco," said Daniels. "He'll be spending more time at your place than ours."

Rem smiled. "I may have to put him through school."

"How about we get him out of diapers first," said Marjorie.

Rem held up a hand. "Hundred percent agree."

Marjorie raised up and gave Daniels a kiss. "Night, Babe."

"Night," he said. "We won't be long. We've got another long day tomorrow."

"Take your time, just don't wake the baby, or you'll know my wrath."

Daniels grimaced. "Nobody wants that."

"Night, Rem." She waved.

"Goodnight, Marjorie. Thanks again for dinner."

"You're welcome. Next time, you cook the tacos."

He raised his beer. "You're on."

She turned and headed up the stairs to their bedroom.

Daniels sat on the couch and Rem joined him. "You're lucky partner. She's a great lady."

"I'm pretty pleased." He glanced over at his weary partner. "How are things with you and Jill? You haven't said much lately."

Rem picked at his label. "Not much to say."

"Since when? Usually I can't get you to stop talking."

Rem shifted on the couch. "I don't know. Ever since this thing with Rutger, I've been hesitant with how to proceed."

"You said it went well when you visited."

"It did. When I went over the holidays, I wanted to tell her about Madison and Henderson, but she was so intent on enjoying the time with me and the family, I didn't want to ruin it for her. I mean, it was her first Christmas in a while where she could relax."

"I get it. It's a hard time to tell someone bad news. But the holidays are over. Why not tell her now?"

"Her dad's health has declined. He spent some time in the hospital and I know she's worried about him. It's why she hasn't come to visit here since she came back down with me for New Year's weekend. I didn't tell her then, and now I wish I had." He rubbed the side of his head and sighed.

"Is that what's keeping you up at night?"

"Well, it doesn't help. That's for damn sure. And now we've got this Jace situation happening, and you know Rutger's somehow involved. It's like a damn penny that won't go away."

Daniels studied his partner. "Is that it?"

Rem frowned at him. "Isn't that enough?"

Daniels finished his beer and put the bottle on the coffee table. "You haven't been sleeping for a while. This Jace thing just showed up today. I get it you're unsure what to say to Jill. It's not easy. But it's not like you to hold back. You sure as hell have never held back with me. What's really eating you?"

Rem paused. "Anyone ever tell you that you can be annoying some-times?"

Daniels pointed. "That lady that just went upstairs."

"I knew I liked her for a reason." He glanced at Daniels who didn't ease up on his stare. "Fine." He paused and put his beer down. "I'm getting a distinct feeling that Jill will likely stay in Seattle, and I'm not moving either, so…"

Daniels nodded. "Basically, it's not likely to move forward if it stays long distance."

"Not likely, no."

"And you're wondering how much to commit if it's only going to result in a break-up."

He stared at his fingers. "Something like that."

"Do you love her?"

Rem shot a look at him, and Daniels waited.

"Maybe," he whispered. "I don't know. We haven't been together long enough to be sure we're even compatible."

"When she was here in Seattle, and you were together, it was during an incredibly difficult time. If you two don't know each other after that, you never will."

Rem picked at a piece of fringe on the couch. "I suppose."

Daniels wondered. "Are you feeling guilty about Jennie?"

Rem offered a ragged sigh. "I always feel guilty about Jennie. I've learned to live with it."

"Jennie wouldn't want you to be alone."

"Well, tell that to the choir, cause the minister's preachin' isn't helping."

"Have you talked to Jill about it? About moving?"

"It doesn't exactly come up in light conversation." He shook his head. "To be honest, I think she's scared to talk about it too."

"So, how do you know there's a problem if you don't talk about it? For all you know, she may well want to move here, but she's worried about what you think, or she's afraid it will push you away."

"Why would it push me away?"

"Exactly. How do you know until you ask?"

Rem groaned and ran his hands through his hair. "God, that annoying factor you have is really...well...way more annoying than I thought."

"It's a skill, honed over many years, plus I learned a lot from my partner. He's pretty good at it, too."

Rem offered him a sideways glance, but didn't say anything.

"You're just scared. Perfectly normal. But you better rip that bandage off or you'll be sitting here three years from now wondering why you didn't do it sooner."

Rem picked up his beer and drained it.

"Let me show you. I'll ask a scary question that's been on my mind."

Rem's eyes widened and he put his bottle down. "What's that?"

"Are you thinking of leaving? Moving away? Going to Seattle?"

Rem stared. He opened his mouth, and seemed uncertain of what to say. "Truth?" he finally said.

"I'm not expecting you to lie."

"I've considered it. But every time I do, I get this hard knot in my gut. As much as I think it would be nice to find someone, get married, have a few kids, I don't know if I can sacrifice my life here to do it. I have roots here. I have you, and family, and my work. I don't want to leave that. I'm happy, and until I'm sure that leaving will mean I can be happier elsewhere, I have no plans to go to Seattle."

Daniels nodded. "If that time ever comes, you know I won't stop you."

Rem chuckled softly. "I know you wouldn't. Just like I wouldn't stop you." He cocked his head up the stairs. "I know you worry about your family and this job. It's tough to maintain them both and stay sane. You know if you ever decide to pursue another calling, you'll have my support."

Daniels felt an unexpected tightness well up in his throat. He should have suspected his partner would pick up on his own fears. "See. Now who's being annoying?"

"You learned from the best."

"Didn't I though?" Daniels eyed the stairs, thinking of Marjorie and J.P. sleeping above. "I'd be lying if I said I hadn't thought about it, but Lozano's done it."

"At the cost of two marriages," said Rem.

Daniels flung an arm over the back of the sofa. "I know. The odds aren't good, but I guess I feel the same way you do. I'm happy, and if I ever find an opportunity where I might be happier, then I'll take it, but for now…" He sighed. "I think you're stuck with me."

Rem smiled wearily. "We're right back where we started, then."

"Not really. We talked. We haven't done that in a while."

"No. I guess we haven't." He stifled a yawn. "Anything else you want to tell me before this touching moment ends and I go home and hit the hay, so we can wake up and go chase bad guys again tomorrow?"

Daniels scratched his jaw. "Actually, yes. I was wondering if you'd go with me to the jewelry store tomorrow. I think I found an engagement ring for Marjorie."

Rem froze for a second before his eyes lit up and he smiled. "I'd be honored, partner. That's fantastic. Does she know?"

"She might suspect. She made a comment a while back when she saw the ring in the window. I figure it's now or never. Plus, I had to save up some money."

"I'm happy for you. She's going to be thrilled. I can't wait till you pop the question."

"Of course, I'm expecting you to be best man. I'd ask J.P., but he might poop when I ask for the ring."

"I promise. No pooping during the ceremony. And you're damn straight I'm best man. I'll fight J.P. for it if I have to."

"Maybe when he can stand on his own. We'll see what Marjorie says."

Rem smiled. "This is great news, Daniels. We needed it. You deserve all the happiness in the world."

"Thanks. I appreciate it."

Daniels' cell rang and vibrated on the coffee table. "Who's calling now?" He picked it up and read the display. "It's Lozano."

Rem's smile faded. "That can't be good."

Daniels picked up the call. "Cap? What's up?"

He listened as Lozano filled him in, his face falling. "You're kidding."

Rem waited. "What? What is it?"

"They're okay?" He nodded. "Yes. Whatever you need. We'll be there." He hung up.

"What the hell is going on?" asked Rem.

"Mel and Garcia. Somebody jumped 'em leaving a bar tonight. They're in the hospital. Mel's beat up pretty bad and Garcia has stitches and a concussion. They'll be laid up a while."

Rem stood. "Are you joking? Who would do that?"

Daniels stood, too, putting his phone in his pocket. "Lozano's got somebody on it already."

"What about us? What do we do? Sit around and twiddle our thumbs?"

"Nope. Lozano gave us a new case. Jace Marlon. As of now, it's all ours." He smacked Rem on the shoulder. "Feel like finding Rutger, partner?"

CHAPTER ELEVEN

Danni stomped into her apartment, almost slamming the door behind her. She didn't want to wake the neighbor. Mr. Miller went to bed early and was a light sleeper; at least that's what he'd told her the few times he'd knocked on her door to tell her the music or TV was too loud.

Frustrated, she slid off her jacket and threw it on the couch. Seymour trotted out of her room and meowed, encircling her legs. She sat on the carpet and petted him, trying to think.

Jace had known that man on the video. He'd frozen when the stranger had looked up and waved. Danni had seen it. But Jace had played it off, saying that he had no idea who the man was, and that he hadn't frozen, but was studying the screen. It was absurd.

Danni had tried to talk to him about it, but he wouldn't engage. He'd turned sullen and moody, saying he needed to get some work done. His insistence on finding the guy had shifted, and she suspected he was looking for a way to get rid of her.

She'd refused to leave, fearful he planned to find the mystery man on his own and get killed in the process. He'd yelled and then she'd yelled, and then Simon had called. Then Jace wanted to call Henry in case he hadn't heard what happened. By then it was time for her shift to start, and he'd jumped at that as a reason to get her out of the office.

Danni petted Seymour, still angry that Jace had kept the bar open. She knew part of it was distraction. He needed to keep busy, and part of it was to keep Danni out of his hair.

Thankfully, he'd had stayed in his office most of the night, so Danni had known he wasn't hunting down a killer. She'd threatened to call the cops if he'd left, which started another shouting match. Thinking about it now, she cursed. Mad at herself and mad at him, she stood and went into the kitchen, grabbing a can of cat food and opening it. Seymore purred at her ankles, and she scooped some out and put it on his dish on the floor. Seymour ate vigorously, and her own stomach growled. She'd missed dinner. The uneaten Taco del Fuego beckoned.

She pulled out her cell and considered calling the cops for the millionth time. They should know what they'd seen on the video. They could find the guy. But Jace had asked for time. Not yet, he'd said. Part of her wondered if he'd kept the bar open to see if the man would return. She had to admit, every time the bar door opened, she'd looked over with a little anxiety, but he hadn't shown. What if he had returned? What would she have done?

Stepping over the cat, she considered warming her taco, sat at her laptop and opened her email, straightening as a new one appeared in her inbox. It was from *BrotherlyLove.* Her heart thumped.

I'm disappointed, Daisy. I paid for a reading from you and have not heard back. I realize you have a lot to deal with, but I'd expected at least an acknowledgement from you. It's unwise to make an angry person angrier. I'll practice patience though, and grant you twenty-four more hours. Do your best not to keep me waiting.

She stared at the email, much like Jace had stared at the video. Something in her thudding heart told her that this was from the man at the bar. The man Jace knew but wouldn't admit he knew. Was he the killer?

She reached for her cell, but stopped before dialing. Who should she call? The cops? Jace? She looked back at the screen. What did she really have anyway? An email request for a tarot reading. He hadn't admitted to any crimes, but he knew her real name, which told her he'd been in the bar the previous night. Odds were, it was the man in the video.

Her finger hovered over the buttons of the phone. Dial or not dial? What would Jace be able to do? Nothing. She should call the police.

But then she had a thought. Why not do the reading? It couldn't hurt and she could choose whether to respond after she pulled the cards. No harm in that, right? Besides, she had to admit, she was curious about what the cards would say. Maybe he was harmless, and the cards would reveal her concerns were unnecessary.

She reached over, grabbed a Rider Waite deck she kept on the table and began to shuffle.

**

Jace drifted. Clouds surrounded him, and he couldn't see a thing. When he reached out a hand, the fog swirled around it. His heart skipped and a twinge of fear made him swallow. He had no sense of location.

Deciding he couldn't stand there forever, he took a step, having no idea where he was going. He took slow deliberate breaths, fighting off his welling panic.

A figure began to take shape in the mist. At first, it was only a silhouette, but then it became more defined, and he saw it was a woman. A second figure appeared, and it also took shape, and stood beside the first figure. Another woman. Their faces were difficult to make out and they were too far away to reach, but Jace tried. He walked toward them in the fog, feeling as if he knew them and that they were important to find; they held the answers he sought.

He moved faster and heard his name called. *Jace.* It was whispered and he couldn't discern the direction of the voice. He picked up speed and began to run, but the women were always the same distance away. *Jace.* The whisper came again.

Another figure appeared. A male. To his right. He sensed the danger immediately. The women were in trouble. He had to hurry. Sprinting, he raced through the murkiness, feeling his fear and worry rise, desperate to reach the women first.

The figure encroached on the female figures. They stood oblivious to the man who Jace knew would hurt them. He called out, screamed, but the man moved fast, and he reached them, but the women faded away in the mist. A laugh erupted from the fog. An evil, deep, menacing cackle. Jace stopped and the man turned, stepping forward, and the mist around his face thinned.

The panic rose, fast and furious, and Jace wanted to run, but he couldn't make himself move. The man moved closer and terror constricted Jace's throat, and the air around him became thick and hard to breathe.

The mist thinned more and the man's face took shape as the fog around him evaporated. He leered, satisfied with Jace's fear. Reaching out, he touched Jace on the chest, and a cold tendril of ice hit Jace's sternum, traveling through his torso and into his arms and legs. He couldn't move and he couldn't speak.

Fog swirled. The man held his gaze, laughed that evil laugh, and took hold of the necklace around Jace's neck. It was the piece of moldavite the woman in the hospital had given him. Rubbing the stone between his fingers, he sneered, and yanked the stone. The cord snapped, and the man, still watching Jace, spoke two words. *Hello, brother.*

Jace startled awake, breathing hard, sweat dripping down his neck. He blinked, trying to get his bearings, and sat up. He was on the couch in his office. After little sleep the previous night, he'd dozed off. Checking his watch, he saw it wasn't as late as he thought. Danni had only left an hour earlier at closing and he couldn't have been sleeping more than thirty or forty minutes. Holding his head, he recalled the dream. *Shit.* It had been a bad one and he tried to catch his breath.

This time the dream had been different though. This time, he'd clearly seen the man's face.

He stood on wobbly legs, but made it to his desk, where he wiggled the mouse on the computer and the screen came to life. He hit a few buttons, accessing the video footage on his surveillance from the previous night. He'd saved it on his desktop and the picture came into view. He hit play and there was the grainy image of the man at the bar. Jace watched as he paid Danni, said something, and turned to leave. Approaching the exit, he looked up, smiled and waved. Jace's breath caught, and the urge to scream returned.

The man in the video was the man in his dreams.

CHAPTER TWELVE

Danni stared at the cards, interpreting the reading. She'd pulled six cards, two for his goal, two for his approach and two for the outcome. For the goal, she'd pulled the Chariot reversed and the Devil reversed. Both Major Arcana cards which indicated long-term issues. The Chariot in reverse indicated a troubled path and the Devil reversed indicated being mired in a damaged place and being motivated by base instincts. So far, not a good start.

The next two cards were for *BrotherlyLove*'s approach. They were the Moon and the King of Swords in reverse. The Moon represented intuition and the subconscious, but also an element of fear. It could reflect bad intentions and secrets. The King of Swords in reverse indicated an expert in his field abusing his power. Danni wondered what that could mean. He'd mentioned abilities. Is that what he was referring to?

The next two cards were the Wheel of Fortune and Justice. These represented the outcome. The Wheel of Fortune meant that the outcome could not yet be known until other things fell into place, and also suggested fate and karma would play a role. Danni assumed that meant that someone would get what they deserved. Did that mean the questioner or someone else? Justice also indicated a sort of karma and that *BrotherlyLove*'s issue would work out as it was supposed to.

Danni studied the cards, trying to understand them. She reread his question, and tried to intuitively apply the meanings. tarot was not just about reading the cards, but trusting your gut to tell you the message they were offering. She decided to pull two more cards to gain more clarification. One for a summary and one for the questioner and his current state. She pulled the Four of Swords and the Magician in reverse.

The Four of Swords represented thinking and planning, so he definitely had some ideas in mind and planned to put them into action. The Magician sent a flutter of anxiety through her. It meant he had the power and skills, and intended to use them even if it meant in a harmful, unfocused way. Was that his intention?

Overall, the cards depicted a man with the potential to use his supposed abilities in a way that could harm others, but that he felt justified in his actions. He'd told her he was angry and she could see it in the cards. This man wanted revenge. If she were to guess, she'd say he'd had a troubled past, and he blamed others for it.

What did that have to do with Jace though? And was this person responsible for Justin's death? Was he out to hurt Jace or did he believe he was helping him?

The outcome cards ultimately suggested change and that everything would work itself out. But what did that mean to *BrotherlyLove*? If his intentions were evil, that didn't bode well for those involved. If he'd killed Justin, did he plan to kill again? Goosebumps popped out on her skin.

Danni wondered what to do next. This reading told her that *BrotherlyLove* was dangerous. But how far should she take this? It was just a tarot reading. The police couldn't arrest someone based on a tarot reading. And she had no proof that this was from the man in the bar, other than he'd used her real name.

Her other option was to respond to him, and tell him the results. Engage him and draw him out. Maybe she could get him to reveal something more. Is that what he wanted? Or would she be making herself a target? He was already mad that she'd delayed her response. Could she be putting herself at risk for not responding?

Studying the cards, she decided to do as Jace requested and give him some time. She'd answer *BrotherlyLove* and tell him what the cards had revealed, and then she'd wait and see. With any luck, *BrotherlyLove* would tip his hand, and then she'd have something to show the police. She ignored the warning bells in her head, telling her she could also be attracting more attention from a potential murderer.

Deciding to take the bull by the horns, she opened her email, hit the reply button to *BrotherlyLove*, and started to type.

CHAPTER THIRTEEN

Rem followed the nurse into the hospital room. The doctor had allowed them five minutes with Devyn Palmer who'd regained consciousness, but was still in ICU. A police officer had been stationed in the hallway outside her room to ensure her safety since she was the only potential witness to her attack and Justin Tenley's murder.

Daniels followed him and they went to her bedside. An array of machines surrounded her, and she had an oxygen tube in her nose. Her wild blonde hair fanned across the pillow, and without the oxygen, she would have looked to be peacefully sleeping.

"Miss Palmer?" asked the nurse, whose name tag read "Rita."

Devyn's eyes fluttered and opened and her gaze was briefly unfocused before she noticed the nurse and then the two men standing by her bed.

"Cops?" she whispered.

"They're here to ask you a few questions. Are you strong enough?" asked Rita.

Devyn swallowed. "Water," she said.

The nurse picked up a bottle with a straw and offered a sip to Devyn. "Just answer a few questions, and no more. You need to rest."

Devyn nodded after drinking the water.

"Miss Palmer?" asked Rem.

She eyed him with intense blue eyes.

He offered his badge. "I'm Detective Remalla and this is my partner, Detective Daniels."

Daniels showed his badge.

Rem tucked his badge back in his pocket. "We know you've been through a lot, but we need to ask about what happened to you."

Devyn's face held a hazy look and Rem suspected she was on some good drugs. "Can you answer some questions?" he asked.

She whispered. "Yes."

"Can you tell us what happened? Do you know who did this?" asked Daniels.

She blinked weary eyes. "I don't know." Her voice became stronger. "It was so fast."

"What did you see?" asked Daniels.

She looked up at the ceiling and her eyes welled up.

"Take your time," said Rem.

"I got up."

"From bed?" asked Rem.

"Yes. It was late, or early. Not sure. I...I..." She squinted. "I heard something."

"What did you hear?" asked Daniels.

"A thump, something falling. I sat up, and Justin wasn't there." She shut her eyes. "Justin," she whispered. "Does Jace know?"

"He does," said Rem. "He found you. Called the police. Probably saved your life."

"Oh, God." She moaned and a tear slid from her eye. "Justin? He found Justin, too?"

"He did," said Rem.

"Is Justin—" She opened her eyes. "Is he dead?"

Rem eyed Daniels. "He is. He died at the scene."

"No," she said. "I didn't know."

"I'm sorry, ma'am. I know it's hard to hear. That's why it's so important to find out what you know," said Daniels.

She cried harder. "I don't know anything. I heard a noise. I sat up and listened. It sounded like a struggle. It scared me. I got up, put my robe on, but…but…" Her face went pale and she gripped the sheets.

"But, what?" asked Rem.

"There was someone there."

"Did you see him?" asked Daniels.

"He came out of nowhere, like he'd been watching me." Her breathing hitched and her breath caught. "I tried to push away, but something sharp hit me, and I…I…fell. I couldn't stand up."

"Did you see his face? Did he say anything?" asked Rem.

The tears fell harder and her breathing came in short gasps. "I'm sorry. I'm so sorry." She shook her head from side to side. "I lied to Jace. I wanted to tell him, but…but…I couldn't. He knew though. He knew."

Rem didn't understand. "Who knew? Jace knew about you and Justin?"

She groaned. "No. No. The man in the room. He knew. He said something." Her crying intensified and a monitor began to beep by the side of her bed.

Rita stepped up. "That's it for now, gentlemen. She's upset. You two will have to come back tomorrow and talk to her when she's stronger."

Rem stayed beside the bed, ignoring Rita. He leaned closer to Devyn. "What did he say? The man who hurt you?"

"Officer, please," said Rita.

"We're leaving," said Daniels. "We just need this one question, and we'll go."

Devyn had the sheets in a death grip and she stared off, tears sliding down her cheeks as she cried. "He said…'I'm doing this for Jace. You're just like all the rest. I should keep you alive to tell him you're sorry. He deserves that.'" Her breath hitched again. "And he's right." Her eyes clenched shut. "I'm so, so sorry." Sobs erupted and the beeping picked up its pace.

"That's it," said Rita. "You need to go." She moved to the side of the bed and Rem stepped back, along with Daniels.

"Thank you, Devyn," said Daniels.

Rem walked to the door. "Get some rest."

They walked out into the hallway and stopped. Rem stood with his back to the room. "Well, what do you think?"

Daniels rubbed his eyes. "I'm not sure. She said she heard something. Like a scuffle. You think she heard Justin being attacked?"

"How's that possible? By her account, the guy was in the room with her, so how is Justin being attacked at the same time?"

"Maybe she didn't hear the attack. Maybe she heard something else. Maybe Justin was still alive, and tried to get up. Knocked something over."

Rem shot out a thumb. "Drugs she's on, there's no telling. She could be remembering a dream about the latest movie she saw."

"Maybe. What do you think about what he told her?"

"Guy obviously knew what she and Justin were up to."

"And knew that Justin and Jace were friends."

Rem nodded. "Well, we know it wasn't Jace. According to Lozano, before Garcia and Mel got jumped last night, they reviewed the video from Justin's lobby and the 911 call and they corroborate Jace's story. He didn't arrive until after Justin was dead."

Daniels pointed. "We need to review that video ourselves. You know who we need to look for."

Rem hooked his thumbs in his belt loops. "A guy who looks suspiciously like a young Rutger Hauer?"

"Exactly."

"You thinkin' that's who it is?" asked Rem.

"You heard what he said to Jace on the phone. It's pretty likely. Who else could it be?"

Rem shrugged. "No idea. We need to talk to Jace ourselves. And Danni, the bartender. Mel said she took off after we left the room. They didn't get a chance to finish the interview."

"She was about to tell us something when we got pulled out, wasn't she? Something about a man she saw?"

"I don't know, but it's time to find out. You feel like checking out Brando's?"

Daniels eyes widened. "A surprise visit?"

"Sometimes those work the best."

"Works for me. Let's stop by Mel and Garcia's rooms on the way out. Check in on them."

"Garcia's supposed to get released today," said Rem. "Mel hopefully tomorrow."

Daniels walked toward the elevator and Rem followed. "Do you recall what Garcia said last night after we visited? He didn't say much about who jumped them in the alley."

"I noticed. You think that was strange, because I sure did."

"It's not like Garcia to be tight-lipped," said Daniels. They stopped at the elevator and Daniels punched the button. "You suspect he knows who it is? And wants to do something about it? Guy worked Mel over pretty good."

Rem frowned. "Well, if that were me, I know how'd I feel. I'd want to kick some ass."

"I hear you, and I wouldn't blame him, but there's another scenario we should consider."

"What's that?"

Daniels looked up and down the hall. "You know what happened to us when we encountered Rutger. We couldn't exactly put it in a report."

Rem held his breath. "You think Rutger did this?"

The elevator dinged and the doors opened. They stepped in and the doors closed. "Think about it," said Daniels, hitting the button to the floor they wanted. "If this is the Jace that Rutger mentioned to us back up at Secret Lake, he may have a reason to want us on this case. We were there when Jill and Madison had their crises. If he's sticking to a pattern here, why wouldn't he want us on this one, too?"

"So Rutger takes out Mel and Garcia, knowing Lozano will give this case to us?"

"Makes sense."

"Shit. That's crazy. He's taking it to a whole other level now."

"But that would explain how he took down two police officers without either of them laying a hand on him. He used those...those...you know."

The elevator slowed. "Extra abilities? Yeah. I know." Rem nodded. "It's hard to forget."

The doors opened. "There is something different with this though," said Daniels.

"What's that?"

Stepping off the elevator, Daniels turned down the hall. "With Jill, we had the Makeup Artist, with Madison Vickers, we also had Karl Scott's death. This time though, there's just Justin and Devyn. There's nobody else to pin this on."

"Then maybe it's time we find this guy and lay the blame where it's due. Sound like a plan?" Rem eyed the hospital doors, looking for the right room.

"Provided we can catch him."

"He wants us on this for a reason. This is leading somewhere. Maybe he wants to get caught, and he wants us to catch him."

Daniels paused in the hallway as an elderly woman wheeled past them in a wheelchair. "I like your cautious optimism."

"It's one of my strengths."

"Along with your paranoid pessimism?"

"That, too. It serves me well."

"How does that work?"

"When we encounter men who move things with their minds, I'm not surprised. I'm prepared."

"Good to know. I'll remember that next time Rutger shows. You can tackle him first."

"If we find him, I'll be on him like butter on toast. He raises those hands; I'll shoot first and ask questions later."

"It's hard to get answers from someone when they're dead."

"It's hard to solve a case when you're dead, too."

Daniels opened his mouth to speak, and paused. "You'd think he'd take it that far?"

"Your theory is he took out Mel and Garcia. If he did that—"

"It's a big jump from assault to murder."

Rem moved out of the way of a passing nurse. "Something tells me that when Rutger's done, he's taking everyone with him, and that includes us."

"You just said you think he wants us to catch him. Now you think he plans to kill us too?"

"That's my paranoid pessimism kicking in."

"I prefer your cautious optimism."

"Me, too, but sadly, the pessimism typically wins."

"Sucks for me."

"Sucks for me, too."

A heavy-set older woman with brown hair and silver roots wearing a flowery dress walked between them. "Excuse me, dears," she said, stopping in the hallway. "So sorry." She opened her large, yellow fabric purse, and dug through it. "Do either of you have a piece of gum? I had some coffee and I can't get the awful taste out of my mouth."

"No, ma'am. Sorry," said Daniels. His eyes narrowed.

"Nope. No gum," said Rem. He watched her pilfer through her purse and something nudged at him.

"Ah, here it is." She pulled out a pack of gum. She smiled at Rem and her eyes creased at the edges. She wore no makeup, and her brown eyes twinkled. "I hate when you can't see something that's right in front of you. Isn't that bothersome?"

"I think we know you," said Daniels, pointing.

The nudge became a shove, and Rem's brain backtracked. He thought of the Makeup Artist and the witness who'd provided the description. "Sonia Vandermere?" he asked.

"Why, yes," she said. "Do I know…wait a minute." She looked between the two of them. "Errol Flynn and Steve McQueen?"

Rem chuckled at the names. She'd compared the two of them to the actors when they'd met during the Makeup Artist case. "Actually, it's Detectives Remalla and Daniels."

"Oh, poo." She closed her purse and slipped the handle over her shoulder. "Such formalities. I prefer Flynn and McQueen. How's that handsome Captain of yours?"

"He's fine, ma'am," said Daniels. He shot a glance at Rem. "What brings you to this hospital?"

"Oh, my poor mother had hip replacement surgery. I was just checking in on her. Thankfully, she'll be just fine. I was just heading to the cafeteria to get something to eat. Would you two like to join me?"

"Uh, no, thanks," said Rem. "We're visiting some friends, and we're working on a case right now."

Her face dropped. "I hope nothing too serious."

Rem rubbed his neck. Something about this woman's appearance nagged at him, but he couldn't place what was bugging him. "Well, we work robbery/homicide, so it tends to be serious."

"Oh, you poor dears. I can imagine. Here…" She opened her purse again, searched through it and pulled out a small vial. "I want you to have this. It's sandalwood oil. It will help you to stay calm and improve your focus. Plus, it smells wonderful on a man, especially handsome ones." She lowered her voice. "That's just between you and me though."

Daniels held up a palm. "That's very kind, but…"

Sonia continued. "Just put some on your pulse points and the back of your neck, and your third eye if you prefer. It will do wonders."

"Third eye?" asked Daniels.

Rem pointed to the area between his brows.

"Oh, yeah," said Daniels. "Listen, that's very…"

"We'll take it," said Rem. "Thanks, Sonia." He took the vial and held it.

"You're very welcome, dear."

Daniels shook his head.

"Well, I should be going. I need to get back to Mom before she starts to wonder where I've gone. She can get a little ditzy sometimes. You know how that goes."

"Yes, ma'am. Nice to see you again," said Daniels.

"Hope your mom is better soon," said Rem, still wondering what was nagging at him.

Sonia took a few steps but turned back. "You say hi to Jill for me. Tell her to hold on to that necklace I gave her. She'll be needing it." She looked at Daniels. "And I hope you're enjoying fatherhood. It looks like it's agreeing with you."

She smiled and headed down the hallway, waving.

Rem and Daniels stared at each other; their mouths open.

"How did she—?" asked Daniels, pointing.

Rem shook his head. "Did she know about me and Jill?"

"How did she know about J.P.?"

"What the hell is going on here?" asked Rem. The nagging sensation suddenly made sense and he snapped his fingers. "That's what's bugging me."

Daniels watched Sonia get on the elevator. "What? The fact that she never actually put any gum in her mouth?"

"No. The fact that we saw her at Secret Lake."

"What? When?"

"At the jail. When we went to see Madison to question her. Remember? She was leaving as we were entering. She was wearing a sunflower dress. I knew I recognized her."

They stood for a second, Rem's mind clicking as he knew Daniels' was.

Daniels face fell. "How much you want to bet if we checked with the nurses' station, that there's no patient here who has had a recent hip replacement?"

Rem glanced down the hall. Sonia had entered the elevator.

"I'll take that bet, provided you want to buy some swamp land in Texas."

Daniels started walking toward the elevator, then picked up his pace. "Hold the elevator."

Rem broke into a run, and Daniels joined him. They dodged a nurse carrying a trey and a candy striper with her cart of magazines, but it was too late. As they reached the elevator, the doors had closed. Sonia was gone.

CHAPTER FOURTEEN

Jace opened the front door to Brando's. After the dream and viewing the video, he'd needed to get away and think. He'd gone home to shower and change and managed a few hours of sleep, then got up, jumped on his motorcycle and just drove. It was early and the light traffic offered a straight shot out of the city and into the hills, where the road twisted and turned, and the cement and lights gave way to trees, hills and large homes on wooded lots. He'd found a secluded overlook that had a view of the city and he'd stopped and sat on the bench, wondering what to do next.

His best friend, who'd been cheating on him with his girlfriend, had been found murdered, and his girlfriend had almost died too. He'd received an ominous phone call, likely from the killer, who'd made Justin apologize to him, before he'd sliced his throat open. And then the killer had spoken to him, saying he'd done it for him.

Jace stared out over the city as the morning dawned and he watched the city come alive. How did life go on as usual? Shouldn't everything stop for a while and take notice? Didn't anybody care?

He thought of the man in the video. The man who'd been sitting in his bar during the card game. The same man who'd appeared in his dreams, night after night, for the past five months. How was that possible? Did his subconscious mind somehow know who this man was and why he'd appeared? Had that man killed Justin, and almost Devyn?

He thought of Devyn and the doctor's remarks. *It was almost as if she was partially healed.* Looking at his hands, he recalled placing them on Devyn, staunching the flow of blood as it seeped through his fingers. What if...? Shutting his eyes, a memory flared from when he was a child. A sick dog. What was his name? Chester. Near death. Jace desperate. Chester had been a rare connection in a solitary world. Jace couldn't lose him. He'd laid his hands on the dog, head down and crying, when he'd felt something. A tingle. Heat. His palms burning. Jace had pulled his hands back, not understanding, but the dog had looked up, eyes bright and shiny. The vet never could explain it. Chester had lived two more years than he should have.

Then, three years ago. He and Justin had been out riding. Justin's bike had hit an oily patch and he'd gone sliding. Scraped up his arm and busted his knee. Jace recalled Justin's grimace of pain and cursing. Jace had held it, Justin yelling, telling him to back off, but then the tingles, and the heat, and Justin had relaxed, the pain subsiding.

They'd ridden back together, the doctor telling Justin it was only a bad bruise, but Jace had known it had been much worse.

Jace laced his fingers together, trying to make sense of it all. Surely it was just the heat of the moment. Strange things happened some times. No big deal. Except it was a big deal. Jace couldn't bring himself to think, much less say, that maybe he'd had some role in healing his dog and Justin, and now Devyn. Could that be possible?

His thoughts returned to the man in the video. Something nudged at him that this man knew something about Jace, and that's why he was here and in his dreams. But did he want to help Jace, or hurt him?

And the two women, who were they? He'd felt tremendously protective of them, although he had no idea who they were.

After taking a deep breath, he expelled it, wishing he had more answers and frustrated he had none. Should he go to the police?

Thinking of Danni, he realized he probably wouldn't have a choice. She knew about the man at the bar, and she'd seen him. It had taken loads of rationalizing peppered with some yelling to get her to hold off from contacting the cops. But that wouldn't last. She'd likely talk to them today. Not that it would matter. They didn't know the guy's name or anything about him. All they had was a grainy image and the fact that he'd been there during the card game. It meant almost nothing.

Once the sun was fully up, he'd driven back into the city, stopped to get breakfast, and went back to his apartment, where he'd showered again and changed. The mail was piled up on the floor and the dishes in the sink remained unwashed. He spent more time at the bar than his own place. He'd never been used to a stable home life and not much had changed. It wasn't like him to get attached to things.

Now, back at the bar, he pushed on the door, and closed it behind him. He wouldn't open for a few more hours, and Danni would arrive in a couple, assuming she didn't quit on him. Considering what had happened and their exchange the previous day, he wouldn't be surprised if she did. One thing he'd realized though, was she didn't scare easy, was resilient, and wasn't the least afraid of him. Jace had the benefit of his size and strength and had used it to his advantage many times. Intimidation worked wonders. But it didn't with Danni, and it frustrated the hell out of him. But it made her unique, and he liked that. Not many women were unique. At least not in his experience.

Walking into the office, he threw his backpack onto the couch, and stopped when he approached his desk. An envelope was propped up on the screen of his computer.

An ice-cold tendril slid down his spine. It had not been there when he'd left. He looked around the office, then walked to the door and eyed the bar. It was quiet. No one was there.

He returned to the desk and sat, picking up the envelope. Nothing was written on the outside. Without thinking, he ripped it open. Inside was a Tarot card. The roman numerals for the number eleven were at the top, and a woman sat on a throne between two pillars, wearing a crown and holding a sword. The word "Justice" was below. And written along one of the pillars in black marker were the words *I did it for you.*

**

Danni unlocked the door to the bar and entered. They opened in two hours and she'd arrived early because she'd needed to talk to Jace. She knew he'd be there because he was always there.

Closing the door, she looked around. It was the same as before except there was a liquor bottle on the counter with a shot glass beside it.

She threw her jacket and purse into a chair and walked up the bar. "Jace?" She picked up the glass and saw it was wet. Someone had used it.

"Back here," she heard.

She put the glass down and headed back toward the office. Jace sat at his desk, studying his laptop. Another shot glass sat by the monitor, half-full. "Starting early this morning?" she asked.

He flipped off the monitor, picked up the glass and drained it. "Yup," he said, smacking the glass back on the table.

She narrowed her eyes. "Are you drunk?"

He belched. "Nope."

"Yes, you are. How long have you been drinking?"

He swiveled in his chair toward her. "Since I was sixteen, give or take a couple years."

"What's the matter?" Since she'd known him, she'd never seen him drink in the middle of the day.

He chuckled. "What isn't the matter?" Sitting back, he pondered the ceiling. "My friend's dead, my girlfriend almost died. They were sleeping together. The cops think I did it. I may be able to heal people. A strange woman in the hospital gives me a necklace, which is nice, but really? What's that all about? A man who haunts my dreams frequents my bar, and may be the actual killer. The killer told me he did it for me, so he must know me in some way. But how?" He threw out his hands and looked back at her. "You see what I'm dealing with here? It's a lot of shit."

Danni stared back. "What exactly are you drinking?"

Jace opened a drawer and pulled out a bottle. "Single malt scotch." He wiggled the half-empty bottle and smiled. "It used to be full."

"Maybe you should slow down."

"I should maybe do a lot of things, but I rarely do, so why start now?" He opened the bottle and refilled the shot glass on the desk.

"Jace, you've had enough. This isn't helping."

"I think it's helping great." He recapped the bottle and put it back in the drawer. "Why are you here?"

"I work here."

"Not for another hour, you don't."

"I need to talk to you about something."

He traced a finger around the rim of the glass. "And what's that?" He pointed a finger. "Oh, wait. Don't tell me. Going to the cops?"

She crossed her arms and leaned on the door frame. "Well, yes, actually. I think I may have some new information."

He glanced over and raised a brow. "I bet you do."

Danni sensed he was more than drunk. He was angry. "Excuse me?"

"You heard me." He picked up the glass and shot it back. "This innocence act is wearing. Don't you think?" He put the glass back on the desk.

"Innocence? You're not making any sense."

"You're sure about that?" He leaned back in his seat, but tipped back too far. His legs flew up and he fell backward. "Shit."

Danni made no move to help him. "You're an ugly drunk. Plus, maybe you better not sit and drink. You're a danger to yourself."

He struggled to stand, but eventually got to his feet. Weaving, he sat on the couch, rubbing his face. "I'm not the danger here. I'm finally starting to figure that out."

She scowled. "What are you saying? That I am?"

His face hardened. "I find it interesting that you showed up two months ago, and all this shit started happening."

"Shit? What shit? This shit happened two days ago. Are you blaming me?" She righted the chair and stood over him. "What? You think I got a job here, to get paid minimum wage, while I sit back and watch you flaunt yourself with an insecure, tacky and mean woman who never hid her dislike of me, while you crack dumb jokes, and run a bar that loses more money than it's worth, so I can devise this mastermind plan to murder your best friend, who happens to be sleeping with this same tasteless woman? Well, call me clever. I'm a regular criminal master-mind."

He shoved himself up from the sofa. "Stop talking about her like that."

"What, did I hit a nerve? How about you stop talking like an idiot? Or is that too big of a jump for you?"

His face turned red. "It's so easy for you to make light of this, isn't it? You stand there, all high and mighty, as if reading pretty cards with pictures on them makes you something special, when your pathetic existence is just as sad and tacky as Devyn's. You just like to pretend you're laid back and cool, when we both know you're just as screwed up as everyone else. Your dad made sure of that."

Danni's heart slammed into her chest and her anger erupted. "You son-of-a-bitch."

"Call me whatever you want, but I saw the card you left me. I know what you did."

"I didn't do anything," she screamed at him.

He walked to the desk and yanked out an envelope from the top drawer. "This. This is what you did."

She shot out a hand. "What? It's an envelope. Not a gun, which is good right now, cause I kind of want to kill you."

"Is that your plan? Kill everyone I love and then kill me?"

Danni shook her head. "What in the hell is the matter with you? What's in that scotch? Meth? Magic Mushrooms?"

"Don't be stupid."

"Me?" She held her hand to her chest. "You want to see stupid? I'll show you stupid." She walked past him, almost shoving him, and went to the drawer. She yanked it open, grabbed the scotch, and poured it into the shot glass to the brim. "Here you go, asshole." She turned toward him and flung the contents into his face. He yelped and wiped at his face. "How's that for stupid?" She refilled the glass. "Should I go for two?"

"Put that down," he yelled.

"What are you going to do, big guy?" She waved the bottle in his face. "Call the cops? Oh, wait. We can't do that, because Mr. Tough Dude here is going to solve the crime all by himself. And what did he come up with? The bartender did it. That's one for the books. You might as well call the press, too."

"I know what you did." He blotted his face with his sleeve and walked up to her. "I may not be able to prove it, but the cops will. And when I'm done, you'll be reading cards for your burly cellmate, wishing you'd appreciated this crappy job and your crappy boss."

Staring up at his hard and shiny eyes, she put the bottle and the shot glass down, and reached for the cell in her pocket. "Call 'em then, Ranger Rick. And when they laugh you out of the building, you can find yourself a new bartender, because I quit." She yelled the word in his face.

He stood there, breathing heavily, as she did the same, neither speaking.

A knock sounded at the door, and she looked over, finding two men. She recognized them from the police station. The dark-haired one spoke. "No need to call the cops, because guess what?" He held out his badge. "Looks like we're already here."

The blonde one cocked his head. "Did we come at a bad time?"

CHAPTER FIFTEEN

Daniels paused, waiting for an answer. Rem gestured with his hand. "You mind if we come in?"

Jace huffed. "Looks like you already have."

"We heard yelling. Thought we might be needed," said Daniels. Flashing his badge, he introduced himself and Rem, and looked at Danni. "Are we needed?"

"Ha," said Jace. "What are you asking her for? She's the one you need to arrest."

Danni's eyes widened. "You honestly think I did this? God. Who raised you? Wolves?"

Jace stiffened and got in her face. "Watch your mouth, Eldridge, or I'll show you who raised me, and we'll both end up behind bars."

"Whoa, whoa, whoa," said Rem, stepping forward. "Let's take it easy here."

"What are you going to do? Are you threatening me?" yelled Danni. She grabbed the filled shot glass from the desk and tossed the contents, but Jace turned as Rem moved in and Rem took the shot of liquid to his chest.

"Hey," he jumped back.

"You see?" said Jace. "She's crazy."

"I'll show you crazy." She advanced on him, but Daniels held out a hand to block her.

"Bring it," said Jace, stepping forward. "You're every bit as unstable as Devyn."

"Hey, hey," yelled Rem, putting his hands up on Jace's chest, but Jace's size required more effort and Rem shoved harder. "Don't make me pull my weapon."

Jace stopped, but he stared at Danni, his chest heaving.

"You two ever think about couple's counseling because you could fill somebody's time," said Daniels.

Danni pointed. "He thinks I did this." She eyed Daniels. "I knew he was stupid, but now I know he's reached Neanderthal stupid." She scowled at Jace. "You get a certificate for that?"

Jace shouted back. "The only certificate you should be worried about is the pretty warrant for your arrest. You can hang it on your cell wall and stare at it while your burly cellmate has her way with you."

Danni's eyes glittered and Jace scowled, and they both started yelling over each other with Daniels and Rem between them. Rem's shirt dripped and he smelled like a distillery.

"That's enough," said Daniels. He moved in front of Danni. "Hey, stop."

Rem yelled. "SHUT UP," and they finally went silent, but stood rigid in the room, faces red and breathing hard. Jace turned and Danni crossed her arms.

Daniels eyed Rem and rolled his eyes.

Danni got a whiff of Rem. "Sorry about the drink. I was aiming for him."

Rem held his shirt. "Guess it could be worse."

"You did have that homeless guy throw up on you once," said Daniels.

Rem blanched. "I'd tried to forget that. Thanks for bringing it up."

"You're welcome." He looked between Jace and Danni, who seemed to be calming down. "You two think you can handle an adult conversation, or do you two need to sit in the corner for a time out?"

Jace kicked at an overturned chair and it skittered across the floor. He weaved a bit and put his hand on the wall for support.

"He's drunk," said Danni.

Daniels noted the half-full bottle of scotch on the table.

"I am not," yelled Jace, but he dropped his head and held it. "Well, maybe a little."

"You better have a seat," said Rem, nodding toward the couch. He smelled his shirt and grimaced. "You got a towel?"

"Bathroom," said Jace, throwing a thumb out toward a closed door.

Rem headed toward it and went inside.

Daniels righted the kicked chair and put it beside the desk. "Why don't you have a seat, too," he said to Danni.

"I'm fine," she said.

He glared at her, and she sighed. "Fine." She sat in the chair.

Rem returned with a wet towel, blotting his shirt.

They stood there and let Danni and Jace collect themselves. "You want to tackle this or me?" asked Daniels.

Rem held the towel against his shirt. "Go for it, Tonto. You're the brave one."

"That's true, I am."

Rem smirked.

"Okay, people," said Daniels. "You want to tell us what this argument is about?"

They both spoke at once.

"He thinks I'm a killer. Can you believe that?"

"She did this. She killed Justin and almost Devyn."

"Stop." He held up his hands. They went still and he pointed at Jace. "You first."

"What?" asked Danni.

Rem put his fingers to his lips. "Shh. You'll have your turn."

Danni pursed her lips, but stayed quiet.

Jace glared at her and Daniels half expected him to stick out his tongue. Jace spoke. "I've been thinking about who could have done this, because I didn't do it, despite what those other two clown cops think."

"Those other two clown cops are Detectives Mellenbuhl and Garcia, and they were just doing their jobs, so be respectful," said Rem. "And we saw the footage at the apartment and heard the 911 call, so you're cleared."

"I told them they were wrong," said Jace.

"As does every other perp who's usually lying," said Daniel. "Let's get back to our story. Why do you think she did it?" He gestured at Danni.

"I didn't think so at first, but then I came in this morning and found that card, and then it all clicked into place. The timing. I hired her a couple of months ago. She hated Devyn, and if she had some sort of thing for me, she could have taken it out on Devyn, and Justin got in the way."

Danni stared and her mouth opened. "Thing for you? Are you kidding me? You honestly think I would kill Devyn because I am in love with you?" She went still for a moment and then smiled and giggled. "That's funny." The giggle turned to laughter. "That's really funny."

"Okay, okay," said Rem. "You said you found a card. What card?"

"It's on the desk. You should ask her. She'll know about it."

Danni stopped laughing. "I didn't leave you any stupid card. Don't tell me, is it a love note?"

Daniels looked over the desk and saw an envelope beside the keyboard. Flecks of liquid dotted the outside. "That envelope?"

"Yes. It was sitting by the monitor when I got in today. I opened it, and I knew it was from her."

"I didn't leave that here," said Danni.

"Yes, you did."

"No, I didn't."

"Be quiet," said Rem. He tossed the towel onto the back of the sofa and came over beside Daniels. "You touch it?"

"Kind of hard to open without touching it," said Jace.

Rem sighed. "Thanks, wise guy." He spoke to Daniels. "What do you want to do?"

"The less contamination, the better." Daniels spied a tissue box on the desk and he pulled one out. He grabbed the edge of the envelope with the tissue and pulled it closer. "You got any tweezers?" he asked.

"Sure, in the bathroom, along with my mascara and lipstick," said Jace. "No. I don't have any tweezers. What does this look like, a beauty parlor?"

"Sorry, he's a grumpy drunk," said Danni. "I've got some in my purse. It's up front."

"Would you mind getting them?" asked Daniels.

Jace stabbed a finger toward her. "What? You're just going to let her walk out of here? What if she makes a run for it?"

Danni stood. "Did you ever stop to think, *moron*, why I would have even come back here in the first place, if I actually left that stupid card that supposedly implicates me?"

Jace stood, too, and wobbled. "Oh, I don't know. Maybe because you planned to kill me, too?"

Danni stepped up to him. "Believe me, I'd consider it right now."

Jace held out his hands. "You don't have the guts."

"Oh, for God's sake," said Rem, turning. "You," he pointed at Danni. "Go get the tweezers, and you," he pointed at Jace. "Sit down and for the last time, shut up."

Danni offered a look of smug satisfaction and left the room. Jace made a pained groaning sound, and sat on the couch.

Daniels held the envelope with the tissue, noting it was open. "Was it sealed?"

Jace looked up. "What?"

"The envelope. Was it sealed?" asked Daniels.

"Does it look sealed to you?" They glowered at him and he sighed. "No. It wasn't sealed."

Danni returned holding her purse. She put it on the desk and went through it, grabbed a smaller bag, and opened that, and pulled out some tweezers. "Here you go."

"Thanks," said Daniels. He used the tissue to hold the flap and pulled out a tarot card. He put it on the desk.

"You see?" said Jace. "Now you know why I think it's her."

Danni stared at the card along with Daniels and Rem.

"Justice," said Rem. He looked at Danni. "One of yours?"

Danni shook her head. "No, it's not."

Jace snorted. "Likely story."

Daniels read the words on the card. Rem read it too, his eyes serious. "What does it say?" asked Danni.

"It says *I did it for you*. You should know. You wrote it," said Jace.

"I didn't write anything. That's not my card. You can check my deck. I'll have the Justice card." She pulled out a small fabric bag from her purse. "Feel free to check."

Jace scoffed. "What, you expect us to believe you have only one deck?"

"I didn't say that. But this is the one I usually carry, but sometimes I switch them out. You are welcome to check the others at home. I have nothing to hide. In fact, that's why I came early in the first place."

"Ha. Sure you did. You came early to take care of me, but that didn't work, so now you're coming up with some story to wiggle out of it." He gestured at the cards. "You probably have a stack of Justice cards at your place."

"That's not how it works, jackass. I don't store Justice cards. That's absurd. And I didn't come here to kill you. Look." She shoved her purse forward. "Look through it. I have a wallet, my cards, some cosmetics, and a pair of tweezers. Better watch out. I may knock you out with my wallet, stab you in the eye with my tweezers, and choke you with my deck." She spoke low. "It's registered as a deadly weapon by the way. Just call me Danni, agent double-o-eight." She narrowed her eyes. "That's right after seven, by the way."

Jace shot out of the sofa. "I should have fired you right after you dropped that bottle. I knew you were trouble." He threw out a hand. "Are you gonna arrest her or what? What more evidence do you need?"

Rem turned. "Just sit down, would you? Give us a second to think."

"Think?" asked Jace. "That seems to be a stretch for you guys."

"You should know," said Danni.

Jace stepped forward. "I don't need you to talk to me…"

Danni straightened. "If you think you're intimidating me…"

They started yelling again, and Rem grabbed the scotch off the table, opened it, and started pouring it on the floor.

"Hey, hey," said Jace, jumped back. "What are you doing?"

Rem stopped pouring. "Getting your attention. Next time, it's going over your keyboard."

Danni smirked and Daniels pointed. "And you. Open that deck. I want to see the Justice card."

Her smirk faded and Jace grinned.

"Fine," she said and opened the deck, taking out the cards. She flipped through them quickly. "It's here. Hold on."

Daniels waited as Rem walked over and put the scotch back on the table. Jace finally went quiet as he watched too.

Danni dealt out the cards. "It must be at the back," she said. "What the hell?"

She got to the end, and Justice wasn't there.

CHAPTER SIXTEEN

Danni flipped through the cards again. "It has to be here." Her heart raced. *Where was the Justice card?*

"Now you believe me?" asked Jace. "Arrest her."

"This is crazy," said Danni. "I don't understand. It has to be here."

"When's the last time you used this deck?" asked Remalla.

"I...I...use it all the time. I did a reading when I got home yesterday."

"When's the last time you saw the Justice card?" asked Daniels.

"I saw it last night—"

"When she put it in the envelope and left it for me to find," said Jace.

"I didn't." Danni put the cards down and tried to think. "This doesn't make any sense."

"It makes total sense," said Jace.

"Sit down," said Remalla. He glanced at Daniels, who offered a raised brow. "Should we tell him?"

Jace shouted. "What is there to tell? The murderer is standing right there. If you don't do something, then I will."

"I'm not a murderer," yelled Danni.

"You," said Daniels, pointing at Jace. "Sit down and be quiet. And you," he looked at Danni. "Take a seat in the chair. We have a few questions."

Jace muffled a curse and sat on the sofa. Danni sat at the desk, wringing her hands.

Daniels scratched his head. "Now, before we go and assume anything about this missing card, we need to clarify something. When we talked to you before at the station, you were about to say something about a man you saw at the bar. But then we got interrupted." He put his hands on the desk. "Who is this man?"

Danni glanced at Jace who cursed again. "He was sitting at the bar during the card game. He barely spoke and he wore a hoodie and stared at his phone for most of the night. He made a few unpleasant comments about Jace and Devyn, and when he left, he tipped me a hundred bucks, saying he thought I might need it soon. And then he left."

"Did you recognize him? Did he pay with a credit card?" asked Rem.

"No to both," said Danni. A small kernel of hope emerged that they believed her. "But Jace knows who it is. He got him on video."

Jace glared at her.

The detectives turned toward Jace. "You want to tell us what you know about this guy?" asked Remalla.

"I don't know anything," said Jace.

"And you're calling me a liar?" asked Danni. "I saw your face. You recognized him."

Jace dropped his head and laced his fingers together. "I don't know why we're talking about a stranger on a tape when the killer is sitting right there." He flung a hand at Danni.

Rem sat on the edge of the desk. "Who's the guy?"

"I don't know," said Jace, his voice laced with frustration.

"Where's the video?" asked Daniels.

"It's on his desktop. He saved it," said Danni, reaching for the mouse. She clicked the file and opened it.

Daniels and Remalla came around to the front of the desk and Danni hit play. A grainy image of the bar came into view. Four men sat at a table, playing their card game. They were further away and harder to see, but still obvious. Danni and the bar were closer and the man sat at the bar as she'd described.

Daniels and Remalla watched with interest as the man, head down and obscured by his hoodie, stood, paid, said something to Danni, turned to leave, and just as he walked out the door, looked up and waved, his eyes directly at the camera. The frame froze on his upturned face.

There was a palpable shift in the air, and both Daniels and Remalla seemed to go still, then glanced at each other, their expressions unreadable, but Danni suspected they were thinking the same thing.

"What?" she asked.

Jace saw it too. He sat forward. "You know him?"

"Shit," said Rem. "That's him."

Daniels straightened, his face pale, and even though Danni had no idea what was going on, her skin prickled. "Is he dangerous?" she asked.

"He's not here for charity work," said Rem.

"Did he say anything else?" asked Daniels to Danni.

"No, other than ordering his drinks."

"And he was there during the card game, watching Jace?" asked Remalla.

"For the most part, yes, but he seemed more annoyed by Devyn." Danni glanced at Jace, who looked away. "How do you know him? And don't lie."

Jace studied his fingers.

"He been in the bar before?" asked Remalla.

"Not that I know of," said Jace.

"You know him from your past?" asked Daniels.

"Nope."

"But you do recognize him, right?" asked Remalla.

Jace hesitated. "Maybe."

Remalla came back around the desk. "We need to find this guy, so you need to tell us what you know."

Jace gripped his hands together. "It's stupid and it's not going to help find him."

"You might be surprised. And stupid in this job is relative," said Daniels.

Jace ran a hand through his messy hair and sighed. "Fine. I saw him in my dreams."

Danni frowned. "You what?"

"In your dreams?" asked Remalla.

Jace stared at the floor. "Crap. Yes. The last five months. I've been having these dreams." He paused, thinking. "Almost every night. They wake me up in a cold sweat."

"The same dream?" asked Daniels.

"Almost. It varies a bit, but for the most part, it doesn't change much."

"What's the dream?" asked Remalla.

Jace cleared his throat. "I'm in a fog or mist. It's hard to see. I'm a little panicked, because I know someone's there, but I can't see them." He swallowed. "Then two figures emerge from the fog. It's two women, and somehow, I know them, but I don't. I feel very protective of them. I try to reach them, but I can't. The harder I try, the further away they get. And then he shows up. A man. Hard to see, but he's there. I can't physically see him, but it's almost like I can mentally see him, although not clearly. He's advancing on the women, and I want to stop him, but I can't. I'm never fast enough." Jace shook his head and closed his eyes. "Sometimes, I'm screaming, sometimes I try to scream but can't. I'm shaking and sweating when I wake up." He opened his eyes. "I don't know what it means."

"Two women?" asked Daniels. "You see two women? Do you recognize them?" He and Remalla exchanged a look.

"No. I don't, but I can barely see them."

"How can you be sure the man in the dream is the man in the video?" asked Remalla.

"Because in the last dream, I saw him clearly. He walked right up to me, and grabbed this." He pulled out a cord with a green stone that hung from his neck. "He yanked it off and I saw him. And when I saw the video, I knew it was the same man."

Danni leaned in to see the necklace. "Why the necklace? Have you had it long?"

"No. In fact, some strange woman gave it to me in the hospital while I was waiting to hear about Devyn. She just offered it to me, and then she disappeared."

Daniels and Rem did that odd thing where they made eye contact again, as if speaking without talking.

"Did she have brown hair with gray roots, and a big flowery dress?" asked Remalla.

Jace's eyes widened. "Yes, she did. How'd you know that?"

Daniels crossed his arms. "Because she's been making the rounds."

Jace squinted.

"She talked to us, too," said Remalla. "She moves fast for an older lady."

"She said she was there to see her mom, who'd had hip surgery, but when I asked, no one had had any hip surgery in that wing."

"Speak of the devil," said Daniels.

"What the hell is going on here?" asked Jace. "Why are strange women giving me necklaces, men in my dreams showing up in my bar, and the people I love being attacked?"

Danni stared at the tarot card on the table. "And why the Justice card? What does *I did it for you* mean?"

Jace's face clouded. "That's what he said to me." He stood and paced. Danni hoped the alcohol was wearing off. "On the phone. That bastard said *I did it for you* before he killed Justin. And now it's on the card." He eyed the card and then Danni. "What do you know about this?"

Danni shook her head. "I told you. I don't know anything about this. This card…I don't know how or why it's…" She paused, thinking, recalling the decks she'd used. "…wait a minute."

"What?" asked Remalla. "What is it?"

Danni's belly flipped, and a cold dread settled over her. "This deck. I switched it."

"You switched what?" asked Daniels.

"I used the other deck last night for the reading."

"What reading?" asked Jace.

"That's what I was trying to tell you, before you accused me of being a murderer. I got a request for a reading after the card game. From someone calling themselves *BrotherlyLove*."

"*BrotherlyLove*?" asked Jace.

"Yes. I didn't think much of it, until he used my real name. Daisy."

"Danni isn't your real name?" asked Remalla.

"You talked about your name at the card game. You told all of us," said Jace.

"Exactly. This guy knew my name. He had to have been there, and he sent me a question through my website and I answered him."

"You think it's the man from the video?" asked Jace.

"Maybe. I can't be sure." Danni held out a hand. "The only other option would be you, Henry, Simon and Devyn. And Justin, of course."

Jace set his jaw. "I doubt it was Justin. He and Devyn had other plans."

"You have this question and this reading?" asked Remalla.

"And what does this have to do with the deck?" asked Daniels.

"I did the reading last night, and I used the deck from my purse. The Justice card was there because it came up in the reading. I grabbed this deck from my table this morning. It's been sitting there for the last couple of days, so—"

Rem offered a hard stare. "So, if this card on the table is from this deck…"

"Then he's been in your house," said Daniels.

CHAPTER SEVENTEEN

"Shit," said Jace.

"Oh, my God." Danni imagined someone in her home, going through her things, or worse, watching her sleep in her bed when she thought she was alone.

"You're sure this deck had the Justice card in it?" asked Remalla.

"I'm sure. There's no reason it would be missing." She leaned over and held her head.

Remalla paced the floor.

Jace tried to assimilate everything. The alcoholic haze was abating and his head was clearing. Had he really accused Danni of murder? It had made sense at the time, but now, with the information coming at him, he began to realize that perhaps he'd overreacted. And hearing now that she might have caught the attention of the man who'd hurt Justin and Devyn, anger bubbled up. He didn't want to lose someone else.

"You two have any ideas, because I'd sure like to hear them. Obviously, this guy's got a bug up his ass for me, but I don't know why. And if he can appear in my dreams, then something is going on." He cocked his head at Danni. "And *BrotherlyLove* means something, because he spoke to me in that last dream. When he yanked off my necklace, he said *Hello, brother*." Jace rubbed his temples as a headache began to bloom. He watched the detectives. "I know you two know something.

Why are you here anyway? What happened to those other two clowns?" They glared. "Sorry. Cops."

Rem stopped pacing. "They're in the hospital. Somebody jumped them last night."

"What?" asked Danni. "Who would do that?"

"Is that why you're here. You think it was me?" asked Jace. "Because it wasn't. They ticked me off, but I didn't touch them."

"We don't think it was you. They didn't say it was you," said Daniels. "They have a vague description of the guy, and it's someone else."

"They're gonna be okay?" asked Jace.

"They'll live, but that's why we're here. We're now investigating Justin's murder," said Daniels.

"We talked to Devyn this morning," said Remalla.

Jace stiffened. "You did? How is she?"

"Still pretty out of it. She's torn up that you found her, and that you know about her and Justin," said Daniels.

Jace set his jaw, and turned away. He felt guilty about not visiting her.

"She ought to feel bad about what she did to Jace," said Danni. "Could she tell you anything about what happened?"

"Not really. She got pretty upset. We had to leave," said Remalla. "She did remember the man telling her that she was like all the rest and that you deserved an apology."

"All the rest?" asked Danni. "What does that mean?"

"We don't know," said Remalla.

Jace turned back. "What do you know?"

Remalla and Daniels were quiet, and they exchanged a look.

"You two keep doing that," said Jace. "You said something earlier." He pointed at Remalla. "About whether or not you should say something. What are you two not telling me?" He turned the laptop so that they could see the man's face on the video. "Do you know who this guy is?"

They were quiet for a second, before Remalla spoke. "This isn't our first run-in with Rutger."

"Who?" asked Jace.

"We call him Rutger because of his resemblance to the actor Rutger Hauer," said Daniels.

Jace looked closely at the video and Danni leaned over. "Yeah, he does actually," said Danni.

"I don't see it," said Jace.

"It doesn't matter what he looks like," said Remalla. "It matters what he's done, and what he's capable of doing."

"Am I gonna need a drink for this?" asked Jace.

"I'd suggest coffee," said Danni.

Remalla perked up. "That's a fantastic idea. You got any?"

"I can brew some," said Danni. "It will help distract me. Everybody want some?"

Jace nodded, as did the detectives. She headed for the door, but hesitated before leaving.

"Something wrong?" asked Daniels.

She chewed her lip. "I'm a little wigged out about this whole thing, and being in the bar by myself, where the card game was, and where he was...I..."

"We'll come with you," said Jace. "We can sit out there."

Her shoulders relaxed. "Thank you."

They followed her out into the bar area and sat at a four-top while she brewed the coffee.

"You open soon, don't you?" asked Rem.

"I'm the owner. I'll open when I want to," He spoke low. "She's okay, isn't she? I know I lost it earlier, but I'm a little more clearheaded now and I know she's not a murderer. But now I'm worried. This lunatic wouldn't come after her, would he?"

Daniels tapped his fingers on the table. "I wish we could tell you what he might do, but there's no way to know. If he actually did go to her place and take the Justice card, then we have to wonder why. Is he targeting her just to scare you, or does he have a more sinister reason?"

"Shit," said Jace, rubbing his head. "She can't stay there. Not if this guy is still out running around."

"We'll figure it out," said Remalla. "We'll check her place next. We might be able to have patrol car sit outside her home."

"Something tells me that's not going to stop him," said Jace.

Danni came over and sat with them. "Coffee's brewing."

"Thanks," said Remalla.

"Okay, so tell us what's going on here," said Jace. "Why am I in this guy's crosshairs?"

Daniels and Remalla stared and Remalla gestured. "Go for it, Tonto."

Daniels leaned back. "You remember the Makeup Artist case, not long ago?"

"The serial killer?" said Danni. "He was killed, right?"

"Yes, he was," said Daniels. "But there was a detective on that case named Jill Jacobs. She worked with us to find him."

"I remember that. She was on the news. Brave lady," said Danni.

"She is," said Remalla.

Daniels gave them a quick rundown of the Makeup Artists crimes. "Long story short," he finished, "one of the Artist's victims was a police officer. He was found in a bathtub, with the words 'I did it for you' written in blood on the walls."

"At the time, we thought it was the Artist's handiwork. The officer and Jacobs were close, and Jacobs was being stalked, so it made sense," said Remalla.

Daniels nodded. "After the Artist was caught, Rem and I got called in to work on a murder investigation up at Secret Lake."

"Secret Lake?" asked Danni.

"It's about an hour from here," said Jace. "Justin and I rode our bikes up there once. Pretty area."

Daniels continued. "A woman who lives there was accused of killing her husband. It looked like a slam dunk, but something made us take a second look. She'd told us a man was watching her. She'd encountered him in the woods and he'd told her, 'I did it for you.'"

Jace stiffened. "The same phrase as the Artist?"

"Yes," said Daniels. "We considered it may have been a coincidence until we met the guy ourselves. We chased him into the woods and he…well…he got away."

"How the hell did he get away?" asked Jace. "You two look like you can handle yourselves."

"Let's just say this guy can handle himself better," said Remalla. "Before he took off, we saw him, which is how we started calling him Rutger, and he spoke to us. He said, 'I did it for her.'"

"We didn't have any evidence, but our guts told us he'd killed the husband, and the wife was innocent," said Daniels.

"So this Rutger guy is running around killing people, and telling their loved ones that he did it for them?" Jace clenched his hands into fists. "Sounds like you have another serial killer on your hands."

"And now he's picked Jace next?" asked Danni. "But why?"

Daniels raised a brow at Remalla. "You want to take it from here?"

Remalla smirked. "You leave me with all the fun stuff, don't you?"

"It's your specialty," said Daniels.

Remalla sighed and rubbed his neck. "Is that coffee ready? I'm going to need a big cup."

"It should be close. I'll check." Danni stood. "Wait till I get back. I want to hear this."

Jace waited for her to leave. "So, this guy kills Justin to come after me? And now he's sending her tarot reading requests?"

"We need to talk to her about that," said Daniels. "Find out what he asked her."

"We can't be sure it's the same guy," said Remalla. "You had two other friends here. Could they have sent the email?"

Jace considered that. "Unlikely. Simon and Henry are stand-up guys. Henry tried to ask her out, but she said no, but Danni turns everyone down. Nothing new. She rejected Justin, too. Simon is engaged to a nice girl he's known since high school. He and Henry have both been super busy. It's tax season for Simon, and Henry's been working long hours on the plans for some big downtown building, but I've talked to both of them since Justin. They offered condolences and whatever they could do to help. They were good friends of Justin's. I'd find it hard to believe they'd do something like that, especially on the same night as Justin's death."

"Well, Mel and Garcia spoke with them, and didn't catch any red flags, but we'll follow up. See what we can find," said Remalla. "What about Justin's ex? What's her name? Liz? What's her story?"

"I didn't know her that well, but she doesn't strike me as a killer. Pretty mild-mannered and quiet, but sweet. I don't see her contacting Danni, unless Justin gave her Danni's card," said Jace. "And I certainly don't see her killing Justin."

"You'd be surprised what might happen, especially if she found out Justin was sleeping with Devyn," said Daniels. "Maybe she showed up at Justin's, and caught them together."

Jace shook his head. "I suppose it's possible."

"We'll check in with Liz and see what we can find out, but the more likely scenario is it's Rutger, messing with Danni, trying to get to you."

Jace groaned. "Son-of-a-bitch. And here I am, accusing her of murder. Some boss I am."

The detectives shared a glance.

Jace pointed between them. "You two do that a lot. This saying something without saying anything look. What are you trying to not say?"

"Is it more than that?" asked Daniels.

"What do you mean?" asked Jace.

Rem scratched his jaw. "Danni's a pretty lady. And you...well...you're you. You two sure fight like a couple."

"There's nothing going on between us. We're friends."

"Maybe Rutger's sensing there's more," said Daniels.

"Well, then Rutger's stupid." Jace stood as Danni came over with a pot of coffee. He took it from her and put it on the table. "I'll get some cream and sugar."

"They're on the counter," said Danni. She put four mugs on the table. "Help yourself."

"You're awesome," said Remalla, helping himself to some coffee. "Thanks."

"Appreciate it," said Daniels. He grabbed a mug and took the pot from Remalla.

Jace grabbed the cream and sugar and put them on the table. Remalla helped himself to both. Daniels kept his black.

Jace grabbed a cup and poured himself some coffee. "So, why me?"

Remalla sipped his brew and sighed. "You make a good cup of coffee."

Danni poured her own cup. "I have to. He's super picky."

Jace smelled his drink, enjoying the aroma. "Bad coffee is like bad alcohol. If you're going to drink a lot of it..."

"...then it better be good," finished Danni.

"Exactly," said Jace.

"Just friends, huh?" asked Remalla.

"What?" asked Danni.

Jace scowled.

"Nothing," said Remalla. He took another sip and sighed. "Okay, let's continue this merry tale. Where were we?"

"A possible serial killer has targeted Jace. Why?" asked Danni, sitting at the table.

Remalla shifted in his seat. "He has killed two people that we know of, and maybe three assuming he killed Justin, but he's not a random killer. He picked you and the other two women for a reason."

Jace went still. "These two women. Do I know them?"

"Jill Jacobs, the one who helped us on the Artist case, is one, and Madison Vickers from Secret Lake, is the other. Ring any bells?" asked Daniels. He accessed his phone and flipped through it. "These are their pictures."

Jace leaned in and looked. "Never seen them before." Something made him stop, and look twice. Chill bumps popped up on his skin. "At least I don't recall if I did."

"You look pale," said Danni. "You sure you don't know them?"

Jace shook his head. "The dream. I'm thinking of the dream. There are two women, but I can't see their faces."

Daniels put his phone away. "Something to consider."

Jace spoke to Remalla. "How do you know he targeted the three of us, and it wasn't random?"

Remalla put his mug down. "Because, during our investigation up at Secret Lake, he said something else."

"When? Was this when you chased him through the woods?" asked Danni.

"It was the second time we chased him through the woods," said Daniels.

"The second time?" asked Jace. "Crap, maybe we need the other guys on this."

"You mean the other guys currently in the hospital?" asked Remalla.

Something connected in Jace's mind. He sat up. "Wait a minute. Do you think this Rutger guy did this to them?"

Remalla glanced at Daniels. "Maybe."

Danni narrowed her eyes. "Oh, my God. He...Rutger...wants you on this case, doesn't he?"

Jace pointed. "Shit. He took out the other two so you two could investigate?"

"We can't be sure of that," said Daniels.

"I think you're damn sure of it," said Jace. "This guy have a thing for you, too?"

"I don't know what he has, but if it's true then he must feel comfortable with us. Why? We're not sure," said Daniels.

"Well, this guy has all his ducks in a row, doesn't he? And I've got two sets of cops who can't take down one lone suspect. Lucky me." Jace gripped his cup.

"I think there's more to this than they're telling us," said Danni. "Something tells me Mr. Rutger is not your average bad guy."

Jace crossed his arms. "Don't tell me. He's Special Forces. Knows all that jujitsu, ninja crap. He was used by a covert arm of the government for their own gain and was part of a secret project that betrayed him and now he's out for revenge."

"I wish it was that simple," said Remalla.

"Would you please tell me what the hell is going on here?" Jace smacked his hands on the table.

The table went quiet until Remalla spoke. "He used your name."

Jace shook his head. "What?"

Remalla leaned in, his expression flat. "Rutger said your name. Told us 'Jace' was next. Said he had to protect his family. Then he yanked the guns out of our hands with no visible means for the second time in as many days, and took off. The guy's a ghost, and if he pulled the same shit with Mel and Garcia, then yes, he's got the upper hand. People who can move shit with their minds typically do." He stared at Jace for a second before sitting back and casually sipping his coffee.

Daniels held his mug and watched Jace who didn't know what to say. "Bet you prefer the jujitsu, ninja crap right about now, don't you?"

CHAPTER EIGHTEEN

Daniels sipped his coffee and waited while Jace took it in. Rem did the same.

Jace finally sat forward. "Are you two out of your ever-lovin' heads? Moving things with his mind? What the hell are you talking about? Sounds like you guys are sampling the products you confiscate."

"Just hear them out," said Danni.

Jace threw out a hand. "Hear them out? They're talking about some kind of paranormal shit. Who is this guy supposed to be, Darth Vader?"

"We'll admit. It's a bit unconventional," said Rem. "If it didn't piss me off so much, I'd say it was cool."

"Vader would have had more friends if he'd used the force for good," said Daniels. "I suspect the same goes for Rutger. I guess they're similar in a way. Their family life sucked and they're not happy about it."

"Look at you and your movie references. I'm impressed," said Rem.

"You should see me at parties," said Daniels.

"I do. That's why I'm so impressed."

Daniels face fell. "You're just jealous because I dress better than you."

"Everybody dresses better than me. It's part of my charm."

"It's also part of your budget, which goes mostly to food."

"Don't forget alcohol," said Rem.

"Are you two finished?" asked Jace.

Daniels cocked a brow. "No, actually, we're just getting started. We're known for this."

Rem raised the side of his lip. "We once made a suspect talk after listening to us for an hour. He begged us to let him out of the room. I still look back on that with fondness."

"Lozano let us go home early that day," said Daniels.

"That's right." Rem held up his coffee. "I forgot."

Jace leaned over and held his head. "I think I'm in the Twilight Zone."

"Or Candid Camera," said Danni, looking around the room.

Daniels turned serious. "All kidding aside, we know how this looks. It took us a while to absorb it too, and it actually happened to us. I know what you're thinking, but we don't take this lightly. There's something unique about Rutger. And to be honest, maybe Rem and I would have told ourselves that maybe we were crazy, except for the fact that we didn't just see it with him. We saw it with Madison Vickers, too. She wouldn't admit it, but she did something unexplainable that likely saved our lives. And Jill Jacobs. She has some sort of wonky psychic ability that allowed her to get inside the Makeup Artist's head, and maybe Rutger's. So, you put all that together, along with this whole 'family' thing Rutger mentioned, and these dreams you're having, and he spoke to you and said 'Hello, brother.' It makes me curious."

Jace looked up. "Curious about what?"

Daniels took a second. "If Jill, Madison, and Rutger are all connected, and now, so are you, what are your superpowers, Wonderboy?"

Jace froze and the color drained from his face.

"I'd say you hit the bullseye, partner," said Rem.

Jace stayed quiet.

"Dead center. Cat got your tongue, Marlon?" asked Daniels.

Jace's face clouded. "This is ridiculous." He stood. "This whole thing. Serial killers. Superpowers. Stupid dreams. Tarot cards."

"Jace…" said Danni.

"No. I'm not done. I can't believe you had me buying this whole charade. Well. I may be a little slow, but I'm not that slow."

"Jace...," Danni, said again.

"No, Danni. You can listen if you want, but I'm done. You two enjoy your coffee but this conversation is over. I'll be contacting your Captain and asking about getting sane cops on this case. Cops who know what they're doing."

"Jace...Detectives—" Danni stood, staring toward the front.

The coffee pot slid across the table, flying off of it, and clattered on the floor, liquid flying everywhere. Daniels stood and jumped back and Rem flew out of his seat. Jace cursed, and Danni yelped. Her cup, which had been on the table, flew up and across the room, smashing against the back wall. Jace's mug veered up and out in the opposite direction, crashing and breaking against the bar's door.

"What the—" Jace stammered.

Danni pointed. "It...It's him."

They turned to look and Daniels saw a man in a hoodie at the window, peering in. It was Rutger. He offered a quick wave and smile before turning and running.

Rem took off in a sprint, and Daniels followed. "Stay here. Lock the door behind you," said Daniels, running out the door, following Rem.

The streets bustled with activity, and they dodged people on the sidewalk, and Daniels narrowly avoided tripping over a dog's leash. Rutger moved fast, but Rem kept pace and Daniels was right behind.

A car horn blared as Rutger ran against the light and tires screeched as Rem dodged traffic. A utility truck came close enough for Daniels to smack the hood as he passed. Rutger kept running, dodging more cars and people, and thankfully, making the next light.

Rem slowed briefly, avoiding an older lady, and Daniels yelled "Police," but most didn't hear or see them in time. He barely skirted past a toddler who'd run in front of him on the sidewalk.

Rutger kept going, ran across another street, and headed toward a construction site. A chain link fence surrounded the area with "No

Trespassing" signs posted. Rutger leapt up onto the fence, climbed up and over, and landed on the other side like a monkey, where he ran into the construction area. Rem jumped up, too, scurried over the fence and hit the ground hard, but jumped up and kept going, yelling "Police. Stop." Daniels scrambled up the fence, reaching the top and gripped it, feeling a sharp sting on his palm. Ignoring it, he pulled up and flew over the top, landing on the dirt below. He ran after Rem into the half-constructed building, hopping over and around piles of wood and stacks of bricks. Sprinting inside, he stopped when he saw Rem, breathing hard, in a partial room with framing and sheetrock. There was a doorway to the right and an unfinished wall to the left.

Sweat dripped down his back. "Which way did he go?"

Rem shook his head. "I don't know. You take that way. I'll take the other."

Daniels headed for the unfinished wall and Rem took the door. Walking through, Daniels only saw more framing and sheetrock. The building looked to be about fifteen floors, and half-finished. He could see Rem moving through the other side of the building as he passed through incomplete sections still under construction. No workers were around.

Daniels began to think Rutger was long gone when someone spoke from above.

"Hello, gentlemen."

Daniels looked up to see Rutger watching them from the third floor. How the hell had he gotten up there?"

Rem came closer and joined Daniels in what would be a future lobby area. It was open, and they could see the floors and scaffolding above. Rem's breathing slowed but sweat glistened on his face. "Come on down. Let's talk."

"I like where I am. Not that it matters, but I'm glad to see you're not waving guns at me this time. I think we've made progress."

"We don't want to shoot you. We just want to talk," said Daniels. He wiped sweat from his forehead with his forearm, and realized his hand was bleeding. "I'm guessing you do, too. Otherwise, why show your face?"

He stared down at them. "Tell your policemen friends that no harm was intended, but I prefer you on the case. Our history makes it beneficial."

Rem scowled. "You did that to Mel and Garcia?"

"I had no choice. But it could have been much worse. I think you know that, Detective."

Daniels considered what to do next. The only idea was to keep him talking. "Why Justin Tenley?"

"You know why. He deserved to die. Jace understands that now."

"And why Jace?" asked Rem. "You his brother?"

Rutger went still for a moment. "My family issues are not your concern. I only need you for certain things, and when you need to know more, you'll know more."

"And what do you need us for now? We know it was you who killed Justin. There's no one else to pin this on except you," said Daniels.

Rutger smiled. "Tell Danni her reading was accurate. She has a gift. She reads the cards well. Tell her she might want to consider a reading on her and Jace. That could be interesting. It wouldn't hurt if she did a reading for herself too."

"We don't have time for readings, Rutger," said Rem.

Daniels scanned the area, looking for a way up. Seeing a staircase against a back wall, he assumed that's how Rutger had accessed the upper floors. He took a few steps toward it.

"I like the name you've given me. It's catchy." He paused. "It's the only name I've ever had. I was never given one at birth."

"Really? Why's that?" asked Rem.

Rutger gripped a pipe. "You'd have to ask—" He hesitated. "Never mind. That's not important."

"But I'm curious. There's a reason you're running around like Spiderman, throwing shit around, and killing people you don't like. There's a story there, and somehow I think you want to tell it," said Rem.

Daniels took another step, nearing the staircase.

"There's a story, but time will tell if you'll ever hear it. Those who do know it, know I'm coming for them. This is just the start. When I'm done, they'll all regret what they did, and they will know who I am. Name or no name."

"You mind if we keep using Rutger?"

"Your attempts to near the staircase are pointless, Detective Daniels. I do have peripheral vision." Rutger shifted his gaze toward Daniels.

Daniels stopped moving.

"Besides, you wouldn't catch me anyway." Rutger narrowed his eyes and shifted his gaze. 'You're bleeding, Detective."

Daniels looked at his hand. Blood had dripped from the cut and onto the concrete floor. "I'll live."

"You should talk to Jace. He has certain skills."

"Jace?" asked Daniels.

Rutger chuckled. "You've only scratched the surface. In some ways, my brother has more power than me. Too bad he doesn't know it."

A voice spoke from behind them. "Then why don't you explain it to me."

Daniels and Rem turned to see Jace standing beside a sheetrock wall near where they'd entered the lobby area.

"Jace, what the hell are you doing here?" asked Rem. "Where's Danni?"

"I followed you." He was breathless, and somewhere along the way, he'd discarded his jacket. His muscular arms and shoulders bulged beneath his shirt and sweat made it stick to his back. "Danni's fine. I told her to lock herself in the office and call 911."

"You shouldn't be here," said Daniels.

"Oh, I think I'm exactly where I need to be." He stepped further out into the open, looking up at Rutger.

Rutger stared back, his eyes flashing, but his face expressionless. "Hello, brother," he said.

Jace stopped in the middle, his face paling. "Who are you?" he asked. "Did you kill Justin?"

Rutger relaxed his grip on the pipe and leaned against it. He stared for a moment before answering. "I knew this time would come. I guess I expected it to be...more rewarding." His eyes gleamed in the light.

Daniels took another step toward the stairs.

"Why don't you come down here and I'll show you how rewarding it can be," said Jace.

Rutger offered a smug look. "I think you may find that I'm more formidable than I look. You may have the brawn, but I have the brains. Plus, I'd hate to hurt my big brother, especially at our first meeting."

"I am not your brother," said Jace.

Daniels inched closer to the stairs. He didn't know what he'd do if he actually made it to them, because Rutger would see him, but he had to try, or at least be ready if Rutger took off.

"Oh, but you are. I'm sorry to tell you, but your background is just as unique as mine, you just don't know it yet."

"You're lying," said Jace. "Why would I believe you? You killed my best friend, and almost killed my girlfriend. You're just another messed up psychotic with nothing better to do but destroy people's lives, and then pretend that you're doing society a favor."

"I couldn't give a shit about society," said Rutger. It was the first display of anger he'd shown. "And society couldn't give a shit about me. The only ones I care about are the ones who made me what I am. You want to blame someone? Blame them."

"Everybody wants to blame the world for their problems," said Jace. "Well, get with the program, Jack. Life sucks. For everyone. Get over it."

Rutger glared. "It's not the world, or life, I'm pissed at. When I say they made me, I'm not speaking figuratively. These people *made* me, created me." He paused. "Just like they made you."

Jace opened his mouth to speak, but seemed uncertain what to say.

Daniels eased closer to the stairwell, but a cold tingle erupted on his back. A force sucked the air out his lungs and he flew backwards, hitting the sheetrock. It gave way and cracked and the air whooshed from his lungs.

"Daniels," yelled Rem, who ran over.

Daniels held his chest, trying to catch his breath.

Rutger spoke from above. "I told you I could see you. You'd think the first time we met would have been a lesson."

"I'm okay," said Daniels, sucking in air as Rem squatted beside him. "Help me up." He groaned as Rem grabbed his arm and helped him stand.

"You sure?" asked Rem.

Daniels straightened and winced. "Just great. Feel like a million bucks." He stretched his achy back.

Jace returned his attention to Rutger. "Did you leave the Justice card? On my desk?"

Rutger smirked. "I felt it left the appropriate message."

"You took the card from Danni's deck?"

"Any other card would have had far less impact."

"Is Danni in danger? Are you threatening her?"

Rutger raised the side of his lip. "That is entirely up to her. The world is a dangerous place, full of weirdos and outcasts, just like me. Who knows what could happen?"

Jace took a step forward. "You touch her, and I'll kill you."

"I'd expect nothing less. You are my brother, after all."

Jace set his jaw. "Who are Jill and Madison? How do they figure into this?"

Rutger went still. "I think you know."

"I want you to tell me."

Rutger pushed off the pipe. "That's for another time and place."

"You got somewhere to be?"

Rutger stepped to the edge, smiling down at Jace. "We're playing this game my way, not yours. And when you need to know, you'll know. For the time being though, I have other tasks to complete. There are those who need to be reminded."

"Reminded?" asked Jace.

"They know I'm out here, biding my time, preparing. They are much like Danni, cowering behind closed doors, waiting for help, but 911 can't help them. Now it's time to come calling. It's time for them to reap what they sowed."

"Who?" asked Jace.

Rutger cocked his head. "You know one of them. So do you, detectives." He eyed Daniels and Rem. "A sweet little lady with round eyes, who looks like Mrs. Claus, but who is distinctly not. She gave you that nice necklace."

Jace reached at his neck and grabbed the stone that dangled from it. "This?"

Rutger grinned.

"Her? You're going after her? For what? Burning your pancakes?" asked Jace.

Rutger squatted with his elbows on his knees. "You want answers? Well that lady has them. Sonia probably knows more than I do." He stood. "But you better hurry, because if I get to her first, well..." He shrugged. "Then it's gonna be hard to talk to a dead woman." He turned, but looked back. "Good luck, brother." He took off in a run.

Rem sprinted to the stairs, taking them two at a time. Daniels had caught his breath, and followed. Jace ran up behind Daniels.

They made it to the second floor and then the third, racing to where Rutger had been. Daniels went to one corner and Rem to another, looking. Jace searched the various rooms separated by sheet rock.

"Anything?" yelled Daniels. He returned to the section where Rutger had been standing.

"Nothing," said Rem, joining him.

Jace came back from checking a room. "He's not here."

Rutger was gone.

CHAPTER NINETEEN

Peter sat outside in the living room, occasionally hearing a raised voice from the office where Sonia and her visitor were speaking. He bounced his knee, wondering what they were discussing, although he knew the topic. What he couldn't be sure of was the outcome.

Since Peter had been assigned to assist Sonia six months ago, he'd become fond of her. Her outward sweetness, kind eyes, gentle nature, and her need to ensure his well-being through a constant supply of lotions, creams and a good cup of tea implied a genial and easy-going temperament. But he'd realized over time that she didn't wilt. Her twinkling eyes belied her determination and grit, and when he'd thought he could sway her, he was typically wrong. Sonia would not back down until they'd caught the man who'd wrought so much pain on others. If Peter made any mention of stopping or easing up, those merry eyes would turn to steel, and all she had to do was tilt her head, and square her shoulders, and he'd known he'd lost. No matter what the toll on her, how little she slept, or how disturbing her meditations, she did not intend to quit. She had to stop this man until he stopped her first.

Peter knew the guilt ate at her, which was her main motivation. Sonia had not enlightened him with the details, but her connection between her and this man is what kept her, and Peter suspected, even the man, going. And they likely wouldn't let up until one of them was dead.

That's what had forced Peter's hand. He'd called in the big guns because he knew Sonia wouldn't do it. Peter had sensed the shift in Sonia after Justin Tenley's death. More withdrawn, and quiet: less appetite and sleep. Something was off and she would admit to nothing: telling him only that he was over reacting, and here, have some chamomile tea.

Now that Justin was dead, Peter suspected the worst. The man the two detectives called Rutger had done what he'd set out to do and Sonia could logically be next. But she'd remained quiet, only going about her business as usual, which was mainly watching and waiting. Regardless of Sonia's attempts to reach out to Rutger, he'd remained elusive. Whenever she got close, he'd shut down, and she could never determine his location. She did her best to follow Jace and the two detectives. Her knowledge of them helped her to keep up with Rutger, and although it couldn't stop him, she could at least keep her presence known, and stay involved. Peter wondered though, if she had something else up her sleeve. Something to maybe draw Rutger out, but she had shared nothing with Peter, perhaps to protect him. He had no idea what either of them could do if they actually found Rutger. Talking him down seemed unlikely.

Weighing his options, Peter had taken the unorthodox step of asking for help, knowing Sonia would be displeased, but realizing he had little choice. If he didn't and something happened to her, he'd never forgive himself.

The voices from the opposite side of the door had gone quiet, and Peter fought the urge to press his ear against the wall to listen. Checking his watch, he saw that they'd been in there for almost an hour. How much longer would it take?

The door opened and Peter jumped in his seat. The woman who'd come to visit walked out, stately and elegant, wearing a perfectly tailored navy suit and white scarf, her silver hair swept up into a smooth chignon.

Peter stood, his heart thumping. Her astute eyes and imposing nature always made him nervous.

"Peter," she said.

"Ma'am," he answered.

"Keep me up to date, would you?"

"Yes, ma'am. Did you have any luck?"

She picked up her small leather purse from the sofa and tucked it under her arm. "I don't believe in luck. Persistence is the key to success, don't you agree?"

"Yes, of course."

"That being said, Sonia is a stubborn woman, but always has been, which is why I called upon her for this job, plus her unique connection to this case makes her well suited for the task."

"I suppose," said Peter.

"You think otherwise?" Her eyes studied him, and although they were of similar height, he felt much smaller.

"I worry about her."

"Worry is a waste of time and serves no purpose. I've dealt with many difficulties in my life, and worry never helped with any of them." She straightened the cuff of her jacket. "And you know what?"

"What?"

"Almost everyone survived, and we are the stronger for it."

"Almost everyone?"

He caught the flicker of hesitation. "Sometimes, Peter, sacrifices are made for the greater good. It cannot always be avoided, no matter how hard we try." She shook off the melancholy and squared her shoulders. "Loss is painful, but considering our circumstances, sometimes we cannot escape it. Sonia understands that."

Peter shook his head. "So, she's expendable?"

She paused, her piercing eyes narrowing. "No one is expendable, Peter. If that's the message I implied, then I apologize. If I could take her place then I would. I've known Sonia a long time, and I consider her a friend, no matter how much we may disagree. I don't wish her harm any more than you. But if this man wishes us all ill-will, and she's the only one who can stop him, well…"

Peter set his jaw, his chest tightening. "I can't stand by and watch him hurt her."

Sonia entered the room. "No one's asking you to do any such thing, Peter. If you are uncomfortable with this assignment, then you may leave at any time. I know what it's like to watch someone you care for struggle, to know they're in danger, and have no idea how to stop it."

Peter shook his head. "I don't want to leave. I just think there has to be other options."

Sonia sighed. "I want other options, too. Should they appear, I'll be the first to consider them, but until that time comes, we go with what we have, and that's me. Unfortunately, even that is not a guarantee. You've seen what he has done, and know what he can do."

"And I also know that we've dealt with other dangerous people who've wished us harm, and we survived. Can't those experiences help us with this one?" asked Peter.

Sonia stepped closer. "This is not their battle. It's mine, and mine alone."

"That's where I disagree," said Peter. "Sometimes asking for help is the most courageous thing you can do."

Sonia regarded the other woman, and the two shared a knowing look, before the woman spoke. "And that's exactly what you have done. I am apprised of the situation. I know what we're facing, and I will take it back to the others. But for now, we stay the course. I trust Sonia's judgement." She tossed the edge of her scarf over her shoulder. "Is that all you need from me?" She looked between the two of them.

Peter dropped his jaw. "That's it?"

"Just one more thing," said Sonia. "Please come to me first, Peter, if you have a concern. If you choose to go behind my back again, and contact anyone else, I'll ask that you be reassigned. I like you, Peter, but I can't afford your doubt. We are treading a thin line here, and I need one hundred percent of your support, no matter what your opinion is of my decision making."

Peter dropped his shoulders. Sonia had never chastised him.

"His intentions were honorable, Sonia," said the woman. "Give him that much."

"I am astutely aware of that, but my intentions were honorable as well, and look where it got me," said Sonia.

The older woman adjusted her hold on her purse. "Which is exactly why Peter was assigned. We must learn from our mistakes. Peter is willing to do what you are not. Maybe you should consider that an asset."

Sonia's eyes didn't waver. "Thank you for your insight. Is there anything else?"

The woman held her ground, and Peter swallowed. "I think I've said all I need to say. You know where I stand."

"I do, and thank you for the offer."

"It stands whenever you may need it."

They stared, and Peter sensed them sizing each other up.

The older woman pulled out a pair of sunglasses from her jacket pocket. "Until me meet again, then." She glanced at Peter. "Good to see you, Peter." She put on her sunglasses and walked to the front entry.

Sonia followed. "You, too. Until we meet again." She held the door, and watching the woman leave, closed it behind her.

**

Rem opened the door to Danni's apartment, and looked around. After checking behind it, he walked back to the bedroom and bathroom, inspecting the kitchen along the way.

"All clear," he said, returning to the front room, and dodging the cat that jumped out from beneath the sofa.

Daniels entered with Danni and Jace behind him. "Just get enough stuff for a few days," Daniels said to Danni.

"Are you sure we need to do this?" asked Danni.

"Yes," said Jace. "We're doing this. Get your stuff. We'll wait out here."

Danni hesitated.

Rem petted the cat. "It's for the best, and to be sure you're safe. Daniels and I are going to try and catch this guy, and we don't trust that a patrol car outside is enough. If you disappear for a few days, we can ensure you'll be okay."

"You honestly think he'll come after me?" she asked.

"He requested a tarot reading from you, didn't he?" asked Jace.

"And took a card from your deck. I think that's enough to know he's a threat," said Daniels. He gestured toward a shelf near the dining table. "Is that where you keep your cards?"

"Yes. I do the reading at the table, but then put the cards on the shelf when I'm done with them."

"We'll get somebody in here to dust for prints. Maybe we'll get lucky. You have a spare key?"

"Really? Dust for prints?"

"It's a long shot, but we'll try," said Rem. "Before you pack, pull up that reading you sent him. We need to look at it."

Sighing, Danni walked to the table with the laptop. After she hit a button, the screen brightened, and she typed and opened her email. "There. Have at it. You can scroll down to see the other messages from him."

"Thanks," said Daniels, sitting at the table, trying not to touch anything. He angled the computer with a pencil so Jace and Rem could read it, too. Danni disappeared into the bedroom.

Rem read the email. "Interesting. Sounds like she got a good read on Rutger. That Magician card is accurate, and the karma stuff, let's hope that works in our favor."

Jace finished reading and groaned. "Shit. This guy's a psycho. How the hell are we going to stop him?"

Rem glanced at Daniels. "*We* aren't going to do anything. You and Danni are going to disappear for a few days."

"Your best chance to find him is through me," said Jace. "You heard what he said. He thinks he's my brother."

"You sure he isn't?" asked Daniels. "We checked your background. You grew up in foster care. You could have a slew of relatives you know nothing about."

Jace opened his mouth to speak, but stopped.

Daniels stood. "You just need to hole up for a few days. Let me and Rem do our job. We'll look for Sonia. Hopefully we'll find her and get some answers."

"Any ideas how?" asked Rem. "She keeps popping up without anybody else's help. We just need her to pop up again."

"We've got her last name from when she was a witness on the Makeup Artist case. Should have her address too," said Daniels. "We'll find her."

"Something tells me she may have lied about her address," said Rem. "Maybe even her last name."

"That's why you need me," said Jace. "She visited both of us in the hospital. Maybe if we go back, she'll turn up again."

"We need you to watch Danni. That's just as important, and Daniels and I can't be in two places at once," said Rem. "You said you have a place you can take her?"

"Yes," Jace nodded. "It's safe."

"Where?" asked Daniels.

Jace paused. "I think it's better I don't tell you."

"What? You don't trust us?" asked Rem.

Jace's face hardened. "I don't trust Rutger. I've seen what he can do. If he got a hold of one of you and used his skills, he could absolutely get you to talk."

"We're tougher than Rem looks," said Daniels.

Rem frowned.

"And if he's torturing Rem while you watch?" asked Jace. "No offense, but I think you'd sing like a canary."

"More like a moose," said Rem.

"Moose don't sing," said Daniels.

"Exactly," said Rem.

"Are you saying I'd crack under pressure?" asked Daniels.

"No. I'm saying you can't sing," said Rem.

Daniels smirked and shook his head. He spoke to Jace. "We get your point."

"Then don't tell us, but make sure you're reachable, and stay in touch," said Rem.

"What do you want to do about the reading?" Daniels bobbed his head at the laptop.

Rem shrugged. "Don't know. We could have our tech guys check the email address. See if we can track it back to the sender, but something tells me that's a long shot. We could have her reach out again and see if he answers. Maybe we can use that to draw him out?"

"He'll see through that," said Jace. "I don't want to involve her any more than we have to."

"We'll have our guys look at it. See what they can do. In the meantime, don't be surprised if he gets in touch. He'll likely do it because he knows he's getting to you." Daniels reached for his phone, but winced, holding his injured hand.

"We need to get that checked," said Rem. "You probably need stiches."

"It's fine. I cleaned it," said Daniels.

"Using soap and water and wrapping it in a bandage will only work for so long. You don't want it to get infected," said Rem.

Daniels held his hand against his chest. "It won't get infected. Besides, we don't have time to see a doctor."

"We'll make time," said Rem.

"Let me see it," said Jace.

Daniels pulled back. "I don't think so. You'll probably pour a bottle of tequila over it."

"I don't have any tequila," said Jace.

"It would probably help disinfect it. Maybe Danni has some," said Rem.

Daniels eyes flared. "Don't you dare."

Jace reached out. "Let me see it."

Daniels hesitated. "Why?"

"Because. That's why," said Jace.

Rem shrugged. "Seems like a good enough reason."

Daniels paused and reluctantly held out his injured palm.

Jace held Daniels' fingers and gently unwrapped the bandage. Daniels sucked in a breath and grit his teeth.

"Take it easy," said Jace. "You need a new bandage. This one's a mess."

Rem stepped closer and could see the blood. "I thought you said it stopped bleeding?"

"It did, but this little inspection isn't helping any. Ouch," he yelped.

"Stay still," said Jace. He hovered his other hand over the wound. "I want to try something."

"What are you doing?" asked Daniels.

"You asked me a question earlier at the bar," said Jace, his voice quieting.

Rem watched Daniels' expression change from pain to curiosity. "What question was that?" asked Rem.

Jace focused on Daniels' palm, his face serious. "About what I could do."

Daniels looked up at Rem. "It's getting hot."

"I'm comfortable. Maybe Danni turned on the heat," said Rem.

"Not the room, bonehead. My hand," said Daniels. His eyes widened. "Really hot. Wow. What are you doing?"

Jace continued to focus. "Just a little experiment." He took a deep breath and put his free hand over Daniels, covering it. He took a few more breaths and released Daniels' hand. "How does that feel?"

Daniels stared at his palm, and opened and closed his fingers. Rem leaned over to look.

"The pain is almost gone," said Daniels.

"It still looks gross," said Rem.

"You should clean it again," said Jace.

"What did you do?" asked Daniels.

"Not exactly sure. I think it's an energy thing."

"An energy thing?" asked Rem. "Now you sound like Jill."

"Jill?" asked Jace. "The lady detective? We still need to talk about her. Madison Vickers, too. If you're assuming they're my sisters, how come they don't know me? Unless they grew up in foster care, too?"

"No, they didn't. That's another mystery on the list to solve, which is only getting longer as we speak," said Rem.

"Tell me about it," said Daniels, wiggling his fingers.

Danni walked into the room with a small bag and a backpack. "Here's an extra key." She handed it to Rem. "I've packed some clothes and toiletries. I just need to get Seymour set up with some cat food and fresh litter. He should be fine for a few days, but if it's longer than that, I can ask the neighbor to check on him." She reached past Rem for her laptop.

"Hold up. Leave your laptop," said Rem. "We're going to have our tech guys look at it, see if they can trace the email, plus dust it for prints."

"But I've used it," said Danni. "Any prints are likely ruined. And why would he look at my laptop?"

"For the same reason he came in here in the first place. Intimidation. Knowledge is power," said Daniels.

Danni shivered. "I'll need it though. I still have a business to run."

"There's a computer where we're headed. You can use that," said Jace.

Danni sighed reluctantly. "Okay. You guys read the email?"

"We did. It seems you know your stuff," said Rem.

"I just read what the cards tell me."

"He may contact you again. If he does, let us know," said Daniels.

"Fine. I'll tell you."

They watched her add food and water for the cat and head into the bathroom to take care of the litter. "Where exactly are we going?" she asked from the bathroom.

"You let me worry about that," said Jace. "We'll stop at my place and get a few things and then we'll take off."

She poked her head out. "You're sure about this? Why don't you just drop me at a motel? Nobody will know where I am."

"Because I don't like it," said Jace. "This guy is dangerous. You shouldn't be alone."

"We don't like it either," said Rem. He eyed Jace. 'You sure this place of yours is safe?"

"Completely," said Jace. "Nobody else knows about it but me."

Danni came out of the bathroom and gave Seymore a scratch on the head. "I'll be gone for a few days, boy, but I'll have Margie check in on you."

The cat purred and strode off, unconcerned.

The doorbell rang, and Rem went still. Jace and Danni didn't move either.

"You expecting someone?" asked Rem, quietly.

"No, I'm not," said Danni.

Daniels stood, waiting, when the doorbell rang again. He checked the peephole. "Who is it?"

"Delivery for Danni Eldridge," said a male voice.

Rem stepped up to Daniels. "What do you think," he whispered.

Daniels cracked the door and Rem stepped to the side, his hand on his weapon.

The voice came again. "Flower delivery."

Jace went to stand beside Danni. "You expecting flowers?"

"No," Danni whispered.

Daniels opened the door wider. "Yes?"

"I'm from *Pick your Petals*. I have a delivery," said the man at the door. "You Danni?"

"Nope, but I'll make sure she gets them. He reached out. "What's your name?"

Rem poked his head around the corner and saw a skinny kid with long black hair, a tattoo on his cheek and gauges in his ears. He startled when Rem appeared.

He looked between the two of them. "Ronson." He handed the flowers to Daniels. "I need you to sign for them."

"You have any idea who sent them?" asked Rem. He took the offered phone from Ronson and signed with his finger.

"How would I know that? I just pick 'em up and deliver 'em."

"I don't know. Maybe you saw someone come in to the shop." Rem held the phone, waiting for Ronson to answer.

"That would be hard. We're online only. All the orders come from the website."

Rem handed the phone back. "Figures. You got a record of who sent these?"

"I don't take the flower orders. I'm just a delivery guy. You'd have to check with my boss."

"Got it. Thanks, Ronson," said Rem.

"Take it easy," said Ronson.

Daniels closed the door and put the flowers on the table. It was a bouquet of daisies in a glass vase.

"Shit," said Jace. "Is there a card?"

"Yes." Daniels reached for it.

"Could there be fingerprints?" asked Danni.

"Not if it's from the flower shop. Whoever sent them didn't touch them," said Rem. "What's it say?" he asked Daniels.

Daniels studied the card. "Thanks for the reading. Can't wait to get to know you," read Daniels. "It's not signed."

"Oh, God," said Danni. "Is it from him?"

"That's it," said Jace. "We're out of here. Get your stuff. Let's go." Jace grabbed Danni's small suitcase and headed for the door.

Danni picked up her backpack, and Daniels put the card down. "You head down to the car. We'll be right behind you," he said.

"Fine," said Jace. "Come on."

He walked out and Danni followed.

Rem saw Daniels' face. "What is it? You think the flowers are a threat or a wild goose chase? Guy sent daisies, so he knows her name. He's messing with her, and Jace."

Daniels shook his head. "It's not the flowers. We'll deal with those. It's this."

He held out his injured palm, and Rem stilled. "What the…?"

Daniels' wound was gone, and fresh, pink skin with a slight scar was all that remained.

CHAPTER TWENTY

Danni followed Jace into the small house. "Is this yours?"

They'd taken Danni's car and after leaving Jace's place, they'd driven up into the countryside outside the city and stopped here, on a small property with a few trees and soft, green grass. A wooden swing on the porch swayed gently in the breeze. Danni admired the idyllic surroundings.

"No. It's not. It's Justin's." He walked in and threw his backpack onto the sofa and the car keys on the small dining table. "I'll put your stuff in your room." He headed into a door on the right.

Danni admired the pretty house. The kitchen was small but tidy. There was a couch and coffee table across from a small TV mounted on the wall. She could see another bedroom across from where Jace had disappeared and a bathroom in between.

Jace emerged from the room. "The place is clean and there are fresh sheets on the beds and fresh towels in the john. Don't know about the food situation. We may have to run to the grocer down the road and pick up some stuff."

"This was Justin's? How come it doesn't look like a man cave?"

"Justin's home is…was…his man cave. This was his escape. He could come here and get away. Have the place to himself. Most of the time, though, after a ride, we'd come up here, drink a beer, and shoot the shit. He gave me a key. Told me to use it whenever I wanted."

"This is really nice." She ran her hand along the top of a dining chair. "Justin keeps surprising me."

"Yeah, me, too," said Jace. "Don't know what will happen to it now that he's..." he paused, "...gone. Guess that will be up to his family."

She walked into the kitchen and looked out the window, seeing the neighbor's porch and enjoying the view of the trees in the backyard. "Have you talked to them, since..."

"Briefly, at the hospital." Jace pushed back his windswept hair. "His parents have never been big fans of me though. Back in school, they always thought I was responsible if Justin ever got into trouble. I told them what happened to Justin and I'm pretty sure they're blaming me for this too. I'm wondering if they'll even want me at the funeral." He sat at the dining table.

Danni walked over. "You know what happened to Justin isn't your fault, right?"

Jace studied the table. "I'm not too sure about that. If it hadn't been for Justin's connection to me, he'd be alive."

Danni sat next to him. "You didn't kill him. This man, this Rutger, he's sick. If he hadn't targeted you, he'd have targeted someone else, and he has targeted others. You're not the only one. That's not their fault any more than it is yours."

"When you're sitting in my shoes, it feels a lot different."

Danni clenched her fingers together. "I have sat in your shoes. I know what feeling guilty is like. It takes time and therapy to work through it. It doesn't happen overnight, but it will happen." She put her hand on his wrist. "Good friends can help."

Jace sighed and cleared his throat. "What happened, back at the bar, was dumb. I was drunk, and stupid, and I said things I shouldn't have said. I'm sorry I implied you were responsible for this mess. And I'm sorry for what I said about your dad."

Danni nodded. She stood and walked away from the table. The house was quiet and it felt safe. She slid her jacket off and threw it next to Jace's backpack. "We both said things we shouldn't have said."

Jace stifled a yawn, and Danni figured he was starting to wind down after a couple of difficult days. He stood, went over to the couch and sat. "You didn't accept my apology."

Danni glanced out another window with a view of the rolling hills. "I accept your apology."

"Thank you." He leaned back against the cushions.

She exhaled a deep breath. "So what do we do now?"

"You hungry?"

"Not really."

"You want to get cleaned up? Take a shower? Then maybe we can go get some groceries?"

"Sure, that sounds good."

"Okay. Bathroom's all yours. I'll go after you." He looked up. "Also, Justin has a laptop in the closet. It will need to be charged, but you can use it."

Danni walked over to the couch and stood beside him.

"What?" he asked. He rested his head back, stifling another yawn and his watery eyes twinkled.

"Why did you bring me here?" she asked.

His brow furrowed. 'That's a stupid question. To keep you safe."

"You know very well that you could have used one of the safe houses the detectives offered, or taken me to a motel. Or I could have left town. Any of those would have worked fine."

"No, they wouldn't."

"Why not?"

"Because this guy is different. I considered leaving you, and trying to find him myself, but I know the likelihood of that happening is slim. I figure we give it a couple of days, and see if Daniels and Remalla can find him. If not, then we'll figure out what to do next. Either way, though, I don't want you to be alone. If this guy shows, he'll have to get through me first."

"That's very courageous of you, but you know what he can do. We both saw it. If he wanted, he could walk right in here and do whatever the hell he wanted."

"He won't do that. At least not yet anyway."

"Why not? How do you know that?"

"Because, he wants something first." He stared up at the ceiling.

"What's that?"

Jace set his jaw. "A reckoning."

"A reckoning? With who?"

"I'm not sure."

"And he needs you to do that?"

"He needs all of us."

Danni hesitated. "All of us? Who's all of us?"

He looked away from the ceiling and focused on her. His intense stare made her cheeks color, and she shifted uncomfortably. He smiled softly. "Go take your shower." He rested his head back and closed his eyes. "And don't use all the hot water."

"Jace..."

"We'll talk later. Right now, I just need to rest."

Danni nodded, understanding. The shower beckoned, and she walked around the sofa and into the bathroom where she flicked on the light. The bathroom was small but clean and brown towels hung from a rack on the wall.

She turned the nozzle and the water sprayed. After adjusting the temperature, she walked out and headed toward the bedroom. Hearing a soft snore, she saw Jace was asleep. Smiling, she moved closer, watching him.

Recalling her circumstances, her smile faded. She and Jace could both be in danger. Were they crazy to stay here in this charming house, and hope for the best? Was she dumb to stay with Jace, the object of crazy Rutger's attention? Wouldn't it make more sense to get as far away as possible?

Everything had happened so fast; she hadn't had time to think. She spied the car keys on the table. She could leave right now. Then no one would know where she was. Wouldn't that be the safest option? Her heart fluttered and it surprised her. What was stopping her? Why hadn't she told them she could take care of herself, and left town?

Listening to Jace's soft snores, she swallowed, admitting the answer. Through all of this insanity, she'd developed a fondness for him. She dared not say crush, because she wasn't a school girl, and that was silly. Jace was imposing, rude, crude, and self-absorbed. He spoke without thinking, and yelled more than talked. And his taste in women was horrible. She certainly wasn't his type. He liked the flashy girls like Devyn.

Shaking her head, she decided she'd do as he asked. They'd give it a few days, and if nothing happened and Rutger remained a threat, she'd hop in her car, and get the hell out of Dodge, Jace and her feelings be damned. No man was worth getting killed over.

Satisfied with her decision, she hurried to get in the shower.

**

Daniels walked out to the car and where Rem leaned against the passenger door. "Well?" asked Rem.

Daniels looked back at the apartment building. "No longer lives here and they have no forwarding address for Sonia."

"Wonderful."

Daniels leaned on the car next to him. "What now?"

"I called Lozano. There's nothing in the system on her, or at least that name. He'll put out a missing person's report. I just hope that doesn't hurt more than it helps."

"I suppose we don't have much of a choice."

"Yeah." He saw Daniels flex his fingers. "How's your hand?"

"Good as new. Unbelievable."

"These guys have some spooky gifts. And I don't think it's an accident."

Daniels nodded. "You heard what Rutger said. That he was somehow made. You think that's how he can do what he does? And what Jill, Madison and Jace can do?"

Rem shook his head. "I don't know, but they don't teach you to expect this crap at the police academy."

"You think it's time we come clean with Lozano?"

Rem pushed off from the car. "We're going to have to tell him something. He's expecting an update on our progress."

Daniels nodded. "We need to put out an APB on Rutger."

"That ought to be interesting. Looks like Rutger Hauer, runs like a deer, and throws shit without touching it."

"I think we may have to leave that part out," said Daniels.

"You think?"

"Problem is, if anybody spots him, they'll never catch him. It might even endanger them."

Rem hooked his thumbs in his jean pockets. "I doubt Rutger would hang around long enough to bother. I think we're the ones he wants to deal with. Besides, even if we do a sketch, we'll be getting tips on every good-looking Tom, Dick and Harry with blonde hair and blue eyes. I don't know if it will do any good."

"Well, we have to do something. He's our only suspect, and we know he did it. How else are we going to find him?"

Rem ran a hand through his long hair. "Something tells me Sonia is the key. We find her and Rutger will come calling."

"You think that's what he wants?" asked Daniels.

Rem frowned. "You mean he's making us do his dirty work? We find her and he kills her?"

"Something like that."

"That could work against him. If we do find her, then we need to be prepared for him to show, and maybe we take him down instead."

"You have any ideas how we're going to do that? He has the upper hand with those parlor tricks of his."

"That's because it's always been on his terms. Maybe if we draw him out, we can set a trap and spring it on him."

"What kind of trap is that? How do you stop someone who can do what he does?"

Rem shook his head. "I don't have all the answers, you know. But somebody out there does."

"Who would that be?"

"You are just full of helpful questions, aren't you?"

"I am, especially ones I don't have the answers to." He straightened and kicked a stone. "This is a big problem. How do you catch a guy who can't be caught? Without getting yourself killed in the process?"

"He said something about not having a name," said Rem.

Daniels pointed. "That's right. That doesn't make any sense either. Who doesn't have a name?"

"We've got to find Sonia. I bet she'll have some answers for us. Maybe she'll know how to stop him."

Daniels furrowed his brow. "Maybe we can get her to come to us."

Rem crossed his arms. "How do you plan on doing that?"

"Think about it. Why did she show up at the hospital? Why did she talk to us? If she'd laid low, we'd have never thought twice about her. But she deliberately came out in the open. Maybe she wants to help us. Maybe she wants us to find her."

"Well, she's not making it easy," said Rem. "We could make it an APB on her, instead of missing persons."

Daniels shook his head. "I don't like that. Not if we don't have to."

Rem shrugged. "Then what?"

"She showed up for Jace, Jill and Madison. And us. She's obviously keeping tabs on us." Daniels paced, thinking. "What else do we know about her?"

Rem snapped his fingers. "Doesn't she make her own stuff? Is it lotions? She likes jewelry too. Wears that big clunky stuff. She gave Jill a necklace."

"Jace, too," said Daniels. "And how much you want to bet she gave something to Madison?"

"So, where do you buy this stuff?" asked Rem. "If she's just buying it online, or any random store, it's not much help."

"No, it's not," said Daniels. "But does Sonia strike you as someone who buys cheap stones?"

"Unlikely."

"There's a few shops in town that sell that stuff. Marjorie's been to a couple. How about we check them out. Flash her picture around. See what falls out. Maybe we'll get lucky."

Rem tipped his head. "It's worth a shot."

"Then let's do it." Daniels started to open the car door.

"You forgetting something?" asked Rem. "Don't you want to stop by a certain jeweler? Make a certain purchase?"

Daniels paused. "We're kind of busy on this case. I figured the ring will still be there tomorrow."

"Uh, uh. Nope. We're going. It won't be longer than an hour, at most. You already know what you want. Besides, he's a jeweler, right? He'll probably know what shops to hit for Sonia's rocks. Might as well kill two birds with one stone."

"You got a point, there. You're sure?"

Rem opened the car door. "Do I look like I'm joking? Get your butt in the car. You're buying that ring. No more putting it off."

Daniels smiled. "You ready to marry me off?"

"Ready? I've been trying to get you off the market for years. Less competition for me."

Daniels chuckled. "Okay, partner. You need all the help you can get. Let's go buy a ring."

CHAPTER TWENTY-ONE

Danni flipped on the coffee machine, and listened to it hum to life. Glancing outside the window, she saw a bird fly by and land on a branch on a nearby tree. She'd slept better than she'd expected for being in an unfamiliar place, and considering her unusual circumstances. Jace had not emerged from his room. After her shower the previous night, he'd remained asleep on the couch. Not wanting to wake him, she'd grabbed the laptop from the closet and plugged it in. After a minute, it had hummed to life and she'd reluctantly checked her messages, and had been relieved to not see a reply for *BrotherlyLove*. Hopefully, she'd heard the last from him, and the detectives would solve this case before he contacted her again.

There had been a reply from *Lovelorn52* requesting a follow up question, and a new question from a user name called *Livininrio*. Rio had a financial question regarding a potential investment and would it be worth the risk. *Love* wanted to know if she pursued the relationship, which had potential, according to the first reading, would it be success-ful?

Danni had pulled out a deck she'd brought from home which was different than the deck that Rutger had stolen from. The detectives had taken that, although she doubted they would get anything from it. Danni didn't really want it back. Just thinking about how that man had been in her apartment without her knowledge made her shudder. She thought of Jace in the other room and was glad he was here.

While Jace slept on the couch, she'd done the reading for Rio, telling them the investment would not be wise to make. The cards revealed the source could not be trusted, and to look elsewhere for a smart investment.

This morning, she planned to answer *Lovelorn*, but first she needed her coffee. After doing the reading for Rio, Jace had continued to sleep. She'd covered him with a light blanket and gone to bed. This morning, when she'd emerged, Jace had been gone, and she could hear light snoring from the other room. The man was obviously exhausted. He likely had slept little since this ordeal began, and the alcohol and grief hadn't helped.

They'd never made it to the grocery, and there was little to eat, but she'd found some bread in the freezer the previous night and she'd left it out to thaw. She'd found some peanut butter in the pantry, as well as some coffee grounds and filters. There was no cream, but she would make do without it. As the coffee brewed, and her stomach rumbled, she made some peanut butter toast.

Once the toast and coffee were ready, she sat at the dining table and opened the laptop. She felt a sliver of anxiety when she opened her email again, wondering if *BrotherlyLove* would be in her inbox, but he wasn't. She wondered if there ever would be a time when she wouldn't hold her breath when she checked her mail.

Picking up her coffee, she jumped when Jace's bedroom door opened. Jace stepped out, looking bleary eyed and still half asleep. His hair was a mess and he still wore the same clothes from the previous night.

"Mornin'," He rubbed his face.

"Good morning," she said.

He pointed. "Shower." He walked into the bathroom and closed the door.

"Obviously not a morning person," she mumbled and sipped her coffee.

She focused on *Lovelorn*, shuffled the deck, and pulled three cards for the follow up. Based on her reading, she pulled two more cards for clarification, and she responded to *Lovelorn*. They indicated *Lovelorn* should look inward for happiness, not towards another. Sometimes the cards did that – took you in a new direction. Although *Lovelorn* had asked about the relationship's success, the cards suggested that true happiness came from within, not externally. She told *Lovelorn* that if she pursued the relationship, and it didn't work out, then that would be okay too. Either way, there would be benefit.

She typed out her response, wanting to be as clear as possible. She liked to provide a picture of the cards pulled, and provide a good explanation of what each meant, to ensure the questioner knew why she'd come to the conclusion she'd reached.

Midway through her response, she heard the shower turn off. She sipped her coffee, considering her next words, when the door opened and Jace stepped out of the bathroom with only a damp towel wrapped around his waist. His long, wet hair hung down to his shoulders, and his damp skin, muscled chest and strapping arms glimmered in the sunlight from the window. His tattoos covered his chest and ran down his back and she tried not to stare. Without acknowledging her, he walked into the bedroom and closed the door.

Danni lost her train of thought, her mind wandering. Suddenly thirsty, she returned to the kitchen to get some more coffee, still seeing Jace wrapped in that towel.

"So what?" she said quietly to herself. "It's not like you haven't seen a man's chest before." Her skin warmed, but she blamed the coffee.

Refocusing, she returned to her laptop and continued her response. A few minutes later, Jace reemerged from the bedroom, wearing jeans and a t-shirt, his hair still damp, but now brushed. "Hey," he said.

"Hey," she answered. "Feel better?"

"Like a new man, considering. You sleep okay?"

"Better than expected. The bed was comfortable."

"You can thank me for that. I told Justin not to skimp on the mattresses. Nothing's worse than a lousy mattress."

"True."

"Is that fresh coffee?"

"It is."

"Bless you. You find something to eat?"

"I managed. There's bread and peanut butter."

"Great. That ought to get us through till we get to the grocery. Sorry I conked out on you last night."

"You needed the rest."

He helped himself to the coffee and popped some bread in the toaster. "You doing the card thing?"

"You mean a tarot reading? Yes."

"Not for anyone weird, are you?"

"If you're asking if it's for *BrotherlyLove,* no it's not. It's for someone asking about their love life."

"That's pathetic."

She'd almost picked up where she'd left off, but stopped. "Excuse me? Why is it pathetic?"

He found some sugar in the cupboard and added it to his mug. "Why does someone need to go to a tarot reader for their love life? It sounds to me that they're just too scared to jump in. They want the cards to tell them what to do. It's like going to a fortune-teller who tells you exactly what you want to hear and then takes your money."

Danni stiffened. "Is that what you think I do?"

He added coffee to his generous helping of sugar. "I'm not saying you're not honest about it. But you are just reading some cards."

"I'm not just reading some cards. I wouldn't do this if I didn't think this was actually helping. These cards, if you take it seriously, can offer some real guidance and assist with difficult decisions. And it doesn't *tell* them what to do. A person can make whatever choice they want."

"I think it's hogwash."

Danni set her jaw. This was the typical opinion of most. She'd learned to deal with it over the years, but Jace seemed to be someone who could easily get under her skin. "Hogwash? People ask for help in a lot of different ways. I've seen these cards touch on issues and reveal subjects that people never expected and probably wouldn't discuss in a shrink's office after months of therapy. If a person is willing to open up and listen, they can be a valuable tool."

He sipped his coffee and leaned against the kitchen counter, looking relaxed in his jeans, t-shirt and bare feet. "Now you're comparing yourself to a shrink?"

"I didn't compare myself to a shrink. I'm simply saying different methods resonate with different people. And if these cards resonate with you, then there's a reason why, and a good tarot reader who's intuitive can be a helpful advisor. Life is hard. Why not ask for guidance?"

His toast popped out of the toaster. "I still think it's silly."

Danni drummed her nails on the table top. "The cards read you and Devyn pretty accurately."

He paused in mid-reach for the toast and looked back. "What?"

"The reading for you and Devyn at the bar."

He stared for a second before grabbing his toast and put it on a plate. "I don't remember."

She shook her head, deciding not to push. He likely didn't want to remember. "I don't know why, after what you saw yesterday at the bar, that you can't believe the cards can read someone. I'd think after seeing that coffee pot fly off the table, anything's possible."

He slathered peanut butter on his bread. "I've experienced too much crap in my life to ask a deck of cards to tell me anything, much less advise me." He shook his head. "And now this weird Rutger guy shows up, doing crazy things that make no sense, and I can somehow—"

"You can somehow what?"

"Nothing." He put the dirty knife in the sink. "You mean to tell me that if I'd asked for a reading, that the cards would have told me all of that?" He chuckled. "If that's true, then you should be charging a lot more."

"I'm not saying they would have been that specific, but they might have revealed that big change was coming, that maybe the people around you were not as they seemed. To be careful who you trust. There's a lot they could have revealed. You don't know unless you ask."

He picked up his plate and mug, brought them to the table, and set them down. "All right. Then let's ask. Let's see what the cards say about our present situation."

"Seriously?"

"Seriously."

She hesitated, then shook her head. "No."

His face fell. "No? Why not?"

"You're just looking for an excuse to make fun of me."

He put his palm over his heart. "I promise. No making fun. I'm curious. God knows we don't have much else to do around here."

She narrowed her eyes.

"Come on. Let's see what you got. I want to know how this situation resolves itself. Ask the cards. What do I have to do to deal with this guy?"

Danni considered it. Should she do it? She took a breath and went quiet, listening to her own internal guidance, which surprisingly felt positive. "Okay. Let me finish this response." She held out a finger. "But no joking around. You make fun, and I'm taking my cards and going home."

"No, you're not. At least not until it's safe."

"You know what I mean."

He took a bite of his toast and peanut butter smeared on his lip. "I'm serious. Let's do this." He wiped it off the peanut butter with a finger and licked it off.

Danni finished her response to *Lovelorn* and sent the email. She closed her computer as Jace took his last bite of toast. She put the laptop aside and he slid his plate back, and she grabbed the cards. "You ready?"

"As I'll ever be. Show me what you got." He rubbed his hands together.

Danni hesitated, questioning the usefulness of this. He'd likely laugh off whatever the cards said. But she still felt the nudge to do it. She put the cards in front of him. "Here. Shuffle."

"Okay." He started to shuffle.

"I'm going to warm up my coffee. You want more?"

"Sure. Thanks. Add some sugar, will you?"

She shook her head, and went to the kitchen, where she refilled both mugs and added more sugar to Jace's.

Coming back to the table, she gave Jace his mug and sat beside him.

"Here. All shuffled." He slid the cards back to her.

"Cut the deck first."

"All right." He cut the deck.

Danni took the cards and held them. "I am going to fan them out and you can pick the cards as we ask. Sound good?"

"You're leading this charge. Whatever you say."

She fanned the cards out on the table. "Ask your first question. Then pick two cards."

Jace rubbed his jaw. "What should we do about this situation?" He pulled two cards and put them in front of Danni.

"Okay," said Danni. "We have the Hanged Man and the Ten of Cups reversed. The Hanged Man suggests hanging back and letting others handle it, so that might suggest the detectives. Let them handle the case and you stay out of it."

"Huh. Don't know if I like that. I'm antsy enough as it is."

"The Ten of Cups is about family. Parents and children. Reversed it suggests upheaval and vulnerability. So, an unhappy family is involved, and maybe trying to fix whatever's wrong."

Jace shifted in his seat. "Family, huh?"

"Yes. Make sense? This guy thinks he's your brother. Maybe there's some merit to that."

"Maybe."

"You want any clarification on that?"

He looked at her, his eyes serious. "What's going to happen?"

She nodded. "Okay. Let's pick two cards for that."

He grabbed two cards and placed them on the table.

"We have the Page of Swords and the Nine of Swords. Hmm." She tapped her finger on the table.

"What?"

"The Page of Swords is a messenger, and the Nine of Swords indicates worry and anxiety. You're obviously worried, and maybe more is coming for you to worry about."

"That's helpful. What else could I be worried about? Haven't I dealt with enough?"

"Pull another card. Maybe that will help clarify things."

He took another card from the deck and placed it with the others. It was the Five of Pentacles. "That doesn't look promising." The two people on the card looked helpless, walking through a frozen field outside a church, one of them on crutches.

"Well, it's not great. It suggests losing money or health. It also suggests deception."

"I don't have any money. At least not enough to worry about losing." He frowned. "Could that mean someone might get hurt?"

Danni sighed. "It could. And you might not see it coming."

"This reading is going downhill fast."

"I agree. It's a little unsettling."

"Aren't there any rainbows and fairies in this deck?"

"There are. You just haven't picked them."

"Just my luck." He held his coffee cup, but didn't drink. "Is there anything can I do about it? With all this deception, is there anyone I can trust?"

"Pick two cards again. Maybe you'll get your rainbow."

He pulled the first card. It was the Two of Cups.

Danni tapped it. "Interesting. That suggests a partnership. Either working or romantic. Pull the second card."

"A romance. That's just what I need right now." He pulled the Queen of Cups.

Danni felt her face warm, and didn't look up.

"What is it?" Jace studied the card. "Don't know much about the lady on the card, but she's cute."

"It's the Queen of Cups."

"I can read. What does she mean?"

Danni cleared her throat. "It suggests an intuitive woman."

"An intuitive woman? Is that who I'm partnering with? Who do I know—" He paused. "Oh, wait…"

Danni looked up and he held her stare.

"You're blushing," he said.

Danni held her face. "Maybe a little." When Jace pulled that card, the sensations that hit her were unexpected. The Queen of Cups had always been the card that had spoken to her and the one she'd related the closest to. It was talking to her now, confirming Danni's suspicions. The card suggested she and Jace work together and perhaps do more than that. "Any other questions?"

Jace continued to study her. "Those cards are smarter than I thought."

"They have their moments." She nervously gathered the deck although he hadn't said whether or not he had another question.

"Danni," he said.

"What?" she asked, pulling the deck back together.

"Danni," he said again, putting his hand over hers. "Stop."

She stilled, the deck still a mess, and met his gaze. An electric current traveled up her arm from where he touched her.

"Jace…like you said. It's just cards."

He leaned in, his brown eyes warm and soft, and her heart thumped. "Thanks for the reading," he said quietly.

"You're welcome." He continued to hold her hand and heat traveled into her chest. She held his gaze, unable to look away.

His thumb moved over hers and his eyes turned a deep chocolate brown. "Maybe we should...have you ever considered..." he started.

She swallowed. "Maybe we should...what?" Her voice came out wispy.

For a moment, they held the look, and she half anticipated him to lean in and kiss her, and she mentally prepared for it. But then his eyes shifted, and he blinked, and leaned back. "Maybe we should go to the grocery store." He stood and took a sip of his coffee. "We're going to need more than peanut butter."

CHAPTER TWENTY-TWO

Remalla sat at his desk and tapped a pencil on a notepad. He waited for Daniels to get off the phone. Swiveling in his seat, he saw Lozano in his office, talking on the phone. They were due to give him an update on the case, and they still weren't sure what to tell him.

Mel and Garcia had both been released from the hospital and would be at home for the rest of the week. Devyn had been upgraded to serious condition at the hospital, and they'd gone to see her that morning. She hadn't offered much more to help them. Her memory was fuzzy but she still remembered what the man had told her. She'd asked about Jace, but they'd said only that he was fine. She'd gone quiet after that, and they'd left, ensuring an officer was still stationed outside her door.

They'd also reviewed the videotape in Justin's lobby, and confirmed Jace's arrival. A man matching Rutger's description, wearing a hoodie with his head down, had entered about forty minutes prior to Jace's arrival. He'd dodged around a delivery man carrying a box and seemed to try and hide behind him. They'd never seen him leave, though and suspected he'd somehow left out the back and into an alley.

Daniels hung up the phone.

"Anything?" asked Rem.

"Nothing from the email. It's impossible to trace without a warrant. Privacy issues. Maybe Lozano can help with that."

"Maybe. But that will take time."

"Anything about the prints from Danni's or the deck of cards?" asked Daniels.

"Nothing yet, but I'm not expecting much."

"No, I know." Daniels held the bridge of his nose.

"Headache?" asked Rem.

Daniels sighed. "No. Just perpetual stress."

"Here." Rem opened his drawer and pulled out a small, squishy ball. He tossed it to Daniels, who caught it.

"What's this?"

"It's a stress reliever."

"Does it work?" He squeezed the ball.

"Not in my experience."

"Then why are you giving it to me?"

"Maybe it will work better for you. You look like you need to squeeze a ball." He grinned.

Daniels smirked. "I'm shocked this didn't work for you."

"That's not the ball I need squeezed."

Daniels raised the side of his lip. "Missing Jill?"

Rem shifted in his seat. "I am. She was supposed to visit, but with this case…"

"You don't think she should come?"

"I don't know."

Daniels narrowed his eyes. "You still haven't mentioned any of this to her, have you?"

"Nope."

"You should. And it may not be a bad idea for her to be here when you do."

Rem resumed his tapping with his pencil. "She'll think I'm crazy."

"That's nothing new." He leaned forward. "But it's not like I'm not going to back you up. We can both verify what happened."

"I'm worried. Part of me thinks I don't want to involve her. What if Rutger goes after her?"

"She's a big girl. She can take care of herself. You know that."

"I know. But she's been through a lot. That Makeup Artist put her through the wringer. She's finally on stable ground."

"How's her dad?"

"So-so. Out of the hospital. He's getting stronger."

"That's good news. But there's never going to be a perfect time to tell her what happened to Henderson."

Rem scratched his head. "Maybe we should see if we can find Rutger first. If we take him down, and then I tell her, it will be a lot easier."

"What if we don't take him down?"

Rem dropped the pencil. "I guess I just don't understand how bringing her into this can help. I mean, what about Madison? If we bring Jill in, shouldn't we tell her too? Her husband got murdered by Rutger."

"Maybe we should."

Rem paused. "You serious?"

Daniels rubbed his chin. "Why not? Think about it." He sat up. "Rutger came after all of them. Jill, Madison, and Jace. Now what? What's he got up his sleeve, other than going after Sonia?"

"You think if we bring them all together, it will flush him out?"

"I think it's something to consider."

"Or it's a great way for him to have all of them in one place. Maybe that's what he wants. To kill them, and maybe us, too."

Daniels fiddled with a folder on his desk. "Well, we can't just sit here, twiddling our thumbs. We have to make a decision. Take the offensive, or sit back and wait for him to make the next move."

Rem groaned. "If we could find Sonia, that might help."

"We've put the feelers out. We just have to hope she gets the hint."

"None of those shops we visited yesterday afternoon knew who she was. Your jeweler Maxwell's suggestions didn't pan out either."

"He said he'd do some checking. See if could talk to some of his dealers who work in gems and stones. We might get lucky."

"You feeling lucky right now?"

"With this case? No. But I did just buy an engagement ring, so that helps."

Rem offered a soft smile. "That's true. When's it ready?"

"Couple of days. I'll pick it up after it's sized."

"Any ideas how you are going to pop the question?"

Daniels shrugged. "I don't know. I figure 'Will you marry me?' is sufficient."

"You know what I mean."

Daniels nodded. "I know what you mean. I figure a nice romantic meal. Glass of champagne. Maybe a horse-drawn carriage. Something like that."

"If you need me to jump out of a cake, let me know."

Daniels chuckled. "I'll keep that in mind."

"I'm also available for bachelorette parties. Tell Marjorie."

"I think she'd prefer someone sexy."

Rem deflated. "I'll have you know I've jumped out of a cake or two in my time."

"I don't think drunkenness qualifies as experience."

"Well, it certainly didn't matter to the ladies."

Daniels' brow furrowed. "Was that the party where you tossed your cookies in someone's lap?"

Rem sat back. "I told you about that?"

"You got no secrets from me, partner."

Rem resumed his tapping with his finger. "It was still a fun party."

"From whose perspective?"

A male voice spoke. "Daniels. Remalla."

Rem turned to see Lozano sticking his head out of his office.

"Time for that update," Lozano said with a wave.

Rem stood. "Actually, Cap, we were about to head out. We've got to question, um…" He looked at Daniels, who stood too.

"Another jeweler. We may have a lead," said Daniels, pushing his chair in.

Lozano scowled. "Don't give me that crap. Get your butts in here." He swung the door wide.

Rem regarded Daniels, who offered a wide-eyed look. "Okay, Cap," said Rem. He mumbled to Daniels. "What are we going to tell him?"

"I don't know. Guess we're about to find out," said Daniels.

Rem walked into Lozano's office and Daniels followed. They sat in the chairs across from his desk. Lozano shut the door.

"Why do I get the distinct feeling that you're avoiding me?" asked Lozano. He took the seat at his desk.

"That's a nice tie, Cap. Did Sheila pick that out?" asked Rem.

"Stop blowing more smoke up my skirt, Remalla. Where are we on this case?" He leaned back and put his hands on the armrests. "You still think this is the guy that caused Henderson's and Donald Vickers' deaths?"

"It's still the guy," said Daniels.

"Any idea where he is?" asked Lozano.

"Well, you read the report. We chased him into a construction zone," said Daniels.

"And he disappeared on you. How the hell did he do that?" asked Lozano.

"Rutger's faster than he looks," said Rem.

"I thought you ran track. You had the fastest time in your cadet class at the academy. And you're telling me he's faster?" asked Lozano.

"Guy ran through traffic and into a construction area. It wasn't an easy chase," said Daniels.

"This guy took out two of our own," said Lozano. "And he's running around out there making us look stupid."

"We're working on it, Cap," said Rem. "We're looking for Sonia Vandermere. She may have information vital to finding him."

"I remember her." Lozano pointed. "She was a witness in the Makeup Artist case. How the hell does she play in to all of this?"

Rem shot a look at Daniels, who squirmed in his seat.

Lozano narrowed his eyes at both of them. "Is one of you going to tell me what the hell is going on here?"

"We still think Jace Marlon, Jill, and Madison Vickers were targeted by Rutger."

Lozano frowned. "I know that much. Did you figure out the connection?"

Rem picked at some dust on his jeans. "Rutger believes he's Jace's brother."

"Really?" asked Lozano. "Why's that?"

"We don't know," said Daniels. "That's why we need to find Sonia."

"And how would she know?" asked Lozano.

"Because Rutger knows her," said Rem.

"What? How?" asked Lozano.

"Sonia has showed up in each of these cases," said Daniels. "She was a witness to the Makeup Artist, she visited Madison Vickers in jail, and she met Jace Marlon in the waiting room while his girlfriend was in surgery."

"Plus, she bumped into us at the hospital," said Rem. "We didn't think much of it at first, but now we're seeing the bigger picture."

"Then please explain it to me," said Lozano. "Why is this guy running around, killing people connected to him in some way, while a sweet, older lady with dimples and lotions is visiting his victims?"

"Because we think they're all related," said Daniels. "They may be siblings, and Sonia somehow knows that."

"Siblings?" Lozano took a deep breath and let it out. "What the hell?"

"I know, Captain," said Rem. "We have reason to believe Sonia's life is at risk, which is why we need to find her. We don't think Rutger wants her to talk to us."

"And you're sure she knows the actual connection between all of them?" asked Lozano.

"He, Rutger, implied it," said Rem.

"Is there any evidence they could be siblings?" asked Lozano.

"Not that we know of. Jace grew up in foster care, so he probably wouldn't know. Jill and Madison have no idea of Rutger's existence, nor of each other's existence, so how that plays out, we're not sure," said Daniels.

Lozano nodded and loosened his tie. Pushing back from his desk, he crossed his arms, studying Rem and Daniels.

Rem put his knee on his ankle and fiddled with his shoelaces, uncomfortable with Lozano's stare. Daniels smoothed his shirt and played with a button on his lapel.

"What are you two not telling me?" asked Lozano.

Rem offered a blank stare. "What do you mean?"

Daniels held out a hand. "What wouldn't we tell you?"

Lozano huffed. "I don't know which of you is worse at lying to me. Remind me of that the next time I ask you to do an undercover assignment."

Rem shared a look with Daniels. Neither spoke.

"You've talked to this Rutger twice, that I know of," said Lozano.

"Actually, now it's three times," said Rem.

Lozano leaned in. "And he's still walking around. What are you doing next? Inviting him to dinner?" His voice rose.

"Well...," said Daniels.

"I guess...," Rem paused. He gestured to Daniels. "You make a mean Chicken Marsala. Maybe we should consider it."

"Remalla," yelled Lozano.

Rem sunk in his seat.

Daniels sighed. "It's hard to explain."

"How about you try?" asked Lozano.

"He's kinda, sorta, well, not your average guy," said Rem. "He's...he's..." He looked to Daniels for help.

"He's—" Daniels started to speak when his cell rang. "You know...talented." He reached for his phone.

"Don't let us disturb you, Daniels," said Lozano.

"Sorry, Cap. It's Marjorie. Hold on." He answered.

Lozano glowered at Rem, who offered an anxious smile.

"Marjorie?" said Daniels. His face fell. "What's wrong?"

Rem sat up.

Daniels straightened too, and then stood. "No. Stay where you are. You did the right thing. Go to the neighbors. We'll be right there."

Rem stood also and Lozano's anger faded, his brow furrowed.

"It's okay. Take J.P. We're on our way." He paused. "Love you, too." He hung up.

"What's wrong?" asked Rem.

"Marjorie just got home with J.P. When she went to the front door, it was open. She's out in the driveway. Doesn't want to go inside."

"Go," said Lozano. "Make sure she's okay. Keep me posted."

Daniels was already out the door with Rem right behind him.

CHAPTER TWENTY-THREE

Jace opened the door and swung it wide with his foot. With several grocery bags hanging from his arms, he carried them into the kitchen and set them on the counter.

"I'm not helpless you know. I can carry some groceries," said Danni, coming in behind him and closing the door.

"I got it. It's fine." He started going through the bags and emptying them.

Danni came into the kitchen. "Here. Give me a bag."

He pulled the one she reached for away. "I got it. Go sit. Read your email. Do a reading or something."

She put a hand on the counter. "What is the matter?"

He put a can of beans in the pantry. "Nothing."

"You've barely spoken since this morning. Is something on your mind?"

"Nope." He dug through a bag and pulled out a box of macaroni and cheese.

"Why did we buy all this food? How long are we going to be here? I thought it was only going to be for a few days."

"You never know. We should be prepared."

"Prepared for what? Armageddon?"

He sighed. "Danni, you seem to forget what we're dealing with. This guy is out there. He was in your place. He took a card from your deck. If those detectives don't find him, we could be here a while."

"How long is that? We can't stay here forever."

Holding a jar of mayo, he swiveled. "I don't know. Stop asking all these questions. I just want to unload the groceries."

Danni opened her mouth, but stopped. "Fine."

"Fine," he said. He put the mayo away.

Danni walked away and sat at the laptop. Jace focused on putting the food away. Ever since the reading that morning, and that moment they'd shared over the Queen of Cups, he hadn't been able to stop thinking about her. Some switch had been flipped on and he was trying his darnedest to flip it back off.

The moment he'd seen her blush and he'd touched her hand, intense heat had bloomed and traveled throughout his body. The desire to lean and kiss her had almost overtaken him, but he'd forced himself to pull back. He'd thought of Devyn and how she was recovering in a hospital, and he'd thought of why she was in a hospital. Because of him.

Various thoughts swirled at once, and he knew it would be wrong to start anything with Danni. He couldn't understand where all this lust had come from. She wasn't his normal type, and until this morning, he hadn't had any romantic thoughts about her, except for the usual male appreciation of the female form. He'd always noticed how good she looked in jeans. They hugged all the right places, but he noticed those things in most women.

He'd spent the rest of the day trying to distract himself. The grocery store was a welcomed errand. He had to get out of the house and try not to spend too much time with her, but now that they were back, that would be almost impossible. They were staying together in close quarters. How was he going to avoid her now?

He pulled out a small bottle of tequila from a paper bag and left it on the counter. It was the only idea he could think of. Maybe a drink would calm him down.

"What's that?" asked Danni, peering from the dining table. "Did you buy alcohol?"

"Sure as shit did. You want some?"

She stood. "Are you serious? Are you going to get drunk?"

Jace squeezed his eyes shut. "Danni, please. Don't start. I just need a drink."

"What do you need a drink for? Didn't you have enough the other day, when you thought I'd murdered Justin?"

He opened his eyes. "Oh, come on. I told you I was sorry. What was I supposed to think? There was a damn tarot card on my desk."

"And just because it was a tarot card, that means I did it? Maybe if you hadn't been so drunk, you would have seen reason."

"I got drunk after I saw the card."

"Oh, that makes is so much better. Why didn't you just pick up the phone and call me?"

He threw out a hand. "Why would I call a murderer and ask them if they'd murdered someone? In my experience, they tend to say no."

She cocked her head. "Oh, so you have experience with calling murderers?"

"You know what I mean."

"I'm not sure I do."

He pulled out a carton of eggs, opened the fridge, and tossed them in with some force, before slamming the door shut. "What are you trying to say?"

"Let's be honest. I don't know you. You could have associated with anyone in your past. God knows what you may or may not have done. Maybe Justin's parents have a good reason for blaming you."

He tightened his jaw and went rigid. "I think you've said enough." He grabbed the tequila and twisted the cap. "And who are you to judge me? You aren't an angel, either. There's a reason you're estranged from your dad." Jace opened a cabinet and pulled down a glass, cracked the tequila bottle open, and poured some.

"You are a bastard."

He held up the glass. "Sure you don't want some?" Holding up the drink, he cheered her, and then knocked it back.

Her eyes were darts. "I'm not staying here."

"The hell you're not."

She turned and grabbed the keys from the table where Jace had dropped them. "I'm leaving."

Jace dropped the glass back on the counter. 'No, you're not."

"How are you going to stop me?" She headed for the door.

Jace ran past her and blocked her exit.

She glared. "Get out of my way."

"No."

"Fine. I'll go out the side door." She turned away.

Jace grabbed her arm. "You are not leaving."

"Don't touch me." She pulled her arm back. "How dare you? Who do you think...," She blinked. "...you think..." Her face drained of color and she held her chest. "Oh, God." Her breathing escalated.

"Danni, what's wrong?"

Her face paled and she sucked in ragged breaths, but couldn't seem to fill her lungs. "I can't...I can't breathe."

He came up beside her. "Sit down." He guided her back to the couch, where she fell back against it. "Take it easy."

She leaned over, her breathing labored. Sweat beaded on her skin.

Jace took her pulse. Her heart raced and her skin was clammy. "What can I do?"

She tried to speak. "Bag. I...need...a bag."

Jace realized she was hyperventilating. "Hold on." He raced into the kitchen and grabbed the paper bag from the tequila and ran back to the couch. "Here. Breathe into this."

She took it, and put it over her mouth, breathing rapidly into the bag.

He put his hand on her back. "Breathe slowly. Calm down."

It took several minutes, but she began to gain control. Her breathing still came in quick gasps, but it sounded less desperate. Her face began to regain some color.

"There you go. Just slow it down."

Her posture straightened, and her gasps became breaths and became slower and easier. Finally, she lowered the bag.

"How are you?" he asked.

"Better." She held her head and rubbed her temples.

"You want to lie down?"

"No. I'm okay."

"I don't think you're okay."

"Yes, I am. Just give me a second."

"You sure you don't want some tequila?"

She glared at him.

"It might help."

She twisted away and tried to stand, but wobbled.

"Whoa," said Jace. "Sit back down."

Reluctantly, she did. "Crap," she said.

"I'll get you something to drink." He ran into the kitchen and grabbed one of the bottled waters. He opened it and returned to the couch. "Here."

She looked up, took the bottle and drank some. "Thanks."

Jace sat beside her. "Has this happened before? Did I cause this?"

Danni stared at the ground. "It's...yes. It's happened before. It's been a while though, but now, with everything going on, I guess it's been triggered again. And no. It's not your fault."

He debated asking more, but decided to wait. "You should lie down."

"I don't want to lie down. I want to leave."

Jace paused, his concern for Danni after her attack subsiding. He suspected the tequila shot had helped. "I'm sorry. I did it again. I acted like an ass." He began to wonder if the heat he was feeling was not from the alcohol, but from sitting next to Danni. He shifted slightly away from her.

"You did." She sighed. "But I made a crack about Justin. I egged you on."

"That's true."

She offered him a sideways glance. "Why are we so mean to each other?" She shifted to face him. "And why are you so grumpy?"

Jace stared at his hands. "I have my moments. And I don't think we're mean to each other. I just think we're…"

"We're what?"

He considered using a different word, but it popped out before he could stop himself. "…passionate." His mind flashed and he briefly pictured Danni in his bed, moaning and arching against the sheets. "Shit," he said audibly.

"What?"

"Nothing," he rubbed his face. He considered another shot of tequila.

Danni put the bag to the side. "Passionate is not a word I would use to describe me. I just get mad."

Jace almost chuckled. "Passionate people get mad all the time. Hell, Devyn and I could get into screaming matches, but then we'd…uh…never mind." How was he continually finding himself in sexual hell?

"Yes. There's no need to tell me. I can only imagine."

"You can?"

"Can what?"

"Imagine?" he asked.

"Of course."

"What do you imagine?" He glanced at her, wondering why he was asking.

She fidgeted. "What kind of question is that?"

"I guess I'm just curious. Do you ever imagine us?" He held his breath.

"Us…what?" Her voice lowered.

"Us together." Her face reflected a myriad of emotions and he couldn't read her, until her cheeks turned pink like they had when she'd pulled the Queen. "You're blushing again."

She put the back of her hand against her forehead. "Jace, I don't think…this isn't…I mean, come on…it's crazy."

"So you have thought about it?"

"Have you?"

He decided to be honest, otherwise the rest of their stay would be miserable while he tried to avoid her. "Oh, yes. Ever since you pulled that stupid card."

"But we're not each other's type. I'm certainly not Devyn."

"That's probably a good thing." He raised a brow. "And I'm not your type?"

"Well, I mean…" She gripped her water bottle. "You're…you're…"

"I'm what?"

Her cheeks turned a deeper shade of red. "You're a bad boy."

He smirked. "I'm a what?"

"Oh, please. Look at you. The hair, the body, the tattoos, the motorcycle, the attitude and ooze of sexuality. I mean, come on, you're a walking romance cover."

He dropped his jaw.

She raised a hand. "I know how this works out. I had my bad boy years, and thankfully, they're behind me."

He shifted to face her. "How does it work out?"

She sighed with impatience. "It's always fun in the beginning, and then, once the initial heat fades, some other pretty thing comes along and…" She flapped a hand. "…that's it. Thanks, babe. It's been fun. Have a nice life. Oh, and by the way, if you love me, you'll rob this store for me."

That threw him a curve ball. "Excuse me? Rob a store?"

She took another sip of her water and put it down. "I may have shoplifted once because I thought I was in love. I was so stupid. I thought Mickey would take me away and solve all my problems. Instead he just created new ones."

"Mickey, huh? He drive a motorcycle?"

She nodded. "Sure did."

"Long hair?"

"Longer than yours. He even had a motorcycle jacket."

"Don't tell me. It had a bald eagle on the back of it."

"Actually, it was the American flag."

He smiled. "Nice."

"So you see, I can't date a motorcycle guy."

He studied her; her focus still on her hands. "Danni. The motorcycle wasn't the problem. Nor was the jacket. Or the hair. You could have a dude in a three-piece suit, with slicked back hair and a six-figure paycheck and he could still treat you like shit."

Her face tightened. "Sounds like my dad," she whispered.

Jace debated what to say next, but she'd opened the door, so he stepped through. "You've never said what happened with your dad. You told me you were estranged. What happened?"

She went still and didn't answer at first, and he thought she wouldn't, but then she spoke. "He and I...we don't...I don't...," she sighed. "I don't want anything to do with him."

"Does he want a relationship?"

"Yes. Lately, he's been trying. I've been ignoring him."

"What happened between you two?"

She rested her head in her palm. "He...he...basically...he killed my mom."

Jace frowned, unsure he heard right.

"When he was young, he, my dad, was a good guy. Handsome, smart, well-dressed. Came from a good family and had a good job. From what I know, he and my mom were happy when they met and fell in love. They got married, and had me. Then things changed. I'm not sure what happened but dad started drinking, which led to drugs. My mom got hooked too, but it was worse for her. My dad could be functional, but not her. She spiraled down. I was six when it finally caught up to my dad. He lost his job, the money disappeared, and we lost our home. Ended up staying with my grandparents. My mother fell into a depression, and my dad started sleeping around." She rubbed her temples. "I can still remember their fights. The screaming..."

Jace clenched his hands together. Her memories mingled with his own – growing up with more than one foster care family, most of whom argued and drank more than they walked and talked.

"Eventually, Dad left. Just disappeared one day. My mom went to bed and didn't come out, except to get a drink or meet up with someone to buy drugs, until one day she didn't wake up. My grandmother found her." Danni balled her hands and swallowed. "I still remember that day. My grandmother picking me up early from school, and having to tell me..." She stopped. "My dad never even came to the funeral."

Jace nodded, but didn't say anything. He figured listening was what Danni needed the most.

Danni took a deep breath. "So, my grandmother raised me. When I was a teenager, my dad reached out, but I wouldn't talk to him. I was so angry and I felt so guilty about my mother. Some part of me thought I could have saved her but I was wrong. I started acting out, dating bad boys, and shoplifting for them. I think that's when I started having panic attacks. My grandmother told me to pull it together or I'd end up like my mom. That scared me. I started to see a shrink. I wanted to figure things out and get my life straight. I stopped seeing bad boys, and tried taking care of myself for once. I discovered tarot and started doing readings for people, and I could see how it helped and it made them, and me, feel better. Plus, I was good at it." She bit her lip and shook out her hands. "Didn't help much with my anger though. My father, he hasn't given up. I hear from his dad, my grandfather, that he's gotten clean, and turned his life around. He's remarried and even has another kid."

Jace felt like an ass. He'd been throwing her relationship with her father in her face, never knowing the true story. "Have you considered talking to him?"

She looked over; her eyes narrowed. "Why the hell would I do that?"

"Because he's your dad."

"Doesn't mean he deserves to be in my life."

Jace carefully chose his next words. "If he was still being an asshole, sure. But if he's not, then what's the harm in talking?"

"I don't want to talk to him. He ignored me for years. He made his bed."

"That's all true. I get it. But how will you feel ten, twenty, or thirty years from now, when he's gone? Will you look back and wonder, what if?"

"No. I won't."

"You sure? What if one day you have kids of your own?"

"Then I'll tell them the truth. Their grandfather is dead. He died the moment my mother died in that bed, all by herself. Lonely and miserable."

"Danni..."

She stood. "I'm feeling better." She grabbed her water. "I'm hungry. You want something to eat?"

He took a hold of her wrist. "Don't. Don't do that."

"Do what?"

"You're not hungry. You're pissed."

She stared down at him; her face unreadable. "I don't want to talk about it."

"I get it. You're angry, and you're scared. You're terrified that if he comes back into your life, he'll hurt you all over again."

She tried to pull away, but he held on. "But what you have to understand, Danni, is that you're not that scared six-year-old, or ten-year-old, or sixteen-year-old anymore. You're all grown up, and you can set the rules. You can tell him how furious you are, and you can tell him what he did to you and your mother, and how he made you feel. You can tell him straight to his face." He stood and faced her. "And that is what you should do, or he and those memories of yours are going to haunt you for the rest of your life."

She froze, her face anxious.

Jace stood beside her. "And it won't matter if it's a bad boy or a man in a designer suit, they'll all be your dad."

Her eyes welled, and a tear escaped and slid down her cheek, and she wiped it away. She spoke softly. "Jesus, maybe you should have been my shrink."

He let go of her, but she didn't move. "I've seen enough dysfunction in my life to know that this stuff will drag you down into the mud until you deal with it. It's why I left home at eighteen. I couldn't do it anymore. Putting up with people who didn't give a shit about me. I told them who I was and what I expected, and when they didn't bother to care, I left. They know where I stand, and if they don't like it, they can eat shit and die." He looked away. "It cost me a few relationships, but Justin and I hung together. And at least I know I made the effort. I can't afford to live like death is more welcome than living, and just waiting for that last day to come." He paused. "You need to come clean with your dad. Tell him how you feel. His reaction will tell the tale. He'll either stand up and be a man, and try to make amends, or he'll cower like a fool. And then you'll know."

"Jace, I don't think…"

"He's your father, Danni. If I had one shot to get to know my dad, I don't care if he'd killed Justin, I'd still talk to him. I'd give him a chance. I know you think you gave him one, but people screw up. They make terrible mistakes. God knows I've made them. But when you know better, you do better, and you try to make it right. He should have that chance with you."

Danni bit her lip, and another tear trickled down her cheek. Jace reached up and wiped it away.

"And don't cry," he said softly.

She sniffed and dabbed her face with the back of her hand. "Why not?"

"Because it makes me want to kiss you, and I shouldn't, because now is not the time." More tears spilled over her lashes and he almost groaned.

She nodded. "Okay." Taking a deep breath, she reached for a tissue from a box on a side table. She wiped her face and blew her nose. "You're right," she said.

"About what?" he asked.

"I'm not hungry."

He couldn't help but smile. "You're not?"

"No. I think I'd like to take a shower though."

"Will you think about what I said?"

She nodded. "I will."

"Good. That's all I ask." He tipped his head toward the kitchen. "I'll finish putting everything away. Go get your shower. Make it hot, and relax."

"Okay." Tears surfaced again. "I think I just need a good cry."

"Shower's a good place for that."

She glanced up at him, her eyes shiny, and took his hand. "You surprise me, Jace Marlon."

Tingles traveled up his hand and arm from her touch. "I surprise myself sometimes."

She pursed her lips, wiped away another tear, and let go of his hand. She headed for the bathroom. "I won't be long."

"Take your time. We'll have hamburgers tonight. I'll make the patties while you're in there."

She expelled a breath. "Thanks."

He nodded and watched her disappear behind the bathroom door and heard the shower turn on. Scratching his head, he groaned inwardly, wondering how he was going to get through these next few days with her. Her vulnerability only made her more attractive to him, and it had taken a supreme act of will not to swoop her up and carry her into the bedroom when she'd taken his hand.

Needing a distraction, he went into the kitchen, finished with the groceries, and pulled out the hamburger meat. Keeping busy is what he needed. He'd make the patties, and then when she was done, he'd go take a cold shower. Seeing the tequila on the counter, he considered another shot, but then thought better of it, and put it away.

He kicked off his boots and socks, preferring to be barefoot when he was home, and opened the meat. He found some salt and pepper and a few other extras and put together four patties, then covered them and put them in the fridge, ready to cook for dinner. Seeing the pack of beer he'd bought, he pulled one out, popped the top off and took a swig. The shower stopped, and he mentally prepared himself.

Wondering how long they might be there, he took a second to shoot a text to Detective Remalla to see if there'd been any progress on the case. Maybe they'd be able to leave sooner rather than later.

From the kitchen, he heard the bathroom door open. It was quiet for a second, but then he heard her.

"Jace, can you come here for a second?" Her tone sounded taut and he wondered if something was wrong.

He left the kitchen and seeing the bathroom door open, he walked closer. "Danni? You okay?" He stopped at the entrance, looking in, and froze. She stood there wrapped in her towel, the steam from the shower making her skin shine, and her combed, wet hair framing her oval face perfectly. His heart leapt up into his throat, and his voice wouldn't work.

She fidgeted nervously, her shy gaze darting around the room until it settled on him. "I was wondering…uhm…well…if…it's a good time for you to kiss me now." Her almond eyes rounded, and she waited for his response.

A rushing sound flooded his ears, and he tried to think, but his brain had short-circuited. Whatever logical thoughts that were trying to fire were not making it up the highway. Heat flushed his body and he stood there, his heart pounding.

She bit her lip. "It's okay if it's not…"

He took three steps into the bathroom and wrapped his arm around her, pulling her close. She sucked in a breath as he lifted her, cupping her bottom, and rested her on the edge of the counter beside the sink.

Her breath brushed his cheek, and he tried to control his own, but it was picking up fast. Her legs went to either side of him, and he held her gaze, her eyes round and dark, and ensuring she was secure, he brushed her hair back with his fingers. Her skin was flushed and her lips were barely an inch from his own. He couldn't stop looking at her.

She nervously fiddled with the towel and whispered. "I know I'm not like Devyn."

He realized she was self-conscious. "I don't want Devyn. And you are absolutely perfect right now." His voice was gruff and he forced himself not to rip her towel off.

She nibbled her bottom lip again, and he groaned. He slid his hands down her neck to her shoulders, feeling her silky skin, and her fingers found the hem of his t-shirt.

"I shouldn't be the only one naked," she said, lifting his shirt.

He raised his arms and helped her pull off the shirt and toss it aside. Her fingers touched his skin and he sucked in a breath and moaned when she trailed them over the tattooed ridges of his chest and abdomen.

"Definitely right off a romance cover," she breathed in his ear.

He couldn't take it anymore, and with his fingers on her arms, he trailed them up her shoulders and neck, where he cupped her face, and grazed his mouth against hers.

She made a sound of ache and need and her hands gripped his ribs. Her forehead touched his own. "Please," she pleaded.

It was all he needed to hear, and his hungry lips descended over hers. He kissed her hard, unable to be gentle, but she responded in kind, giving back everything he gave. She pulled him against her and he marveled at the feel of her skin against his. Her mouth and tongue were like delicate instruments that he wanted to play again and again. She tasted like strawberries and the noises she made as he ravaged her mouth drove his desire higher and he imagined the sounds she'd make later in the bedroom.

Her hands traveled and he felt her nails dig in to his back as their kiss deepened. Dragging his lips away, he trailed kisses down to her neck, where he nipped and sucked at her nape.

She reached for her towel, prepared to pull it off, when he stopped her.

"No," he said, raggedly. "I want to."

She dropped her hand, and he raised his, finding the edge of the towel where it held around her breasts, and he pulled on it. The towel dropped, and he groaned audibly. "My, God." He found and held her gaze, both of them breathing hard. "You're beautiful."

She slid a hand around his neck and pulled him in, raising her lips up to his, and they resumed their kiss. His palms found her breasts, and he delicately slid them over her most sensitive parts, and she cursed against his mouth, moving closer, wanting to be touched.

He savored her body, wanting to claim everything and make it his own. Everything about her was glorious. He couldn't get enough of her.

Impatient, she moved her hands and slid them down his chest and abdomen, and found the button on his jeans, where she undid it and slid down his zipper.

His control slipping, he grabbed her hand, and held it. He kissed his way to her ear. "Let's get more comfortable." He lifted her and held her against him, while she nibbled his neck and wrapped her arms around him. He walked out of the bathroom and into his bedroom, where he laid her down against the sheets. Kissing her, he explored her body with his fingers and she arched, whimpering, and clinging to the sheets, just as he'd imagined.

Writhing against him, she whispered. "Take those stupid jeans off. Now."

He smiled lasciviously. "With pleasure." He slid off of her and reached for his waistband, but paused. "You're sure? I am a bad boy."

Her eyes twinkled with desire. "God, yes. The badder, the better."

He dropped his jeans and stepped out of them. Her eyes widened, her gaze traveling over him.

"Good to know," he said, and he returned to the bed, intent on giving her exactly what she wanted.

CHAPTER TWENTY-FOUR

Daniels took a hard turn into the driveway and stopped abruptly, the car coming to a jerky stop. Remalla jumped out of the car and Daniels scanned his house and saw Marjorie step out of the neighbor's front door. He left the car and met her on the neighbor's porch. Rem jumped up and surveyed the Daniels' front entry, checking and looking inside the windows.

"You okay?" he asked Marjorie. He gave her a hug. "How's J.P.?"

"Yes, I'm fine. J.P. too. He's inside, sleeping."

"You go back in. Rem and I are going to check it out."

"Please be careful."

"I will. It might be nothing. Maybe the wind blew it open."

She frowned. "That door was locked when I left. I'm sure of it. I know how nerdy you are about security. It wasn't the wind."

He eyed Rem who still stood on the porch. "Did you see anything? Or anyone?"

"No. Nothing. I looked in the windows, but nothing looked disturbed."

He nodded. "Okay. Go be with J.P. Rem and I will be back in a second."

She took his hand. "Don't do anything stupid."

He squeezed her fingers. "Me? I'm as calm as a cucumber. It's Rem I have to keep an eye on."

"Not when it comes to us, you're not. You're pissed. I can see it on your face."

Daniels made an effort to project quiet confidence, although she was right. Inside, he was raging. "I promise. Nothing stupid." He gave her a quick kiss. "Now go inside."

She sighed, and let go of his fingers. After a quick glance at Rem, she went back into the neighbor's house. Daniels ran across the lot and joined Rem up on his own porch.

"Anything?" he asked. He spied the open door.

"Nothing that I can see. It's all quiet."

Daniels unsnapped the holster of his gun and pulled out his weapon. Rem did the same. "You ready?" he asked.

"As I'll ever be." Rem stood to one side of the door and Daniels stood on the other. He reached over and pushed the door in and it swung wide. Pointing his gun down, he looked around the side and saw the inside of his home. The front stairs led up to the second floor and the potted plant on the table in the foyer greeted them in silence. He stepped around the frame and into his house. Rem followed.

"I'll take the kitchen," he said, stepping right.

"Okay," said Rem, stepping left.

Daniels walked past the stairs, checking a small guest bathroom, before stepping into the kitchen. A plate with crumbs sat beside the sink and he saw his coffee cup he'd used that morning beside the toaster. The breakfast table and the high chair were clean and undisturbed. He walked back and checked the laundry room, seeing only a stack of folded clothes. He returned to the front entry where he met Rem.

"It's clear," said Rem.

"Same here," said Daniels. They both looked upstairs.

Rem took the stairs first, aiming his weapon in case anyone appeared from above. The house held an eerie quiet, and Daniels didn't know if it was because it was empty and his senses were on high alert, or if something sinister waited for them above. He followed Rem, keeping his gun pointed down. Once they crossed the halfway point, he swiveled and faced backward, aiming his gun at the banister on the second floor, protecting their backsides. Nothing moved and he saw nothing suspicious.

At the top, Rem stopped and Daniels stepped up next to him. "I'll take the master," said Daniels.

"Got it. I'll check the nursery."

Rem headed down the hall and Daniels walked into his bedroom; gun raised. The bed was unmade, and Marjorie's robe was lying across the foot of it. He remembered her wearing it that morning while he'd drunk his coffee before going to work. He'd given her a kiss, told her he'd loved her, snuggled J.P., and left, never thinking he'd be doing this hours later.

The bedroom was empty, and nothing seemed out of place, and he walked into their bathroom. There were two sinks. Toothpaste, aftershave and a razor sat beside his sink and he saw Marjorie's hairbrush, lipstick and curling iron beside hers. The room smelled like her perfume, which sat beside her lipstick. Everything looked as it should, and he began to wonder if maybe the wind did open the front door. He did a quick check of the toilet area and closet, but nothing jumped out at him. He heard Rem from the other bedroom yell, "All clear."

Daniels began to relax, and started to holster his gun, when he spied something on the mirror, tucked behind a tissue box and Marjorie's makeup bag. The hairs on his skin raised and he walked over, looking closer.

Rem entered the bathroom. "Nothing out here. You good?"

Daniels leaned in, and pointed. A shiver ran up his spine, and something primal moved through him, like an ancient, dormant anger that sparked only when your family was threatened. "Look," he said.

Rem stepped closer. His brow knitted. "Shit." He took out his cell and snapped a few pictures.

Daniels grabbed a tissue, and pulled the Tarot card from where it was tucked, and looked at it. It was the Ten of Pentacles. Along the side, written in black ink, were the words *Nice family, Detective.*

**

Another black and white, lights flashing, pulled up to Daniels' house.

Daniels cursed. "Is the whole force coming?" Three more black and whites, plus a forensics van, and a fire engine were in his street. The neighbors were out on their lawns, pointing and talking. Marjorie was still in the neighbor's house where he'd asked her to wait. "I mean, why do we need a fire engine?"

"You know Lozano. He's not taking any chances," said Rem. "What did you do with the card?"

"Ibrahim's got it."

"Good. Maybe they'll find something on it."

Daniels watched the activity around his house. Yellow tape had gone up around his porch and through the windows, he could see Ibrahim's forensics team dusting for prints. Two sets of police officers were talking to the neighbors, hoping to find someone who'd seen something. "Does it matter?"

Rem raised a brow. "What do you mean?"

Daniels scowled. "We know who it is." He pointed. "That man was in my house, Rem. Rutger was in my damn house." He balled his hands into fists.

"I know." Rem's face went flat. "He's trying to get to us." He watched the activity. "What do you want to do?"

Daniels shook his head. "I want to kill him."

"Me, too, but I mean with Marjorie and J.P. You guys can't stay here."

"I'm going to talk to her about taking J.P. and staying with her sister and her family. They live two hours away."

"Good idea. Get them out of town until this is over."

Daniels narrowed his eyes. "And how long is that going to be?"

"Good question." He eyed his cell. "Marlon texted. Wants to know if we have any updates."

Daniels rubbed his neck. "Nothing he's going to like."

"I looked up that Tarot card, the Ten of Pentacles, on the web."

Daniels looked over. "And?"

"It's about family. Supporting and taking care of your loved ones. Or something along those lines."

Daniels kicked a stone and it flew across his lawn.

Rem put a hand on his shoulder and gripped it. "We'll get him."

Daniels cursed again. "That bastard. He's playing with us. And it's working." He thought of him, Marjorie and J.P. sleeping, eating and laughing in his home, and how Rutger had casually strolled through it, seeing and touching his possessions, as if they were his own. The violation felt visceral. Although he dealt with victims all the time, he hated being one. Another thought occurred to him and he stiffened. "We should consider something."

"What?"

"If he's after the both of us, it's not just my home he might have hit. He might have visited yours too."

Rem's face fell.

**

Danni stared up at the ceiling, replaying everything that had happened in such a short period of time. She thought of her shower, and how she'd been rinsing her hair, and thinking of Jace, and what he'd said to her, and how she'd taken his hand and he'd wanted to kiss her. And then it was all she could think of – his hands on her body, his lips on her skin, and when she'd turned the shower off, she'd known what she was going to do. Her mind warred with her, but she didn't listen, and she'd called him, and asked him to kiss her, and he had, plus much more.

She closed her eyes, remembering their amorous afternoon. The heat began to build again, and she marveled on how her body could react over and over to him. It was like the sun had ascended and brightened the day, but then refused to descend.

Listening to his deep breathing as he slept beside her, she remembered his lips and teeth caressing and nibbling her above and below, and she shifted in the bed, much like she'd writhed beneath him. Sighing, she opened her eyes again, and looked over at him. His left arm was slung over his eyes and the sheets were at his waist, revealing his trim waist and muscled torso. A tattoo of a twisty, green vine traveled down his side and ended at his hip. Danni remembered teasing and tasting it with her tongue.

Deciding to think of something else, she recalled their present situation, and reality set in. What the hell was she doing, starting something with a man she barely knew, who was being targeted by a killer? The same killer who'd likely broken into her apartment and taken a card from one of her decks. Her plan had been to take the car and leave, and let the police and Jace figure it out. But now...

She moaned. How in the hell could she leave now? This man beside her had some kind of sexual hold on her, and she didn't see it abating anytime soon. Taking a deep breath, she tried to think logically. It was just sex, right? It's not like this would turn into something, would it? She and Jace were just two people caught up in an intense, emotional and stressful situation, and they'd temporarily found comfort in each other's arms. Happened all the time. Once it was over, they'd return to normal. He'd go back to the bar and find another Devyn, and she'd...well, she wasn't sure what she'd do. Go back to her cards and find another part-time job. She sure as hell couldn't be his bartender and watch him with other wo...

Oh, hell, Danni thought. I'm already jealous. Shit. Maybe she was in deeper than she thought. She went back to staring at the ceiling.

"You awake?" His gruff, sleepy voice startled her.

She looked over, and he moved his arm and peered at her. Her heart started hammering. "Yes."

"You okay?"

She swallowed. "Sure."

He shifted in the bed to face her. The covers moved lower to reveal more of his bare hip. She tried not to notice.

He stared for a second, and she felt the heat rise on her skin. "What are you thinking?" he asked.

She wondered what to say. It was one of those moments where she doubted herself. What if he didn't feel the same way? What if his desire for her was over, and he got up to make the hamburgers, and that would be it? Or maybe he would tell her she should leave, since there was a murderer out there and he couldn't afford to get involved. Or maybe after their time together, he'd decided Devyn was more his type of gal.

Danni chewed her lip.

"Be honest. After our conversation earlier, I need you to tell me the truth. I can take it. I'm a big boy." His face revealed its own tension, as if he worried she might say something he wouldn't like. Maybe he was fearing rejection just as much as she was.

She rolled in the bed to her side, facing him. "Tell me about your childhood."

His face furrowed. "What, now? Why?"

"Because I showed you mine, now you show me yours. Plus, I'm curious."

He hesitated, and for a moment, she wondered if he would do it. An expression of doubt clouded his face, but then he answered. "I don't know much about it."

"You were in foster care, right? From what age?"

"Since forever. I was left outside a fire station when I was two. Apparently, I just walked right in, asking about the fire trucks. There was no adult with me, and no one ever came forward to claim me. They knew nothing about who I was, other than I could tell them my first name, and there was a piece of paper in my pocket with my date-of-birth, but that was it."

Danni pulled her covers up. "They never found anyone who knew you?"

"Nope. And I have no memory of it. I went into an orphanage for a while, and then foster care after that. Apparently, I was a bit of a handful. Stayed a few places, some longer than others. Sometimes with good people, and others not so good. I began to realize that an adoption may not happen, and that I may have to go it alone. After that, I only became more rebellious. If nobody wanted me, then I didn't want them either."

Emotions played across his face, and Danni imagined how hard that must have been, to have wanted a real family, and never gotten one. "When did you meet Justin?"

He groaned and rolled over on his back. "High school. He'd been in a similar boat, although he'd been adopted at fourteen, and we bonded. Became the bad boys as you say. His parents hated it. They didn't like me and didn't want me hanging around their son. Just made us better friends though." He chuckled softly. "He and I actually got our first tattoos together." He pointed to his forearm, and she saw a tattoo with the word *brother* and a drop of blood beside it. "His parents were so pissed."

Danni could feel his tension and his sadness. She debated getting closer, not wanting to push, but then she told herself to get over it. Sliding closer, she shifted the covers, and came up next to him, putting her forearm over his torso. He moved his arm, letting her rest her head on his shoulder. His hand came around her and he stroked her lower back with his fingers. The sensation was magical.

"I'm sorry," she said. "About what happened to him."

He continued to stare upward. "Justin fought his own demons. I thought, or maybe hoped, he'd conquered them, but I was obviously wrong."

She took a breath. "Why do you think he slept with Devyn?" She stroked his ribs. "And if I'm prying, just tell me."

His hand on her back stilled. "I don't know. He'd always suffered a lack of confidence. His relationships with women were never long, and the moment they threatened a commitment, the faster he'd run." He sighed. "I suspect Devyn may have tipped the scales. She liked making me jealous, and maybe it went too far, and once it started, they didn't know how to turn back."

"I guess there's a certain element of thrill when it comes to betrayal, no matter how much may be at risk."

"I suppose."

He stayed quiet, and she continued to caress him. "You've been on your own since you were eighteen?" she asked.

"Yes. Got on my bike, and never looked back."

"You miss it?"

"What?" he asked.

"Family. Someone to come home to?"

"Not really. The people I came home to weren't all that great. I like my peace and solitude."

"You ever get lonely?"

"Sometimes, but it's no big deal. I like my own company." He rubbed his jaw against her head. "What about you? You get lonely?"

"Sometimes, but Seymore helps."

"Your cat?"

"Yes."

"Cats can't do what we're doing right now."

"Seymore snuggles up to me all the time."

He paused. "Does he make you scream and—"

"Okay," she said. "No need to go further. I get your point."

He chuckled.

She tickled a rib with her fingertip and she heard him inhale. "Do you think this Rutger person is your brother?"

He expelled the breath. "Well, that took a turn."

"You have to wonder though, don't you? Considering your background." She looked up at him, her jaw on his chest. "And maybe you have two sisters."

"I don't know. Maybe. It's hard to imagine. It may just be some nut job who's made all of this up in his mind."

She considered that. "I think you sense he's telling the truth, and if he is, he may likely hold the key to who you really are." He gazed down at her. "Maybe you do have a family out there, Jace Marlon."

He moved his hand up and down her spine, causing tingles to travel over her skin. "Marlon isn't even my real last name," he said. "I gave it to myself."

"You did? Why Marlon?"

He smiled, and her heart fluttered against her chest. She wondered if he could feel it since she was lying against him.

"Because I was a fan of Marlon Brando, and I wanted to be like him. Tough, elusive, and wanted by women. So, I became Jace Marlon. And why I named my bar Brando's."

His fingers moved lower and softly slid over the top of her buttocks. His touch made her squirm.

She pushed up, bringing her face to his, and he slid his hands upwards to her breasts. "You asked me a question a minute ago." She kissed him gently as she straddled him.

He kissed her back. "What was that?"

She fought to go slow, enjoying his touch. "You asked what I was thinking." She trailed kisses down his cheek to his neck and shoulder, his growing beard tickling her skin. His hands traveled up and down her torso.

"God, you feel so good," he said.

"Don't get distracted." She nibbled on his collarbone.

"Sorry. What were you thinking?"

She moved down to a nipple and caught it between her teeth and he moaned. She let it go and kissed his sternum, right above a tattoo of a large flame. She traced the tattoo with her tongue and he sucked in a breath. Wanting him, she looked up. "I'm thinking how amazed and lucky I am to be here with you. And no matter what happens, or whatever hell else is going on in the world right now, there's no place else I'd rather be."

His hands moved up to her arms and shoulders and he cupped her face and brought it to his. Sliding his thumbs over her cheeks, he kissed her deeply, and Danni dropped her hips against him, moving suggestively. He groaned, deepened the kiss, and rolled, pinning her beneath him, still kissing her.

Her stomach rumbled, and he broke away, breathing hard. "You hungry?" He rocked against her as she'd done to him. "I can make you a hamburger." He peppered small kisses down her neck.

Her heart raced, and her skin was aflame. "That's the not the meat I'm thinking about right now."

He laughed and her belly flipped. Raising his head, he grinned at her, stroking her jaw. For a moment, he turned serious. "There's no place else I'd rather be either."

Her hands gripped his back and her legs encircled him. "Well, then. You better feed me."

Smiling with a look that told her she would be getting that and more, his lips returned to hers. "As you wish. It's not a hamburger, but I think you'll be more than satisfied."

Kissing him and feeling his body move over hers, his hands and fingers exploring, she succumbed to his ministrations, knowing he was right.

CHAPTER TWENTY-FIVE

Rem checked upstairs, inspecting the bedrooms and bathroom. Everything looked fine. He came downstairs, seeing Daniels come around the corner from the kitchen.

"Looks okay," said Daniels. "Living room, too."

Rem went into the master, seeing nothing undisturbed. "The outside video camera didn't show anything and everything's locked up tight." He checked the closet and bathroom and returned to the front entry. "Looks like he bypassed me, for now at least."

Daniels nodded. His cell beeped and he pulled it from his pocket. "Marjorie and J.P. made it to her sister's."

"Good. They're okay?"

"Considering, yes." Daniels typed a message and returned the cell to his pocket.

"You got your stuff?" asked Rem.

"It's in the car. I'll get it later." Daniels entered the living area, his face clouded.

"You can take one of the rooms upstairs. They're clean. Bathroom, too." said Rem.

"You finally staying in the master?" asked Daniels, pacing.

Rem watched his partner move back and forth. "After Jill headed home, it seemed to make the most sense. Silly to stay upstairs."

"Yeah," said Daniels.

Rem rested against the doorframe, watching Daniels walk like a lion in a cage. "You keep doing that, you're going to wear a hole in the floor."

Daniels rubbed his head. "He was in my house." A muscle in his jaw twitched. "I should have been there."

Rem sighed. "You're not a superhero, no matter what Marjorie says."

"He was in my—our bedroom. J.P.'s nursery." He tensed, stopped walking, and cursed. Looking around the room, his eyes settled on the sofa, and he walked over, grabbed it from below and launched it up and backwards. The sofa tumbled over, landing upside down. Daniels grunted and yelled at the same time.

"Hey," said Rem. "Aunt Audrey bought that at a vintage shop. She'll be pissed if you damage it."

Daniels whirled on him, his face red. "Aunt Audrey is in assisted living. And I think we've got bigger issues than Aunt Audrey."

Rem let him vent and watched him resume his pacing. "Feel better now, after taking it out on my couch?"

Daniels dropped his head, taking a deep breath. "Not really."

"You could toss the coffee table, but I suspect that would be less satisfying."

Daniels eyed the table, and after a pause, he grabbed the edge and knocked it over.

"Or maybe not," said Rem.

"This isn't funny."

Rem straightened, and walked into the living area, lifting the table and putting it back in place. "Believe me, I know."

Daniels stopped, and his face fell. "Shit. I know you do." He put his hands to his face and pushed his usually gelled hair back. "I'm just so pissed."

Rem went over and grabbed the side of the sofa. "Little help here, strongman?"

Daniels went to the other side and helped Rem lift the sofa back up. He walked around the side and sat in it. "Sorry."

"None needed." Rem sat beside him. "We're stressed, you especially, and you needed to get it out. Better the sofa and not me."

Daniels rested his elbows on his knees. "What are we going to do?"

"I find that alcohol helps in these situations. Care for a beer?"

Daniels eyed him. "I can't drink right now. I want to find this guy."

"You can and you will have a drink. Then we'll talk about what's next." Rem stood and went into the kitchen, grabbing two beers from the fridge. He opened them and brought them into the living room, where he handed one to Daniels, who reluctantly took it.

Rem sat and took a swig. Daniels held it for a second and then took his own swig.

"Better?" asked Rem.

"No."

"Take a couple more."

Daniels shot Rem an impatient look, but then took another drink, swallowing a couple of gulps.

"Good. Now try and relax," said Rem. "I don't need that vein in your neck to get any bigger."

Daniels started to speak but hesitated, and he took another pull from his drink. He put the beer down and sighed. "Okay."

Rem sat forward. "Okay." He put his beer down. "Let's look at this logically."

Daniels snorted. "Really?"

"What else do we have to do?"

Daniels shrugged and shook his head.

"Rutger visits your house and leaves a card about family and writes on it. He knows that will get to you. Make you emotional. Why?"

"Because he's an asshole."

"But why now? Why go after you? And why the card?"

Daniels stretched his neck. "It's got to be about family. He's pissed about his, so he's interested in mine?"

"Maybe. Could be jealous. You have what he's always wanted."

"So does that make me a target? I can't give him what he wants."

"Maybe going after you gives him satisfaction. The same way going after Jill, Madison and Jace gives him satisfaction. He's already hurt all of them. He can't find Sonia. Now he needs a new target."

"Great. He's bored, and he picks on me."

"What about the card?" asked Rem.

"What about it?" Daniels took another drink from his beer.

"Where'd it come from?"

Daniels shot a glance at Rem. "Good question."

Rem pulled out his cell and dialed a number.

"You think it's from the same deck as the Justice card?" asked Daniels.

"Let's find out," said Rem. He got a hold of Ibrahim, and asked him to check the tarot deck they'd brought it in earlier, and see if any other cards were missing.

"Even if it is, what's it matter? It doesn't lead us to him," said Daniels.

Rem checked his phone after the call. "That leaves us with Sonia. We still have to find her. Shoot. I need to respond to Jace and tell him what's going on."

"I hope he's having a better time than we are."

"The way those two fight, they're either both dead, or madly in love." He shot out a quick text to Jace.

"We haven't heard anything from the people we talked to earlier who deal in gems and stones. Not a good sign."

"It's still early. Maybe tomorrow."

Daniels rubbed his eyes.

Rem finished his text and put his phone down. "You should get some rest. It's been a long day."

"I'm not tired."

"You're exhausted. So am I, for that matter." He drank from his beer.

"What? No Dracula or monster movie tonight?"

"I haven't checked the TV schedule. I think *The Omen* comes on either tonight or tomorrow."

"That ought to help with sleeping."

"You know that movie?" asked Rem. He held up a hand. "It's a Christmas miracle."

"Watched it when I was a kid. Scared the shit out of me. Aren't there any documentaries on?"

"I could care less about gorillas in the Sudan or tribes in the Amazon who've never seen a human."

"I don't think there are gorillas in the Sudan. Probably a few elephants."

"Wonderful. Happy for them."

"I think poachers are a problem though."

Rem held the bridge of his nose. "Good to know."

Daniels took the last pull of his beer and put it down. "I guess I'll head upstairs. Call Marjorie, take a shower, and maybe by then, I might be able to sleep."

"Good," said Rem. "Feel free to join me for *The Omen* though, if it's on."

Daniels cell rang, and he pulled it from his pocket. "Hey." He swatted a yawning Rem on the arm.

"What?"

"It's Maxwell."

Rem sat up. "Your jeweler?" He checked his watch. "It's a little late to be calling."

Daniels answered and Rem listened. Daniels spoke for a few minutes, his expression shifting from curiosity to surprise. "Sure. Yes. That's fine. We'll be there in the morning. Thanks." Daniels hung up.

"What is it?"

Daniels paused. "The ring is ready."

Rem grabbed his beer. "That was fast. I thought it was going to be a few days."

"I know." Daniels held the phone. "He wants us to pick it up tomorrow at 9:00 a.m." He frowned and opened up his phone, searching for something on the internet.

"Something strange about that, other than the speed?" asked Rem.

Daniels found what he was looking for. "The shop doesn't open till 10:00."

Rem raised a brow. "Maybe he's an early riser?"

"That doesn't make sense."

"How'd he sound on the phone?"

"Clipped. Direct, but friendly. But that's normal."

"Did you ask for a rush on the ring?"

"No." Daniels put his phone away. "You think he has something for us?"

"I don't know, but I guess we'll find out tomorrow." Rem stood. "I'm gonna get ready for bed, have another beer, watch some TV, and hit the hay. We'll plan to leave tomorrow at 8:30."

Daniels nodded. "Okay."

"You feeling all right?" asked Rem.

Daniels stood. "I'm still pissed, but your furniture is safe. Once I talk to Marjorie, I'll feel better. I just want to get this guy, and get back to some normalcy."

"Me, too." Rem's cell rang. He frowned. "Everybody's up late tonight." He checked the display. "It's Ibrahim."

Daniels turned serious and Rem answered. "Ibrahim. What you got?"

He listened and Daniels waited. "Really? You sure? Interesting. Okay. Thanks." He hung up.

"What is it?" asked Daniels.

"They checked Danni's deck. The one missing the Justice card."

"And?"

"The Ten of Pentacles is also missing."

Daniels shoulders dropped. "No big surprise."

"But so's another card. The Four of Cups."

Daniels face furrowed. "The Four of Cups? Do we know what it means?"

"Ibrahim looked it up. It's about missing something. Not seeing what's right in front of you."

"What do you think that's about? What are we missing?"

"I don't know. But I think the bigger question is who is the card for? Who's next on his list?"

Daniels groaned and stretched his neck.

"Maybe I'll have that second beer now," said Rem.

Daniels sighed. "If you don't mind, I'll think I'll join you."

CHAPTER TWENTY-SIX

Danni watched the coffee brew, smiling to herself, her mind traveling back to the night before. She'd never had a more satisfying time with anyone in her life. They'd paused briefly to get out of bed and make sandwiches, before returning to bed and each other. They slept on and off, waking only to savor more of their bodies. The only distraction had been Jace's nightmare. Danni had been awakened by his grunts, and seeing his sweaty skin and grip on the sheets, she'd gently jostled him, and he'd opened his eyes, breathing hard. He'd told her about the reoccurring dream of the man and two females, and how he had to assume it was about Rutger and the two women he'd never met – Jill and Madison.

She'd listened, and they'd talked, but ultimately wound up back in each other's arms, wanting each other again. They'd fallen back to sleep and Danni had woken up early, and slid out of bed, letting Jace rest. She'd taken a quick shower, got dressed and now listened to the coffee percolate. Smiling and staring out the window, she saw the neighbor, an older man in his fifties with salt-and-pepper hair, sitting out on his porch, sipping his own coffee and reading the paper.

Distracted by her thoughts, she jumped when Jace came up behind, encircling her with his arms. He kissed her neck. "Good morning."

Heat traveled down her torso and her heart fluttered. She grinned, desire welling up. "Good morning. How'd you sleep?" She leaned her head back and ran her hands over his.

"For the amount I got, not bad. What about you?"

"Same." She turned in his arms and brought her arms around him. "Want some coffee?"

"I want some of you." He continued to nibble her neck. "I'm going to jump in the shower. Want to join me?"

She sighed against his cheek, and he brought his face to hers, their lips barely touching. "I'm tempted, but I just took my shower, and I know what will happen once we're in there, and that's the last place I want to be when we run out of hot water, which we will." She grazed her mouth against his, and he kissed her softly and chuckled.

"I suppose that's true," he said. "I guess I'll just have to ravish you later. Maybe after breakfast?"

"I think so. I don't have any plans. Do you?"

He smiled and rubbed his nose against his hers. "I think I can fit you into my schedule."

"Excellent." She ran her hands down his back, and almost reconsidered her decision. "Go get your shower."

His hands moved down over her butt where he squeezed and she squealed. "I'll be right back." He kissed her again, broke away and headed into the bathroom. "Hold that thought."

She swallowed, her head spinning from his touch. What the hell had happened to her? Twenty-four hours ago, this was only a distant thought in her mind. Now she couldn't stop thinking of the man. Sighing, she grabbed a coffee cup, added some cream, and poured some coffee into her cup.

Thinking she ought to get something done before he re-emerged and touched her again, she opened her laptop, her stomach grumbling. They would need to get something to eat to keep up their strength. She would scramble up some eggs in a minute but wanted to check her email first. After opening it, she saw a new Tarot reading request, a new response from *Lovelorn*, and stopping on a third one, she froze, holding her breath. It was another email from her father.

Nibbling her lip, she debated what to do. She'd ignored his other emails, but this time, Jace's words echoed in her mind. *You need to tell him how you feel. People make mistakes. He's your father.* Reluctantly, she opened it.

Hi, Daisy.

It's your old man again. I know you want nothing to do with me, but I'll keep trying. I screwed up. I know it. But I want to do better. I am doing better. There's nothing I can do about what happened to your mom. But there is something I can do about you.

If you're willing to give me just a few minutes, I'll take them. I'll take whatever I can get. Please, give me that one chance.

Dad.

Danni hovered her finger over the Delete key, but couldn't bring herself to hit it. Tapping at the tabletop, she debated what to do. The familiar anger flared. His irresponsibility, his ignorance, his treatment of her mother, and how he'd left Danni before and after her mom's death. Frustrated, she stepped away from the laptop, unsure what to think. Needing a distraction, she opened the fridge and pulled out the eggs. She searched the kitchen and found a pan and grabbed some butter and salt. Starting up the stove top, she heard the bathroom door open, and Jace came around the corner, his hair wet and wearing his customary t-shirt and jeans.

She added butter, cracked an egg and dropped it in the pan. "Feel better?" she asked.

He leaned against the wall. "I was feeling pretty good before, but yes, the shower felt good." He watched her crack more eggs.

Thinking about her father, she kept adding eggs.

"You must be hungry. You plan on eating the whole carton?" asked Jace.

She eyed the pan, counting six eggs. "Oh, well, I'm guessing you'll eat at least four." She closed the carton and added some salt. She could feel his eyes on her. "There's some sausage if you want some."

"What's bugging you?"

"Nothing. I'm good." She stirred the eggs in the pan.

"Something has definitely shifted since I went into the shower. Did I do something?"

Realizing she was letting her anger get the best of her, she put the spatula down. "No. you didn't. I checked my email." The eggs sizzled.

He straightened. "Is it Rutger?"

"No." She turned down the heat and faced him. "My dad."

His face softened. "Did you read it or delete it?"

She grabbed the spatula and moved the eggs angrily around the pan. "I read it. He wants to make amends."

He took a second. "Are you going to respond?"

"I don't know. I haven't decided."

He nodded. "You're pissed, aren't you?"

She kept scrambling the eggs, although they were getting close to done. "I...I'm...I don't know what I am or how I feel. He's...he...wants a few minutes, but..." She shook her head, and he came up and took the spatula from her.

"Go sit. I'll finish."

Unexpectedly feeling emotional, she let him take the spatula, and walked to the window, seeing the man on the porch. "Your, or should I say Justin's, neighbor is outside." She needed to talk about something else.

Jace leaned to look out. "Oh, yeah. That's..." He scrunched his face. "Oh, what's his name...Ben. Ben Olson, I think. Nice guy. I met him when he came over once when Justin and I were sitting out front. He asked for some sugar."

"People still do that?"

"I guess around here they do." Jace slowed the spatula and his voice lowered. "I wonder if he's heard about Justin." He turned off the heat and moved the pan to a different burner. "Coffee ready?"

"Yes. Did you want some sausage? I can heat it in the microwave."

He turned to face her. "Sure, but before we do that, do you want to talk about your dad?"

"The eggs are getting cold."

"Danni..."

She crossed her arms. "This isn't easy for me."

"I know it isn't, but putting it off won't help."

Staring at her feet, she asked a question. "Did I ever tell you why I go by Danni?"

"No, why?"

She looked up. "Because when I was a teenager and he...dad...showed back up, he called me Daisy. And I hated it. I hated that he used my name, as if he had any right to." She hugged her elbows. "Right after that, I started telling everyone to start calling me Danni, because I didn't want to be Daisy anymore. I didn't want to go by the same name as the one he gave me."

"Your mother gave it to you, too."

"My mother is dead, and she can't use it anymore."

He nodded. "I don't care what name you go by, and I suspect neither does he. But he's a man who has a daughter out there, and he wants to reconnect. You're a grown woman now, and you don't have to be emotionally thrown by him every time he attempts to get in touch. So, if you can find a way to deal with your anger long enough to meet with him for a few minutes and hear his side, and then you can let him know yours, then you'll have a more stable base from which to make your decision. Then this whole business of you shutting down each time you hear from him will end."

"I don't shut down."

"You don't exactly relax."

"I'm doing just fine."

"Fine sucks, and most of the time, fine means you're not being honest with yourself, or others."

She hung her head.

"I'll shut up about it now. I've said my two cents. Do with it what you want."

Danni sucked in a breath and let it out. There was so much she wanted to say to justify her anger and rage, but something stopped her. At some point, the excuses didn't help anymore. Justifying only went so far. Eventually, she'd have to face her demons. She shook out her hands, and walked to the fridge. "I'll get the sausage."

They ate breakfast quietly, talking little. The fire between them still flared, but Danni felt it had been dampened by their conversation. She pushed the eggs around on her plate.

"I'll think about it," she finally said. "About what you said. I can't promise anything, though."

He put his fork down, his plate clean. "I didn't ask you to promise. Just consider it."

"I will."

"Good." He wiped his mouth with his napkin. "Any other fun emails we can talk about?"

Glad they had moved on; she slid the laptop over and swiped it open. "Uhm, let's see. We could talk about *Lovelorn.* She responded."

"Poor *Lovelorn.* Unrequited love."

She raised a brow. "How'd you know?"

He smiled and sipped from his coffee. "Aren't they all?"

She shrugged. "Sadly, a lot of them, yes." She read the email. "*Lovelorn* says thank you for the help, and she will take the advice. She'll definitely use me again and do I offer phone or in-person readings?"

"Do you?"

"Sometimes. For face-to-face, I have to know the person first. Maybe if I had an office or something, I might do them more often. But over the phone works fine."

"Probably smart to stick to the phone or online. Better to be safe."

"And a new request." She opened the other email and frowned. "A woman wants to know if her husband's cheating on her."

"That's sad. Maybe she should just ask him."

"Maybe she did."

"Then she needs to work on her bullshit detector. In my experience, women usually have excellent ones."

"Sometimes it's easier to believe the lie."

He went quiet and put his coffee cup down, studying her. "Do you believe in love?"

The question startled her. She shoved her laptop back. "Excuse me?"

"You heard me. Do you believe in love?"

She started to answer, but hesitated. Did she? She sensed Jace wanted a serious answer. "I do."

"Even after what happened between your parents?"

The memory of her family's arguments echoed in her mind. "Strangely, yes. Love doesn't just mean romantic love. I loved my mom, and she loved me. There's different types of love."

"What about romantic love?" he asked.

She shifted in her seat. "You're getting deep on me, Jace Marlon."

He rested his chin in his hand. "I know, but I'm curious. There's no right or wrong answer."

Fidgeting, she thought about it. "If you're talking about romantic love that lasts a lifetime, I do believe it's possible. There are people out there that have found love that survives through thick and thin. I don't know if everyone is that lucky, though. Some people aren't meant to be with just one person their whole life." She met his gaze. "Love is complicated."

"That it is." He leaned in. "I, for one, believe in it." He took a finger and brushed a lock of her hair back. "I think it's messy and sloppy and painful, but it's also the greatest force on our planet for good."

His eyes held hers and that familiar heat flared. "You're something else." She put a hand on his jaw and stroked his cheek. "Who are you?"

He smiled. "I am a man who is no longer hungry for food, but for something else."

Her heart rate spiked. "What could that be?"

He put a hand on her thigh and slid it up her leg. "Let me show you." Moving closer, his lips hovered over hers, when his cell phone beeped. He moaned. "Hell."

She pulled him close. "Ignore it."

Groaning, he pulled back. "I need to check it. I texted Remalla last night and I haven't looked at it since. It might be him."

Sighing, she watched him find his cell. Reading his messages, his face fell.

"What is it?"

"Someone broke into Detective Daniels' house. They think it was Rutger."

She stood. "Did he get away?"

"Seems that way. There's another message." He fiddled with the screen and his eyes widened. "Shit."

"What's wrong?"

He slid the phone in the pocket of his jeans and searched for his shoes. Finding them in the corner, he walked over and grabbed them.

"What are you doing?"

"I've got to leave for a while. You stay here and stay put."

Her breathing quickened. "Where are you going?"

His shoes on, he stood. "That woman, Sonia. I got a text. She wants to meet."

Danni froze in shock. "How do you know it's from her?"

"I don't, but something tells me it is. She said she wants to talk to me, and it has to be now. I have to go."

"Jace, you don't know what you're walking into. It's not safe." Danni realized they'd been living in a protective bubble, and now reality came roaring back. "You can't go by yourself. At least contact the detectives."

"She wants to meet alone."

"You can't be serious. That's crazy."

"It'll be okay."

"Do you even know where you are going?"

Jace threw on his jacket and found the car keys. "She sent me an address."

Danni pulled on his arm. "Jace, please reconsider. This could be dangerous. What if it's Rutger?"

"If it were Rutger, he would have told me. I'd still go. I think he knows that."

"Jace, please…"

He stopped, and came up to her. Wrapping an arm around her, he pulled her close. "Don't worry. It'll be okay. I have to do this to figure out what is going on. She holds the keys to my past. I have to talk to her." He kissed her and let her go. "Lock the door and stay inside. It will be okay. I'll text you as soon as I know something."

All she could do was nod. "You better come back to me."

He opened the door, and looked back. "Remember, there's no place else I'd rather be."

"Then stay."

He held her gaze, and she hoped she'd convinced him. "I wish I could. I'll be back as soon as I can." And then he walked out and closed the door behind him, leaving her alone.

CHAPTER TWENTY-SEVEN

Daniels approached the front door of the jewelers. The parking lot was empty. Rem looked around. "You think he's here?"

Daniels checked his watch. "He said 9:00. It's 9:00." He tried the door and it opened. "He must be." He motioned to Rem. "After you."

"Thanks." Rem entered and Daniels followed. The store was quiet, the glass counters and the jewelry within reflecting the sunlight streaming through the windows. The store lights were still off and everything was quiet.

Daniels approached a counter, seeing the bell beside the register. "You think I should ring it?"

"Go for it."

Daniels raised a hand just as a male voice spoke. "Gentlemen."

They swiveled to see Maxwell, tall and slim with broad shoulders, wearing his usual sleek black suit, his trim mustache and hair perfectly groomed, standing beside a door leading to the back.

"Maxwell," said Daniels. "We're here. You have the ring?"

Maxwell nodded. "It's good to see you both. Please come in to my office. We're not open yet. I can help you back here."

Rem shot a glance at Daniels, and Daniels picked up on his suspicion. "You always let clients in this early to pick up a ring?" asked Rem, resting his hand near the gun on his belt.

234 · J. T. BISHOP

Maxwell smiled. "Don't be alarmed, gentlemen. I'm sure in your line of work, you might think I'm about to murder you, but never fear. Dead men don't pay for their jewelry." He stepped aside. "I just think this business might be more appropriately handled out of sight."

Rem raised a brow and Daniels shrugged. "After you," Daniels said again to Rem.

Rem balked. "It's your ring. You first."

Daniels shook his head, and headed for the back room. Passing Maxwell, he saw a dark hallway with an open door on the right.

"First door, please," said Maxwell.

Rem followed Daniels into the hall, as Maxwell entered the store.

"I'll be out here should you need anything." Maxwell slid a curtain shut, leaving Rem and Daniels alone in the murky space.

"Well, this is weird," whispered Rem. "What's with all the cloak and dagger stuff?"

"Why are you whispering?" asked Daniels.

Rem pointed. "Because Lurch out there is wigging me out."

"Lurch?"

Rem rolled his eyes. "Never mind. You going in there?"

"Yes." He tried to look beyond the door, but the room veered left, so he couldn't see into it.

"You're freaked out too, aren't you?" asked Rem.

"Why are all the lights off?"

"I don't know, but I don't like it. This doesn't feel like we're picking up a ring."

Daniels took a step inside. Rem followed close behind.

"I feel like we're in a Stephen King novel," said Rem. "If there's a vampire in here, it's every man for himself."

"I'll keep that in mind," said Daniels, walking past the wall and into the room.

It was an office and the curtains were drawn. Daniels could see a sparse desk with only a paperweight and a letter opener on it, and a couch with two side chairs. As they entered, a silhouette moved and a curtain raised, allowing in some light.

"What the...?" asked Rem, squinting.

"Hello, Detectives. It's so nice to see you."

Daniels recognized the figure. "Sonia?" he asked.

"Sonia Vandermere?" repeated Rem. He visibly relaxed and held his chest. "Shit. You scared the hell out of us."

"Us?' asked Daniels.

"I'm sorry, boys. I didn't mean to startle you, but I have to be careful, and I don't want dear Maxwell to be in any danger either."

"You know Maxwell?" asked Daniels.

Sonia smiled, and her cherub cheeks dimpled. "Oh, my yes. I...we...have a history." Daniels sensed she was blushing. "But that's for another time. I know you've been looking for me. Maxwell knew the minute you asked about me who you were looking for. Isn't it interesting you end up at the same jeweler who happens to know me? Life is funny that way, isn't it?" She fanned herself. "Sorry. This room is so stuffy. I'm going to sit." She took a seat on the couch. "Please, detectives." She gestured toward some chairs in the room. "Relax. I brought some scones. Help yourself."

Daniels, his eyes adjusted to the light, saw the plate of scones on the table in front of the couch.

"What kind of scones?" asked Rem, walking over and perusing the selection.

"Blueberry. I hope you like blueberry."

Rem picked one up and bit into it. "They're good,' he said through a mouthful. "Be better with some coffee."

"Would you like her to do your laundry, too?" asked Daniels, smirking.

Rem swallowed. "I'm just saying, coffee would be good." He took another bite.

"My apologies. I didn't bring coffee. I could ask Maxwell to make some tea," said Sonia.

Daniels waved. "No, thank you." He took a seat across from her. "We need to talk to you about Rutger."

Her face turned serious. "I know."

Rem took the seat beside Daniels. "You know who we're talking about?"

"I know exactly who you're talking about," said Sonia. "He mentioned me, didn't he?"

"He did," said Daniels. "Said you knew things about him. He threatened you."

She nodded, playing with a large pink stone that hung from her neck. "I'm sure he did."

"What's your connection to him?" asked Rem. "And to Jill, Madison and Jace?"

Her eyes widened. "You know a lot. More than I realized."

"I saw you at the jail, where they were holding Madison, and Jace told us you saw him at the hospital," said Rem.

"And you came forward as a witness in the Makeup Artist case," said Daniels. "You spoke to Jill. Something tells me that wasn't coincidental."

"Oh, Detectives." She twisted a large-stoned purple ring on her finger. "I wish I could help you."

Daniels cocked his head. "What do you mean?"

"Rutger wants to kill you," said Rem. "We want to stop him. He's killed three people that we know of, and we're pretty sure you're next." He took the last bite of his scone.

"And he broke into my house," said Daniels. He leaned forward. "We need to find him, Sonia."

She wrung her hands. "I understand. Believe me, I do. But there are things about him that make him very dangerous."

"You mean how he throws shit around with his mind?" asked Rem, reaching for another scone. There was a small dish of butter and he slathered some on.

She visibly inhaled. "You've seen that?"

"Uh, yeah," said Daniels. "He's demonstrated his abilities a few times with us." He held his chest.

"Then you know what I'm talking about. He's not to be taken lightly."

"Sonia," said Rem, holding his scone. "There has to be a way to stop him."

Sonia stared off, again fiddling with her necklace. "There may be a way, but I can't tell you what it is."

"Why not?" asked Daniels.

"It's not legal, gentlemen. You'd have to arrest the responsible parties. Plus, it's not your battle to fight."

Daniels stood. "This man has killed people, and from what we gather, he plans to kill more, including you. Maybe Jace, Jill, and Madison."

"It's possible. Maybe even you, too," said Sonia.

Rem went still, and put down his scone. "I think I lost my appetite."

Daniels' anger flared. "Rutger threatened my family, and you can't help?"

Sonia frowned. "That's not his style. He has no issue with you personally. Or Detective Remalla. At least, none that I know of."

Daniels gripped the back of the chair. "Are you saying it didn't happen?"

"Why kill us if has no issues with us?" asked Rem.

"If you get in his way, there's no telling what he could do," said Sonia.

Daniels scoffed. "I don't understand. You tell us he plans to harm us if he feels like it, and he's a threat to others, that's very clear. But you can't help?"

She laced her hands together. "It wouldn't matter what I told you. It wouldn't make any difference. You two can't catch this man."

"What are we supposed to do?" asked Daniels. "Sit back and twiddle our thumbs?"

"Let me handle it," she said.

Rem chuckled. "No offense, Sonia, but you're not very scary."

Her face stilled. "You have no idea what I'm capable of, Detective. Hence why it would be better to keep you two out of it. Rutger's beef is with me, not you. And to be honest, your involvement only puts you at risk, and I'd rather not worry about someone else."

"It's too late for that. We're involved. He made sure of that." Daniels paced.

"You could always leave. Disappear for a while," she said.

Rem shook his head. "This conversation is definitely not going in the direction I thought it would."

"We're not going anywhere," said Daniels.

Sonia sighed. "I was afraid of that."

"Can we start from the beginning here? My head is swirling," said Rem. He dusted crumbs off his lap. "This Rutger, from what we know, goes after Rick Henderson, who was connected to Jill, then he takes out Madison's husband, Donald, and then he kills Jace's best friend, Justin. Why?"

"Are they siblings?" asked Daniels.

Sonia shifted in her seat. "It's better I not say."

"Too late, Sonia." Daniels walked around his chair and sat. "Rutger called Jace his brother. It's not a big leap that since he targeted Jill and Madison, that they're somehow related too."

Rem nodded. "Plus, they all have some wiggy abilities. Jill's psychic, we saw Madison throw something without touching it, and Jace...he healed Daniels' hand."

"He did?" asked Sonia. "Oh, my." She fanned herself again.

"It's only getting hotter," said Rem. "And I'm not talking about this room."

Sonia stood and walked over to the desk. A purse was perched on the desktop and she dug through it. "I need some of my chamomile lotion. I'm feeling a little stressed."

"You and me, both," said Rem. "I'm pretty sure Daniels, too."

She found a small bottle and squirted some cream into her hands, and rubbed them together, then rubbed some on her temples.

"Sonia," said Daniels. "We need your help."

Her eyes darted around the room, and her normal cheery demeanor faded. "I know you do." She faced them; her face flat. "But I can't give you what you want. I'm sorry."

Daniels stood, his ire flaring and ready to argue with her, when a voice from behind stopped him.

"Then maybe you'll help me instead."

They all turned, and saw Jace standing in the room.

CHAPTER TWENTY-EIGHT

Danni stared at the computer screen, trying to focus on the reader's question. Jace had left an hour earlier, and she hadn't heard from him. Trying to distract herself, she'd responded to *Lovelorn*, telling them thank you for the message, and that she was available for phone readings. Then she'd reopened her dad's email, and reread it, still debating whether to delete it. Unable to decide, she'd moved on to *Ladydesperate*, the woman wondering whether her husband was cheating. She'd done a reading, and was typing in her response, but struggled to answer in detail. Her mind kept shifting to Jace and hoping he was okay.

Deciding to take a break, she stood. She'd made another pot of coffee and she went to get more. Sighing, she checked her phone again, wondering if she'd missed a message from Jace. She hadn't.

Movement caught her eye, and looking out the window, she saw the neighbor walking down his front porch. Watching him, she frowned when he veered toward her house, or rather Justin's. She lost sight of him at a certain point and wondered if he was only heading down to the road for a walk when there was a knock on the door.

Her heart skipped and she held her breath. Did the neighbor want something? Jace had told her he'd asked for sugar in the past. But Jace had also told her to stay inside, and keep the doors locked.

The knock came again, and she put her coffee down and approached the door. It was the neighbor, not Rutger, and not some monster from the black lagoon. Telling herself to calm down, she opened it.

The man from the porch with the salt and pepper hair smiled. "Hi, I'm Ben from next door." He waved.

"Hi," said Danni.

"I'm sorry. I didn't mean to disturb you. I just saw that you guys were here, and, well, I don't know if he remembers meeting me, but I met Jace once with Justin."

"Yes. He remembers you." Determined to be friendly, she offered her hand. "I'm Danni."

He shook it. "Pleasure. Are you Jace's girlfriend?"

The question threw her. "Uh, uhm. We're good friends."

"Great." He shifted from foot to foot. "I don't know if Jace is here..."

"Oh, sorry. No. He left, but he should be back soon."

"Okay, well. I just wanted to convey my condolences. I heard about Justin, and it was just awful. He was a nice guy and a good neighbor. It's terrible what happened."

Danni's chest tightened. "Thank you. Jace would appreciate that."

"Is he doing okay? I know they were close."

"About as well as could be expected. It's been hard," she said. *Especially when a madman is responsible and still threatening you.*

"If you guys need anything during your stay, just let me know."

She smiled. Justin had a kind neighbor. "That's very sweet, but we're okay right now."

"Do they have any information about the funeral arrangements? I've been checking the paper, but haven't seen anything."

"Justin's family's been handling that. I don't think we know anything yet, but I'll let Jace know you'd like to attend."

"I'd like that. Thank you."

"You're welcome."

He pointed toward the house. "I'm actually baking some cookies. I'm going to see my granddaughter later, but I'd love to share some with you guys. There's no way we'll eat all of them."

She waved. "That's very sweet, but please don't go to the trouble."

"There's no trouble. I'll drop them off later."

"You really don't have to."

"Nonsense. Too many people worry about sugar these days, but if you can't have a good cookie when you're down, when can you?"

She nodded. "I guess when you put it like that..."

"Great. I'll bring them by on my way out."

"Okay. Thanks." She hoped Jace would be there to enjoy them.

He turned with a wave. "You have a nice day. Say hello to Jace for me. Hopefully he'll be here when I'm back."

"Hopefully. Thanks again."

He walked off the porch and headed back to his house and Danni closed the door.

"A kind neighbor who asks for sugar, and drops off cookies," she said to herself. "Where am I? Wonderland?"

She returned to the kitchen and found her coffee, watching Ben return to his house from the window. Her mind returned to earlier worries. Where was Jace? Was he okay? She debated texting him, but her imagination played out scenarios where she distracted him at the wrong time, and he died from some horrible wound inflicted by Rutger, all because of her text.

She put down the phone and ran her hands through her hair. *Get it together, Danni. Nobody's dying.*

Thinking of her dad, she went back to her laptop, and opened the email. She read it again, thinking of Ben and his kind words. Life really was short. Was all this anger and resentment worth it? And what was it costing her? Was Jace right? Would she ever be able to have a healthy relationship with a man?

She stared at the email, thinking. Making a decision, she bit her lip, and hit the Reply button.

Hello,

She couldn't bring herself to type Dad. Her mind whirled with what to say. Pleasantries would not work in this situation. She typed, deleted, and then retyped several times. Finally, she decided to be direct.

I'll give you one hour of my time. That's it. We can talk. But after that, I promise nothing. This will likely be the last hour you ever have with me.

Danni

She read and reread it several times, debating changes. Should she suggest a time and place? Should it be by phone or in person? Deciding those details could be figured out later since she didn't even know where the man lived, she took a big breath, put her finger on the button, and hit send. She closed the laptop quickly, as if she might get an immediate response, and she wasn't ready yet.

Tapping her foot, she wondered what to do next. The house remained quiet, and she sipped from her coffee. She almost wished Ben had invited her over, just so she could get out of here. This sitting alone with her thoughts was unbearable.

Spying the cards on the table she'd pulled for *Ladydesperate's* reading, she figured she should at least complete that, and not keep *lady* waiting, especially since the cards didn't look good. *Lady* deserved to know.

She opened her laptop again, telling herself if her dad responded, then she'd stay cool, and take it one day at a time. When Jace came back, he'd help her through it.

After opening up *lady's* draft email, she reread her partial response and picked up where she'd left off. She typed for several minutes, and feeling satisfied she'd answered *lady's* question, she hit send.

Glad that was done, she debated what to do next. She started to surf the web, when a notification popped up that she'd received a new email. Nervous, but telling herself to relax, she clicked over to it, and froze. It wasn't from her dad. It was from *BrotherlyLove.*

Holding her breath, she eyed her phone sitting on the kitchen counter. Should she text Jace? The detectives? *Read it first, Danni. Then decide.* It was just an email.

Nervously, she opened it.

Hello Daisy (My preference)

Just wanted to let you know that I appreciated your reading. Your insight and intuition were accurate and well-received. I like you, Daisy, and wish you no harm.

Jace is lucky to have you. Maybe we'll have the chance to meet again, but, sadly, I doubt it.

To your health,

BrotherlyLove

Danni read it again, holding her breath. What was he talking about? Why would he mention never meeting again? Was that a veiled threat toward Jace? This man was truly insane. Her hands trembled and she shook them out. She needed to contact Jace and tell him. Rutger be damned. She'd waited long enough anyway. She stood and started to head for the kitchen to get her phone, when another knock sounded on the door. Startled, she jumped, holding her stomach.

God, when this over, she thought, *I'm going to drink down that whole tequila bottle Jace bought.* Exhaling a nervous breath, she suspected Ben was returning with the cookies.

She walked to the door and opened it. A man stood there, but it was not Ben.

He smiled. "Hello, Daisy."

Freezing in place, a scream locked in her throat. Terror and adrenaline shot down her spine and into her legs, and some force inside her told, no shouted, at her to move. She tried to slam the door closed, but he blocked it with his foot. With no other option, she turned and ran.

**

Jace walked further into the room.

Sonia stared; her mouth open. "Jace."

"Hello, Sonia. Your friend out front pointed me back here." He pulled the stone out from around his neck. "I'm still wearing your gift."

She spoke softly. "I'm glad. Is it helping?"

"Yeah. Everything's just great."

"Moldavite is a powerful stone, but it doesn't work miracles."

"Too bad."

"When I find a stone that does, I'll let you know," she said.

"Maybe you can keep us in the loop on that one too," said Remalla.

"What are you doing here?" asked Daniels. "Where's Danni?"

"She's safe," said Jace. "I'm here to talk to Sonia. And I could ask you the same thing. What are you doing here?"

"It seems Sonia is the lady of the hour," said Rem. He glanced over. "What do you say, Sonia. Are you going to give up any secrets?"

"You know I can't," she said, nervously rubbing the stone around her own neck.

"Not even to me?" asked Jace.

She looked between the three of them, and took a seat at the desk, looking like a grandmother about to lead a board meeting. "You don't understand."

"No, I don't," said Jace approaching the desk. "How do you know me?"

"I...I...wish I could say."

"Do you know who my parents are?" asked Jace.

Daniels and Remalla listened, seeming just as interested as Jace.

Sonia didn't answer.

"Do you know who Rutger's parents are?" he asked.

She laced her fingers together.

He kept going. "Do we share the same parents?"

She stared at the desk.

"Who are Jill and Madison, and how do they play into this?"

She remained quiet, but a tinge of pink colored her cheeks.

Jace moved closer, and leaned over, his palms on the desk. "Am I related to them? Are we siblings?"

Sonia swallowed, but remained silent.

Jace fought to stay cool. "You can only keep secrets for so long. They always come out eventually. Rutger knows that, and I think he wants you to stay quiet. Or he just wants you dead. He's mad about something, and he's taken it out on all of us. And I want to know why. Why does a man I never knew existed suddenly feel the need to murder my best friend? For what purpose? Have I done something that would warrant that type of revenge? Did Jill and Madison do something equally as bad?"

Sonia looked up at him, her expression somber. "You survived."

Jace set his jaw. "I survived what?"

Sonia dug through her purse and pulled out a vial. "It's peppermint oil. Great for headaches. Anyone want a sniff?"

"No," said Daniels.

"I'll take some," said Rem. "This shit is enough to give anyone a headache."

Daniels rolled his eyes.

Rem took the vial Sonia offered and smelled it as Sonia had.

"Deep breaths," said Sonia.

Rem took a few solid breaths, and handed it back. "It actually helps."

Sonia returned it to her purse. "Where do I get some of that?" he asked.

"Rem…," said Daniels.

"What? I'm curious," said Rem.

"I can get you some," said Sonia.

"If you two are feeling better now, I'd like an answer to my question," said Jace. He kept his voice firm but relaxed, although his insides were roiling. He was determined to get answers.

"Amen," said Daniels.

"What did I, and I'm assuming Jill and Madison, survive?" asked Jace.

Sonia set her purse aside; her face unreadable. Flattening her palms against the table, she sighed. "Jace, listen…" She paused, her head tilting and her face going from doubtful to strained. The pink color in her cheeks faded and she went pale.

"Sonia?" asked Daniels.

She stared off as if hearing some distant call.

"What's wrong?" asked Rem.

She abruptly looked back at Jace; her expression serious. "How did you know I was here?"

Jace frowned, the turn of subject unexpected. "You sent me a text."

Her face fell. "No, I didn't."

"Yes. You did." He pulled out his phone, accessed the message and showed it to her.

"That's not my number," said Sonia. "I didn't send that."

"Then who did?" asked Rem.

"I did."

They turned at the voice and Jace went rigid. Rutger stood at the door, wearing his customary jeans, shirt and hoodie. The hood was down and his blonde hair stuck out like he'd been caught in a windstorm. He leaned casually on the frame, a chilly smile on his face.

Sonia stood, and Daniels and Remalla each moved to either side of her, their hands near their sidearms.

Jace eyed him. "You sent the text."

"I did." Rutger strolled into the room. "Why is it so dark in here?" He walked to a shuttered window and flung the curtains open, allowing the sunlight in. "You'd think you were trying to hide from someone."

He made a tsk-tsk sound. "You should know by now, Sonia, that you can't escape."

Sonia had gone very still, her face strained. "Why are you here? Where's Maxwell?"

Rutger looked out the window. "It's a beautiful day." He turned toward them. "And don't worry about Maxwell. He'll recover."

"You're under arrest for the murder of Justin Tenley, Rick Henderson, and Donald Vickers," said Rem.

Rutger chuckled. "What judge would be put me in prison? Henderson was killed by the Artist, and you already know who's guilty of Vickers' murder, not that he was any great loss to society."

"What about Justin Tenley and Devyn Palmer? You can't pin them on anyone," said Daniels.

Rutger grinned. "Oh, Detective. You and your partner are way behind the curve."

"I'm sure that's what you'd like us to believe," said Daniels. "And thanks for the card, but if you come near my family again, I promise, I will kill you."

"I think everyone in this room wants to kill me, and if they don't yet, they soon will. In fact, I can't really see a scenario where I don't die. But before that happens, I have a few more things to do." He leered at Sonia. "Don't you agree, Sonia?"

"Dean, please…," said Sonia.

His congenial personality disappeared and his face clouded. "Don't you dare call me that."

Sonia went quiet.

"Is that your real name?" asked Remalla. "Dean?"

Rutger's shifted his anger to Remalla. "I'll warn you once, Detective. But just once."

Rem raised his hands. "No problem. We'll stick to Rutger."

Jace tried to decide what to do. Rutger was on the edge and he needed to keep him from jumping. "Since you sent me the text, you obviously wanted me here for a reason. Why is that?"

Rutger eyed Rem, his expression flat, and then Sonia, before his shoulders relaxed, and he answered Jace. "Just doing a favor for someone, plus it gets us all in the same room together. I thought it would be fun." He pointed at Sonia. "Did you get any answers from her yet?"

Jace eyed the detectives, wondering what their play was, but he got the impression they were winging it just like him. "No. She won't tell me anything."

"She's good at keeping secrets. Aren't you, Sonia?"

Sonia stood her ground, but didn't speak.

"Look at her, so high and mighty. Thought she could solve everything. Thought she could—" Rutger paused.

"Could what?" asked Jace. "What is she not telling me? What are you not telling me?"

Rutger grinned and glanced at his watch. "That should be enough time."

"Time for what?" asked Jace.

Rutger's eyes narrowed. "You all are such fools. You should know by now that I always know more than I say and am capable of more than you think."

Sonia sucked in a breath, and she spoke, her voice quiet. "You didn't come here to kill me, did you?"

He smiled.

"Who are you doing a favor for?" asked Daniels, his brow knitted.

An uncomfortable feeling of dread settled over Jace. Something wasn't right. "What the hell is going on?"

Rutger strode through the room, looking confident. "I never went to your house, Detective."

"What?" asked Daniels.

"Who did?" asked Rem.

Rutger leaned against the wall, one ankle over the other. "And I didn't hurt Devyn. She's a wretched woman, but Justin was my target."

Jace's heart thumped and his stomach rolled. "Someone else hurt Devyn?"

He ran a hand down a curtain. "This office could use a little redecorating. It's so boring. You need to tell Maxwell, Sonia."

Jace fought to control his anger. "Tell me what is going on."

Rutger let go of the curtain. "I sent another email to Danni. Told her I appreciated her help. She's a smart lady."

Jace clenched his hands. "You're *BrotherlyLove*."

Rutger faced him. "Too bad you left her alone."

Jace couldn't stop himself. His fury erupting, he advanced on Rutger, grabbing him by his shirt and pushing and holding him up against the wall. "Don't you dare touch her," he growled in Rutger's face.

"It's not me you have to worry about," said Rutger, and he smiled.

Something snapped inside Jace and he slammed Rutger again against the wall and then slid his hands up to his throat. Rutger's face turned red.

"Jace, don't," said Daniels.

Before Daniels could react and as Jace squeezed, the letter opener shot off the desk and at Sonia, sinking deep into Sonia's midsection.

She cried out, holding her belly and falling to her knees.

"Sonia," shouted Rem, kneeling beside her.

"Jace, stop," said Daniels, moving to Jace's side. "He stabbed Sonia. He'll kill her."

"What did you do with Danni?" asked Jace.

Rutger eked out a few words. "Nothing. I didn't do anything."

Sonia cried out.

"Leave Sonia alone," yelled Jace.

"As you wish," said Rutger. Sonia yelled again.

"The knife slid out," said Rem. "We need an ambulance. She's going to bleed out over the floor." He jumped up and pulled a blanket off the back of the couch and put it against Sonia's wound.

Daniels pulled out his phone. "I'll call an ambulance." Holding his cell, he pulled out his hand cuffs. Before he could do anything with them though, the cuffs flew through the air, hitting the wall above the couch.

Jace held on to Rutger, who didn't fight back. Rutger managed a few more words, although Jace suspected he was close to passing out. "You're the only one who can save Sonia, Jace," he said, his voice raspy and his face twisted. "She dies, and her secrets die with her. You'll never know the truth."

Jace's internal battle raged. He had Rutger. He could kill him right now, maybe force him to talk, but Sonia was wounded.

Rutger sputtered a few more words. "You know you can help her."

Jace raged and cursed, letting go of Rutger and throwing him to the ground. He went to Sonia, who was lying on her back while Rem held the blanket against her stomach. She moaned.

"Hang in there, Sonia. You'll be okay," said Rem.

Daniels kneeled beside Rem. "Ambulance is on its way. I'm going for Rutger."

"You can't handle him by yourself," said Rem. He looked at Jace.

"I got it. Go." Jace took Rem's place with the blanket and held it against Sonia's belly. "Be careful."

Rem and Daniels disappeared behind him and Jace focused on Sonia. He knew Rutger was right. He could help her.

"Sonia, relax," he told her.

"Jace," she said, her voice fading.

"I got you." He closed his eyes, letting his hands move over her, until he found the spot that felt right and then he sensed the energy, feeling it build, and he moved it through him and into her as his hands warmed. He didn't know exactly what he was doing, but all he could do was trust his instincts. He heard yelling, and a grunt, then a crack as if something broke behind him, but he didn't let it distract him. This was not his childhood dog, or Daniels' hand. This was Sonia, and her life was ebbing away. He could almost feel it, and he knew he had to hurry. "Stay with me, Sonia," he said.

Her eyes flickered, and she moaned again.

Jace kept working, allowing the energy to move, and praying he could help her in time. If she died, he'd never know the truth.

Rem and Daniels returned, breathing hard. "How is she?" asked Rem, kneeling again beside Sonia. Sirens began to wail in the distance.

Jace took a deep breath and released it. The energy drain he'd felt from Sonia began to slow and then the energy required from him began to lessen. She'd lost consciousness, but he felt sure the bleeding had almost stopped.

He relaxed, sitting back, feeling exhausted. "She'll be okay. For now, at least."

Rem took her pulse. "Steady," he said.

Jace looked over, noticing the detectives. Their faces were red, their hair disheveled, and they were both sweaty. "Where's Rutger?"

"Long gone," said Remalla, sitting back on his heels. "Long gone."

CHAPTER TWENTY-NINE

"Jace, wait," yelled Daniels, Jace ignored him and ran up to the front door. It was partially open.

Remalla caught up to him. "Let us go in first."

Jace seemed frozen, his face stricken, but he pushed the door open and ran inside.

"Damn it," said Daniels.

"We should have left him at the jewelers," said Rem, following Jace.

"We didn't know where this place was," said Daniels. His sidearm in his hand, he went in behind Rem.

They entered a small living area. "Danni," yelled Jace.

An overturned dining chair and a broken lamp were the only items out of place. Jace ran into the bedrooms. "She's not here."

Rem noticed the cracked bathroom door frame. "Looks like she hid, but he broke the door down."

Jace cursed. "How could I be so stupid." He paced, his energy erratic, his hands clutched behind his neck. "I left her alone."

"It's not your fault," said Daniels, holstering his weapon.

Jace pointed, his face a grimace. "Yes, it is. Rutger drew me out. He knew I'd come. I played right into his hands, and now Danni, she's...she's...son-of-a-bitch." He grabbed the bottom of the sofa and flipped it backward, and it toppled over upside down.

Rem jumped out of the way to avoid getting hit. Seeing the sofa, he glanced at Daniels. "You two should start an act."

"It helps more than you know," said Daniels.

Jace continued his pacing. "We have to find her."

"We will. We need to call Lozano. Get forensics up here," said Daniels. "Talk to the neighbors. Maybe they saw something."

"We don't have time for fingerprints," yelled Jace. "This guy will be long gone and Danni will be dead by the time you get a hair you found on the floor under a microscope."

Rem shook his head. "We know this is hard, but if you want find this guy, we have to…"

"Rem…look," said Daniels. He pointed toward the dining table. A laptop and a cup of coffee were the only items on it, plus a deck of tarot cards. On the laptop, though, was a single tarot card, perched between the keys.

Rem came closer, making eye contact with Daniels. "It's our Four of Cups."

"There's writing on the side," said Daniels.

Jace came over. "What is it?"

Rem turned his head to read the writing. "You can't win them all." He looked up at Jace. "You have any idea what that means?"

Jace dropped his jaw. "Was that left by whoever took Danni?"

Daniels nodded. "Danni didn't leave it." He straightened. "The card means we've missed something obvious. There was a card left at my house too, after someone broke into it. It came from the same deck as the Justice card left at your office." He pointed. "This card was missing from the deck, too."

"Rutger took that deck from Danni's, didn't he? So Rutger *is* responsible for this?" asked Jace.

Rem studied the card. "Not necessarily."

"Then what?" shouted Jace. "What the hell do you two do anyway? Don't you know anything? We all thought this was Rutger."

"I know," said Daniels, rubbing his eyes. "We're just as frustrated as you are."

"Are you?" Jace paced again. "Then why are we just standing here like old men at a bus stop. We need to do something." His gaze stopped on something and he walked into the kitchen. "Oh, God. It's her phone."

"Don't touch…," started Daniels, but Jace picked it up. "…it," finished Daniels.

"That's why she didn't answer," said Jace. He gripped her cell, closing his eyes. "I'm sorry, Danni. I shouldn't have left." He opened his eyes. "We have to find her."

"We will," said Rem. He looked at Daniels. "What have we missed?" Daniels scowled, but Rem recognized his partner's focus. "What is it?" Rem asked. "What are you thinking?"

Daniels shook his head. "We've gone too fast on this, Rem. We shot right past something important. We've been so caught up in Rutger and his shenanigans, that we missed the details." He eyed the card. "This wasn't just about Jace."

Jace walked over. "What do you mean?"

"Shit," said Rem. "Maybe this was about Danni from the beginning."

"And Rutger just used it to throw us off-base," said Daniels.

"But how is that possible?" asked Jace. "Are you saying there's a second killer?"

Rem thought about it. "Maybe." He thought back to their first encounter with Danni. "And if there is, how do we find him?"

"We go back to the beginning, and we look for the clues that we overlooked," said Daniels.

"Come on," said Rem, heading for the door. "We'll call Lozano from the car."

"Where are we going?" asked Jace. "What about Danni?"

"You want to find her?" Rem asked. "We do what Daniels said."

"Start from the top and with the basics. If we missed a clue, we'll find it." Daniels tipped his head. "Let's go."

**

Lozano eyed his detectives from his office window. They had files open on their desks and Daniels' laptop was open. Another man, who Lozano realized was Jace Marlon, sat at an empty desk beside them, flipping through a file. Lozano left his office and approached them. "Anything?"

Rem rubbed his neck, and stretched it. His long, dark hair, which Lozano constantly argued with Remalla about cutting, seemed even longer, and was pulled back with a hair tie. "Nothing yet, Cap, but we just now got all the files together."

"You really think there's someone else besides this Rutger you've been chasing?" asked Lozano.

"Seems that way," said Daniels. He typed some keys on his laptop. "I'm going to pull up the lobby footage from Justin's apartment. It will take a second to load."

"I've got Devyn's statement from the hospital," said Rem, "plus the forensics from Justin's apartment and Justin's neighbor's statements that Mel and Garcia put together."

"I talked to the hospital. Sonia's stable and doing well," said Lozano.

"Thanks for checking, Cap," said Rem.

"And I've got an APB out on Danni. The whole force is out looking. Hopefully, we'll get lucky."

"Yeah, let's hope," said Daniels.

"I'm Captain Lozano. You're Jace Marlon?"

"Sorry, Captain," said Daniels. "Yes. This is Jace Marlon. He's helping us review the files."

"Captain," said Jace. He barely looked up before returning to the file in front of him. He flipped a page and he glared. "I don't know why I'm looking at this. It's my statement from that night. I think I know what happened."

"Look at it again. Think back to that night at the bar. Make sure nothing got missed," said Rem. "The smallest detail could make a difference."

Jace groaned. "This is ridiculous. I feel like we're going in circles."

"Welcome to police work," said Daniels.

Jace offered a curse under his breath and went back to the file.

"What makes you think there's a second perp, other than Rutger?" asked Lozano.

"Because Rutger told us there was," said Daniels.

"What? He told you?" asked Lozano.

"Sorry, Cap. We haven't had time to get you up to speed," said Rem.

"Didn't he stab Sonia?" asked Lozano.

Daniels eyed Rem, and Lozano saw Jace look up.

"Yeah, he did," said Rem.

"Don't you think he might be yanking your chain?" asked Lozano.

"That might seem logical," said Daniels, "but Danni was taken at the same time as Rutger showed at Maxwell's. It's hard to be in two places at once."

Rem sat up. "Here. Remember this? Devyn's statement?" He pointed at a paper.

"What about it?" asked Daniels.

"She said a noise woke her. A thump, like something fell. We thought it was odd at the time," said Rem.

"Now it makes more sense," said Daniels. "Maybe she heard Justin's attacker, who we assume is Rutger. She gets up and gets attacked herself."

"Somebody else was in the room with her?" asked Jace. "Rutger is working with someone?"

"It's odd, I know," said Rem. "Rutger's a loner, so why is someone else there, and how does Rutger know him?"

"And how does that tie in to Danni?" asked Daniels.

Lozano watched the back and forth of his detectives. "Can I talk to you two in my office, please?"

Daniels and Remalla looked up. "Can it wait, Cap?" asked Remalla. "We're pretty busy."

"I am aware of your time constraints, Remalla. I'm not blind," said Lozano. He looked at Jace. "Excuse us."

Jace sighed. "Sure. Take your time. Danni's out there with a killer and you guys can have your meeting."

Lozano raised a brow, but stayed quiet, but he offered a look to Daniels and Remalla. "You coming?"

"Right behind you, Cap," said Rem. He stood. "We'll find her Jace. Stay cool."

"Video's up," said Daniels. "We'll check it after." He stood. "We'll be right back. Keep looking through the files," he said to Jace.

"Sure. Take your time." Frustrated, Jace ran a hand through his hair.

Lozano walked into his office and Daniels and Remalla followed. They took a seat.

Lozano sat in his chair. "You two sure about this?"

"We wouldn't be reviewing everything if we weren't sure, Cap," said Daniels.

Lozano rested his elbows in his desk. "I mean about Marlon. Should he be here, reviewing the files? He's not a cop and it's not his job."

"Where else is he going to go?" asked Rem. "His best friend is dead, and his girlfriend may be next."

"Girlfriend?" asked Lozano. "Are they dating?"

Daniels shrugged.

"I think the signs are there," said Rem. "Only one bed was unmade in that house."

"Nice deduction, Sherlock," said Daniels.

"Thanks. I thought so."

"She could very well make her bed and he doesn't," said Lozano.

"Regardless, they're close, and if she dies, he'll blame himself. I have some idea how that feels, so I say we cut him some slack," said Rem.

Lozano glanced at Daniels, who nodded. "Okay. I'll give you two some leeway here, but if you don't find her soon, Marlon's going to have to back off. He's too close to this. He goes off on a wild goose chase and you may have two more dead people on your hands."

"We understand," said Daniels. "We'll keep an eye on him."

Lozano huffed. "You better. You get any hint that he's going to be a gunslinger on this, you cut him loose. I don't care how close he is to Danni."

"Got it," said Rem. "Anything else?"

"I've got forensics at the house where they were staying. They're going over it, plus talking to the neighbors."

"It's a long shot," said Daniels. "They didn't find anything at Danni's or my place. It's unlikely he'll screw up now. All we've got is the cards."

"You never know, maybe they'll find something." Lozano sat back. "I know you haven't had time to fill out a report, but how exactly did Rutger get away from you again at the jewelers? This guy have wings? Or should I say horns? And how did he manage to stab Sonia?"

"Well, Cap," said Rem, looking at Daniels. "It's a long story, and we need to get back to the case." He threw out a thumb.

"Yeah. We'll fill you in as soon as we can," said Daniels.

Lozano scowled and raised his voice. "You two can take two minutes to tell me what the hell—" His phone rang. He eyed the display. "Crap. It's the Chief. I've been trying to reach him all morning."

"You better take that, Cap. Don't leave the Chief hanging." He stood along with Daniels.

"This conversation is not over," said Lozano. "As soon as I'm off the phone—"

"Whatever you say, Cap," said Daniels. He walked to the door.

Rem followed him outside. "See ya, Cap."

Lozano grunted, knowing his detectives were dodging him, and answered the phone.

CHAPTER THIRTY

Daniels walked out of the office, and Rem followed, closing Lozano's door behind him. Rem whistled. "We barely dodged that bullet. Remind me to tell the Chief he has great timing."

"You can mention it at your next lunch," said Daniels.

Rem snorted.

"Where's Jace?" Daniels returned to his desk, but Jace wasn't there.

"Maybe he had to go to the john," said Rem.

Daniels sat and eyed his laptop. He did a double-take. "Rem. The video's been watched."

"What?" asked Rem. "The video from the lobby?"

"Yeah. Look."

Rem came around Daniels' desk and looked over his shoulder. The video was up and it was stopped on a frame from the entry at Justin's apartment building. "That's the shot with Rutger."

Although it was a grainy black and white image, Rutger could be seen entering the lobby, his hood up, and his hands in his pockets, heading toward the elevator. The time code read 3:36 a.m. A delivery driver wearing a vest and baseball cap and carrying a box under his arm had provided partial cover but had not fully concealed him.

"You think Jace watched this?" asked Rem.

"He must have," said Daniels. "Why'd he stop here?" He looked back toward the doors of the squad room. "And where the hell is he?"

"You think he saw something we missed?"

Daniels heart dropped. "If he did, and he took off on his own, Lozano is going to kill us." He glanced at Lozano through the windows of his office. The captain was still on the phone.

"That and the getting himself killed part isn't going to make me feel too great either." Rem straightened. "I'm calling him." He grabbed his cell and hit some buttons, and listened. "Shit. It's going to voicemail."

"Tell him to get his ass back here," said Daniels.

Rem left a colorful message for Jace and hung up.

"So, what did he catch that we didn't?" asked Daniels.

Rem returned to look at the video. He stared at it along with Daniels. "Hell. We're idiots. That tarot card was right. We missed the obvious."

Daniels frowned. "What did we miss? That is obviously Rutger entering the building."

Rem gestured at the screen. "And so is the delivery guy. Who makes deliveries at 3:30 in the morning?"

Daniels face fell. "Son-of-a-bitch. We are idiots." He studied the screen. "That may be our second guy, Rem."

"Maybe. Hopefully. Only who is he? And why did they come in together? Did they plan this?"

"Let's start with the *who* first," said Daniels. "One question at a time." He rubbed his jaw, thinking. "Jace disappeared."

Rem took the seat where Jace had been sitting. "Which means if that delivery man is our bad guy, and Jace recognized him, then that's where he's headed."

"Shit. We better find him."

"I know. If it's somebody Jace knows, then maybe he's right in front of our noses." He flipped through the files about Jace's statement.

A door opened and closed. Daniels looked up to see Lozano approaching, sliding his jacket on. "I'm going to the Chief's office. Should be back in about an hour. Where's Marlon?"

Rem didn't miss a beat. "He's starving. Ran down to the cafeteria."

Lozano pointed. "You remember what I said. Keep him on a short leash."

"Will do, Cap," said Daniels.

"I'll want an update when I get back," said Lozano, heading for the squad room doors.

"Sure thing, Cap. Say hi to the Chief," said Rem, with a casual wave.

The Captain disappeared behind the doors. Rem went back to the files and Daniels slid his chair over. "Remind me to never trust you in a stressful situation."

"Who else are you going to trust?"

"Good point. You see anything?"

Rem reviewed Jace's statement. He went back over the phone call Jace received from Justin's, and Jace finding Justin. Nothing stood out.

"Go to the card game," said Daniels.

Rem found that section and read through it.

"Wait a minute," said Daniels. "Jace won a lot of money that night. Remember what the writing on the four of cups said? *You can't win them all.* You think that's a reference to the game?"

"Maybe. Who were the two other guys at the game? Here." Rem tapped at the file. "Simon Melinger and Henry Hunt. Mel and Garcia gave them the all clear."

"Let's check them out," said Daniels. He slid back to the computer, accessed the database he needed and entered Simon's name. After waiting a few seconds, he read the information that appeared. "Nothing that stands out. No prior record. Works at an accounting firm. No traffic stops in the last year."

"Try Henry Hunt."

Daniels accessed the records for Henry. "Same. No priors. No red flags. Works at a construction company."

"Wait a minute. Jace said something at the bar, about Henry." Rem closed the file. "Remember? Didn't he say Henry hit on Danni, and she turned him down?"

Daniels nodded. "Yeah, he did. That's still a stretch. I'm guessing Danni's turned a lot of men down in that bar."

"Yeah, but not that night." Rem rubbed his head. "That flower delivery to Danni. They were daisies."

Daniels tried to think. "If Rutger didn't send them, then the person who did knew Danni's name, which means he had to be there that night, assuming some member of Danni's family isn't stalking her."

"No, I know." Rem bounced his knee. "We're still missing something. I can't put my finger on it."

Daniels understood the feeling. "I keep going back to that conversation with Jace at his bar, before Rutger showed up and dragged us through the city streets."

"What about it?"

"Why show up then? For what purpose? I know Rutger threatened Sonia, and maybe that's why, but hell he could have called or just walked into the bar. If he wanted to talk to Jace, he could have done it without us chasing him through downtown."

Rem's eyes widened and he snapped his fingers. "Downtown."

"What about it?"

Rem dropped the file back on the table. "Go back to the computer. Pull up Henry."

"He's still up."

"Where does he work?"

"He's an engineer." He looked for the employer name. "Clara Construction."

Rem tapped the screen. "That's it."

"What's it?" asked Daniels.

"That building we were in, when we chased Rutger. You remember the name on the sign outside the area?"

"I was a little busy chasing Rutger."

"I think Rutger running into that area was not a coincidence. He gave us a clue. The name on the sign was Clara Construction. They're putting up that building."

Daniels stilled, recalling that chase. He vaguely remembered seeing a large billboard on the site touting the name of the project and its projected opening date, but he couldn't recall the company name. "You're sure?"

"I am. It made me think of my Aunt Clara with the glass eye."

Daniels pursed his lips. "Of course it did."

"It's still a long shot, but the coffee's getting warmer," said Rem. "We need a picture of Henry."

"Let me see if I can access his driver's license," said Daniels. "He's got one citation for speeding last summer. Here." The picture popped up on the screen.

Rem and Daniels leaned in. "Shit," said Rem.

They returned to the frame from the lobby video. It was grainy, and Daniels had to zoom in, but the image of the delivery man was good enough to see the resemblance. "That's him," said Daniels, a chill running through him. "Son-of-a-bitch, Rem. Henry's our guy."

**

Jace closed the door to the cab, and the driver pulled away. A stiff, chilly breeze blew and ruffled his hair. Jace pushed it back, found a leather tie from his pocket, and pulled it behind his neck and secured it. He looked up at the tall building in front of him. The billboard touted the opening of the Heisen Center in the summer. *Clara Construction* in big italic letters was written beneath it.

The minute Jace had seen the video, he'd recognized Henry and everything had clicked into place. Jace knew Henry worked at Clara Construction. This building was his baby. He'd talked about it a few times at the bar. Jace had paid little attention, and he hadn't made the connection when he'd followed the detectives into this area to chase Rutger. But after seeing the video, and remembering Henry's interest in Danni, it all came together.

After watching the footage, he'd debated whether to tell the detectives, but he couldn't risk more delays. Daniels and Remalla would want to be sure. They'd want to tell their captain, and once they did, Jace would be relegated to the sidelines. Danni didn't have time for delays. Jace had to get to her. He suspected that Danni being taken had something to do with him, and he couldn't help but think that maybe he had somehow triggered Henry. Henry was your average man. Average height, average weight, average job. He had no girlfriend and from what Jace could tell, he was frequently rejected by women. Jace was the opposite in every category. Seeing Henry in that lobby video, Jace had realized that Henry had targeted Devyn, and now he was after Danni.

How Henry had wound up involved with Rutger, Jace couldn't guess, but Rutger had deliberately led Daniels and Remalla to this building on their chase. It couldn't be by accident. It was a risk not telling the detectives. They could be checking out Henry's place and putting out the alert to the police, but some gut feeling in Jace told him Henry was here and time was short. And as much as he hated to admit it, a construction site would be a great place to conceal a body.

Standing, staring up at the building, he watched as the sun descended beyond the hills in the distance. It would be dark soon.

Jace started walking, unsure where to start. It was a several-story building under partial construction. They could be anywhere. But he knew one thing. Henry was here, and he had Danni.

CHAPTER THIRTY-ONE

Danni shivered, her mind slowly becoming aware of her surroundings. A stiff breeze blew her hair back, and she opened her eyes. Blinking several times, she tried to focus. Everything was blurry, but her vision slowly cleared and she realized she was outdoors. The wind blew again, and she could see twinkling lights. Wondering where she was, she moved slowly and moaned. Her head ached, her mouth was dry and her hands wouldn't move. Her mind whirled and her memory kicked in. The house. A knock. She'd answered the door, and he'd been standing there. She'd raced through the living area, and had locked herself in the bathroom, but he'd kicked in the door and dragged her out.

The chair and lamp had been knocked over in the struggle, but something had come down hard over her head, and she'd gone down.

Fear bubbled up and evaluating her situation, she realized she was gagged and her hands bound in front of her with a zip tie. Scanning the area, she saw what looked like a building under construction. Scaffolding, wooden beams, and pipes popping up from the cement floor surrounded her, and sawdust and bits of wood and a few tools littered the ground. Where the hell was she?

Her stiff muscles ached, and her head throbbed, but she pushed herself up into a sitting position. Her head cleared enough for her to figure out that the twinkling lights were nearby buildings. The city was lighting up around her as the sun descended. The only other ambient light shone from a distant wall, which, looking through the maze of beams, appeared to be near an elevator. Another cold breeze blew, and Danni got to her knees, trying to determine her location. Checking behind her, she quickly scooted forward, away from the edge of a very big fall. From what she could see, she was several stories up.

Moaning softly to herself, she began to pull the gag down when someone spoke.

"Before you do that, we need to talk."

She startled and turned to her right, seeing the man sitting on an edge of scaffolding. Forcing her mind to work, the man's name finally flickered to life. Henry. Jace's friend.

He stared for a moment. "Surprised?"

She tried to control her fear, but it exploded anyway. Her body shook and not just from the chilly breeze.

"Maybe next time you'll take me seriously," he said. He wore a baseball cap, and a pair of worn jeans, with a windbreaker over a t-shirt. "You like it here?" He gestured with his arm. "I helped design this place. It's supposed to open in the summer. We're a little behind, but so long as the weather holds up, I think we'll make the deadline." He slid a hand into his jacket and pulled out a knife.

Danni's insides dropped, her eyes welled, and a tear escaped and slid down her cheek. Jesus. She wasn't ready to die. She looked around. Her feet were unbound, but where the hell would she go?

He stood, and a whimper bubbled up and escaped from her throat.

"Ssshh," he said. He came over and squatted in front of her. She didn't move and was too terrified to make eye contact.

He took a hold of her gag, and she instinctively pulled back.

"I'm going to take this off. Don't scream. Even if you do, it won't matter. You're fifteen stories up and your screams will be muffled by the wind. Plus, I won't like it." He yanked on the gag and it came down around her neck. Her tongue felt like sandpaper, but she stayed quiet.

"Good. That's better," he said. "Now we can talk."

Danni doubted she'd be able to say much of anything. It was taking everything she had to not dissolve into desperate tears. She bit her lip and tried to hold it together.

He remained for a moment watching her, and then took a finger and ran it down her cheek, wiping away a tear. Danni cringed and moved back.

"You know why you're here?"

She shook her head.

"Hmm," he said, studying the knife in his hand. "It's not your fault really, although you could have been nicer to me."

Danni sniffed and tried to speak. Maybe talking to him might help. She gathered her courage and whispered. "I'm sorry."

He took a lock of her hair and twisted it around his finger. "You're definitely nicer. Much nicer than Devyn." His face twisted. "I hated her."

Danni grimaced and forced herself to speak. "You hurt Devyn?"

"Yes. I did." He let go of her hair, and sat in front of her, crossing his legs. "It was unexpected, but necessary."

"Why?" Another tear slid down her cheek.

He took a deep breath and faced the wind, "Because, it seemed...needed. There are too many Devyns in the world." He looked back. "I actually hadn't planned to kill her, but then that night, that night...I saw who she really was...and the most extraordinary thing happened. I got help." He smiled and put the knife in his lap. A strong gust of wind almost blew his cap off, and he took it off and put it beside him.

Danni took a breath, trying to stay calm. *Keep him talking.* "Who helped you?"

He put his hands in his lap, looking like an eager child ready to play Duck, Duck Goose. "When I left that night, after the card game. I got in my car and sat there. I was angry. About you and Devyn and Jace. I stared out at the city and at this building in the distance, wondering how much more I could stand. Women are such cruel creatures, but I'd always believed that someone out there might live up to my expectations. I saw you leave and I wondered if it could be you." He gave her a melancholy look. "I took your card from the bar and I went to your website on my phone. I saw Devyn come out with Jace. He groped her and she gave him a sloppy kiss, then got in a car and left. Jace went back into the bar. I decided then to send you an email."

Danni didn't understand. "I…I…don't remember an email…"

He smiled. "I'm *Lovelorn*."

Danni's stomach twisted and she fought the urge to throw up. "You're *Lovelorn*?"

"Yes." He put his free hand on her knee. "My question was about you."

Danni couldn't help herself and averted his touch. "I…I…didn't know."

"I know. That's what made it so exciting. I wanted to see what the cards would say about us if I was anonymous. I thought maybe they would be on my side." He paused. "I no sooner sent the email when a car pulled up and Devyn got out. She ran to another car across the street. Justin emerged and she ran into his arms and kissed him. He got anxious and looked around, and I ducked down. We were across from Jace's bar, and he obviously did not want to be seen. She didn't care though. She was all over him, and they got in the car and drove off." Henry laced his fingers together, his hands clenched. "They were cheating on Jace, and he had no idea."

Danni watched him, her mind reeling, but unable to determine what to do.

"I felt this rage bubble up. This woman, who barely offered me a second glance and who only spoke to me if she had to, was screwing around on my friend, with his best friend. I knew it was her fault. She'd deliberately flaunted herself in front of Justin."

"Justin could have said no." Danni braced herself for an angry reaction. She figured she had nothing to lose.

He remained calm though. "Oh, Justin was a fool. I know that. But Devyn took advantage, and made a fool of Jace at the same time. She was a unique and special slut, and I knew then that I would do something about it. So, I followed them, and went to Justin's apartment building."

Danni stayed quiet, sensing his need to tell her what had happened, almost as if he wanted to unburden himself. Another breeze blew and she shivered again. She wore only a thin t-shirt and jeans, and as night fell, the warmth of the day dissipated.

"When I got there, though, I didn't know what to do. All the pent-up anger grew because I felt helpless. I knew they were in there, laughing behind Jace's back. Behind my back too. And Simon's. We were all fools to them."

"You could have told Jace," she said.

He met her gaze, and her heart pounded. Was she pressing too hard?

"No, I couldn't. What would he have done? Would he have believed me? And even if he had, he'd forgive her, and give in to her weak pleas for mercy. It made me sick to even think about it. No. The more I stood there, the more I realized what I needed to do. Get rid of her."

He picked up the knife and held it, and Danni stiffened. "Henry, please," she whispered.

"I'm not done." He held the knife in his lap. "I was standing there, trying to think of creative ways to kill her, when someone walked up to me. He said something which changed my life forever." He ran a thumb down the edge of the knife. "He said, 'I know what you're thinking, and I can help, if you're ready to accept it.'"

Although Danni suspected who this mysterious benefactor was, she still had to ask. "Who was it?"

He smiled. "I think you know." He laid the knife against his leg. "I wasn't sure what to think at first, but he clarified it very quickly. He said he knew I wanted to kill her, and he wanted to kill Justin. We could help each other out. I hesitated about Justin because he's my friend, but in the end I understood. Sometimes sacrifices have to be made for the greater good, and in the end, Justin deserved it."

Danni shook her head. "Oh, God."

"We made a plan. We walked into the lobby. I wore my baseball cap, and grabbed a box from the back of my car, and he gave me a vest to wear, and we simply walked in like we lived there, and went right upstairs to Justin's floor. He told me what to do and what he wanted me to say to her, and gave me a knife. He said he would take care of Justin, and I would take care of Devyn, and then we would go our separate ways. My heart was racing, but I was excited too. He somehow gained access to the apartment, I'm still not sure how, and before I knew it, Justin came out of the bedroom and into the kitchen. He walked right past me, never saw me, and I entered the bedroom. I closed the door and I heard Justin go down, and so did Devyn. She never saw me in the dark, and when she got up..." he clenched the knife, "...I stabbed her. She collapsed, bleeding, and I told her what he wanted me to, plus added what I thought about her. She was terrified and I watched her succumb." He closed his eyes, as if remembering, and reopened them. "It was the most exhilarating feeling of my life."

Danni shook with cold, adrenaline and fear. She had to get loose or she would die in this building. "Henry, listen."

"Stop talking," he said, his eyes a dead calm. "Afterward, I walked down the stairs with him, the man who helped me, and he mentioned you. He'd seen you at the bar and heard us talking. He told me if I really liked you, that I shouldn't give up. Every risk was worth taking, no matter what the cost. And now that I'd handled Devyn, I was ready for the next step. I told him I'd already contacted you, and he was pleased. He encouraged it. Said he'd requested a reading himself."

He stared off. "I wondered if he liked you too, and I asked him, but he said his issue was with Jace, and that you were all mine." He tilted his head, his eyes cold like the breeze. "The cards seemed to be in our favor. I thought we had a shot, and I even sent you flowers, but then you backtracked on me. I was discouraged." He sighed. "Let me ask you," he leaned in closer and found her knee again, squeezing it. "Did they see this coming?"

A sob escaped her throat and her terror almost made her jump and run, despite his nearness. "Henry, don't do this."

"Do what? We're talking. Nothing's happened yet."

"You took me. They'll be looking for me."

"I know. I'm sure Jace is frantic, wondering where you are." He rubbed his hand on her thigh, and she pulled back again, whimpering. "Tell me," he asked, "did you always like him?"

"He's my boss and my friend."

"He took you away. I think he's in love with you. At least that's what he told me."

"Jace told you?"

"No. The man who killed Justin. He said I'd have to fight for you. Show my strength, and what I was capable of. He gave me tips. I contacted him a few times after Devyn. I took the cards from your apartment. Did you know that? He told me what to do with the Justice card as a favor to him, and I placed the other two cards. One at the detective's house because my friend suggested it. He said the police need to know who they're dealing with, and I put the other at the house you just left, because now Jace knows that I'm in charge, not him. He, my new friend, told me where the house was, too. He knew where Jace had taken you."

Danni's breath caught and her breathing hitched. "I don't understand how taking me helps you."

"It's not for you." He reached out and pushed a lock of hair that had blown in her face away. "I realize that now. It's for Jace. He's not right for you. I finally see that. He deserved Devyn. He doesn't deserve you."

More tears escaped and slid down her face. "Henry, you don't even know me."

He moved closer, and Danni tried to lean back, but he brought the knife up and she froze.

"I know all about you. I've done my homework. I know about your mom and what happened to her. How you were raised by your grandmother, and your poor pathetic dad, who doesn't deserve you any more than Jace does." He placed the tip of the knife on the cement in front of her. "I saw his email to you on your laptop when I was in your apartment. Did you know he lives in Phoenix, Arizona? He has an eight-year-old son and a pretty wife. He moved on without you, Danni."

Danni blinked through her tears. "You know where my father is?"

"Your childhood wasn't much different than mine, except maybe your grandparents were nicer. My grandmother hated me, so I smothered her in her bed when I was twenty."

Danni couldn't hold back a sob. "Henry...please let me go." She could barely get the words out.

He lifted the knife and brought it to her throat, and she cried out. "I don't want to hurt you, Danni. I just want to talk. I want you to see me for who I really am. I know Jace has all the machismo, but I have so much more to offer. Don't you see that now?"

Danni tried to stay still, but the terror flooding her made it impossible. She kept trying to inch back away, but he wouldn't let her get far. "I want to go home," she whispered. "Please, let me go home."

His face shifted and he glared. "No. You want to go back to him."

"No, please. Listen."

"I'm done listening. I've listened my whole life. Now people are going to listen to me." He grabbed her arm and yanked her up to her feet.

"No, please, Henry. Don't." She babbled, trying to figure out what to say or do. He yanked her to the edge of the building, the ground below looming. "Henry, no," she screamed.

A warbled melody interrupted, and Henry stopped. He held her for a moment as if considering his next move, and then pulled her back. The warbling came again, and he sat her against the scaffolding. Danni tried to get a hold of herself, but her body quaked, and tears soaked her shirt.

"You move, you die," he said. "And don't even think of running." He lifted his shirt and she saw the gun in his waistband. "I'm prepared to do what I have to do."

She wiped her face with her arm and sat still, her stomach rolling. Still holding the knife, Henry pulled out his ringing cell phone and smiled at the display. "Well," he said. "Guess who?" He eyed Danni, his eyes dead but his face a sneer, and he answered the phone. "Hello, Jace."

CHAPTER THIRTY-TWO

Jace wandered the first floor, seeing nothing other than construction materials, debris, insulation and wooden framing. It was much as it had been from the previous day. It had rained briefly on and off throughout the afternoon and the deserted site was empty, like a playground after recess. He took a few minutes to wander, and then took the stairs to the second floor, doing much the same as he had on the first floor. Everything was quiet, other than the sound of the whipping wind.

Frustrated, he knew if he continued, he could spend the next hour searching the site, and he could miss them entirely, or worse, be too late. The thought also occurred to him that he could search every floor, only to realize they'd never been here. Images of Henry holding Danni at some unknown location plagued him. What if he was wrong, and his impulsive actions cost Danni her life?

Trying not to think the worse, he debated again calling Daniels and Remalla. He should tell them what he'd discovered and where he was. Pulling out his phone, another idea popped into his head. He stopped for a second, considering it. It was either incredibly stupid, or incredibly smart. Deciding on the latter, he pulled up Henry's number and dialed. Jace doubted he'd answer, but if he did, then maybe he could talk him down. If Jace was his real target, then he might let Danni go. Or maybe Jace could determine where Henry was holding her. The odds of it succeeding were slim, but Jace had to try.

The phone rang three times and Jace heard it pick up. He went still, and was surprised when Henry spoke his name. He didn't know what to say. A shiver ran through him. "Henry," he replied.

Wind on the line made it hard to hear, but the noise indicated that Henry had to be outside. The odds that he was at the construction site rose, and Jace looked around, wondering if he was nearby. Not seeing anything, he headed to the stairs. "Where are you?" he asked.

Henry chuckled on the line. "I hear the wind on your end, Jace. I take it you're somewhere below?"

Jace's heart rate zoomed higher. Henry was here. "If you're at the Heisen, I am." He raced up the stairs, taking them two at a time.

"You're smart, Jace. I should have known you'd find us."

Us. "Where's Danni? Is she here?" He got to the third floor and kept going. Something told him Henry was further up.

"Sitting right beside me."

"Let her go."

"I can't do that. You know I can't. I finally have her to myself. Why would I let her go now? Especially with you charging after her for the rescue. In fact...," he paused. "...this is playing out nicely. Where are you?"

"Fourth floor."

"Good. I'm on the top floor. Come and get me." The line went dead.

Jace raced up the stairs, but stopped, seeing the elevator. He ran over and hit the button, hearing it whir to life from below.

**

Danni listened to Henry speak. Her eyes darted around, looking for anything to use as a weapon or somewhere to run, but didn't see much to help her. Where was Jace, and what was he doing? Hearing Henry's words before he hung up, her belly constricted. Jace was here and on his way up. But Henry had a gun, and a knife. He would kill Jace.

Terrified, she tried to think. What could she do? Could she somehow warn him?

Henry hung up and grabbed her by the arm. "Get up. Now."

Shaking, she stood. "What are you doing?"

He shoved her back toward the edge, and she screamed, but he stopped just short of the drop-off. "You stand right there and don't move."

"Henry, don't do this."

"Turn around. Face the other way."

"Henry, please. Think about what you're doing."

"I said turn around," he yelled at her, and she swiveled, facing outward, looking over the city, and prayed the wind wouldn't blow her off balance. He leaned up against her, gripping her arm, and spoke in her ear. "Don't move and don't scream. You do, and I'll kill him the minute he steps onto the floor, and then I'll find your father, and I'll kill him and his whole family. You want an eight-year-old's death on your hands?"

She fought not to step back against him, and moaned. "No."

"Then don't move. Remember. I have a gun. This can be over very quickly. If you care about him, then do as I say."

Danni quivered, praying for help. "Henry—" But then he moved and was gone.

**

Jace jumped on the elevator and hit the number fifteen. It was a temporary elevator and the wind whipped through the slats. It moved slowly and Jace cursed, wanting it to move faster. He remembered his initial plan to call Daniels and Remalla and grabbed his phone again. He'd heard their earlier voicemail but had ignored it. Now, he called Remalla back.

Remalla answered on the first ring. "Jace, where the hell are you?"

"I'm at the Heisen Center, downtown. It's Henry. He's got Danni."

"We know. We're pulling up below. You need to stay put. We'll be right behind you."

"He's got her on the top floor. I'm on my way up."

"Jace. Listen. Wait for us. You go up there, and you'll get yourself killed. Danni, too."

"I can't sit and wait. I'll stall him until you guys make it up."

"Don't be stupid. He'll kill you."

The elevator approached the fifteenth floor and began to slow. "I'm here. I'm going in."

"Jace, wait—"

Jace hung up.

**

Daniels came to a screeching halt in the parking lot. Rem cursed and hung up the phone. "Jace's up there. On the top floor. So's Henry and he's got Danni."

After identifying Henry on the video, they'd called his employer and learned Henry had taken the day off, then they'd issued an APB, and sent a team to Henry's home. They headed to the construction site, assuming it was a potential place to take Danni.

"Seems like our long shot just hit the golden buzzer. I'll call for back-up," said Daniels.

Rem jumped out of the car, looking up. There would be no way they could wait for back-up to arrive. Everything would be over by then. He spied the elevator above, stopped at the top of the building, and then watched it begin to descend. Rem wondered what Jace was confronting. Daniels exited the car, and looked up too. "They're on their way." He hesitated. "Shit. You thinking what I'm thinking?"

Rem nodded. "Yup. Sure am. Let's go."

They slammed their doors shut simultaneously and ran toward the building, slipping through an opening in the fence, and passing a large cement hole in the ground.

"Interesting place for a pool," said Rem as he darted past.

"I think that's a fountain," said Daniels, racing beside him.

They got to the elevator, breathing fast.

Rem slammed his palm on the button. "Come on," said Rem, hitting it a few more times. The elevator continued its slow descent.

CHAPTER THIRTY-THREE

Jace stepped out onto the floor. The sun had fully descended and the only illumination was a light beside the elevator and the dim lights from the surrounding buildings. He looked around, seeing the wooden framing, beams and scaffolding. A pile of bricks sat beside the elevator. The wind whipped harder up here and chill bumps popped out on his skin.

He searched for Danni, but didn't see anyone. The elevator closed and began to descend. Daniels and Remalla would be up soon. He hoped they wouldn't scare Henry off, or endanger Danni. Moving further onto the dark space, he stepped around a pile of metal rods and wood, and tried to look around the beams. Ambient light cast strange shadows on the concrete and he was reminded of the haunted house he and Devyn had visited last Halloween. He half expected a demented clown to pop out at him.

Staying alert, he kept walking, nearing the far end of the building, and that's when he saw her. She stood near the edge, facing away from him. "Danni," he yelled.

She turned and yelled his name back. Shaking her head, she said something else but the wind carried it and he didn't hear her. He picked up his speed, running past and around beams, while also watching for Henry, who had to be nearby.

Getting closer, he yelled again. "Danni."

She took a step forward, her face red and stained with tears. "Jace." Her hands were bound and there was something around her neck. She moved closer. "Be careful. He's here."

Jace stepped into the framed room where she stood near the edge, his heart pounding with relief. "Come here." He headed toward her, but something sharp slashed him in the right arm, and searing pain tore through his shoulder.

"Jace," screamed Danni, running toward him.

Caught off balance, Jace shifted toward Henry. His face contorted; Henry held a knife with the blade buried in Jace's arm. He'd somehow hidden in the shadows, and Jace had walked right past him.

Jace cried out, the pain traveling down his arm and he swiveled to grab the knife just as Henry kicked out, aiming for Jace's knee. Jace's leg buckled and he went down, the knife wrenched from his shoulder. Blood spurted and raced down Jace's arm.

Danni screamed and ran, but Henry caught her, stopping her in her tracks and dragging her back toward the edge.

"No," Jace yelled.

Danni struggled against Henry, but he didn't break his hold and pulled her against him. The wind whipped her hair, and she screamed again. They were close enough to the edge for her to look over and Jace could hear her sobs.

"Henry, don't." Jace reached out, and slowly got to his feet, his knee throbbing, and his shoulder aching, but he ignored the pain, and took a hobbled step closer. "Let her go."

Henry stood there, a strange smile on his face. He held Danni right at the edge and she cried out and grasped at his jacket, desperately holding on. Jace struggled to reach them. "No, stop," he said.

"Let's see how big a hero you are now." Henry pushed, Danni shrieked, and Henry let her go.

**

Henry swiveled with the force of the hold Danni had on his jacket. For a moment, she hung there, clinging to him, and realizing she was about to pull him over with her, he yanked back. The jacket ripped, and she lost her grip.

Jace shouted, racing forward. He got to the edge just as she fell, and reaching out, he grabbed for her. Scrambling for anything to stop her fall, Danni's hands caught the edge, but her momentum took her over. Henry watched in surprise as Jace got to her, catching her hands and latching on to her wrists and the zip tie, but her weight almost toppled him, and he fell to his knees and ended up leaning over the side of the building, holding her while her body swung from his grip.

She made a piercing scream, her terror billowing from her lungs.

"Hold on," shouted Jace, his voice strained. "I got you."

He'd grabbed hold of a pipe with his other hand and used that for leverage, but his injured arm held her, and blood ran down his tricep and forearm and into the hand that gripped her. He struggled to pull her up.

Henry imagined the pain Jace had to be feeling, both in his shoulder and in his inability to stop her fall. It was just a matter of time before she slipped from his grasp.

Henry encroached and squatted beside Jace. "Looks like you have a problem."

Jace grimaced under the agony of trying to pull Danni up. "Henry, help me." His voice quivered and Danni screamed again, her legs dangling.

Looking down, Henry could see what would eventually be the impressive water fountain entry below. For a moment, everything went quiet, the wind died, the air was still and Henry smiled. He couldn't have planned it more perfectly.

And then he heard the elevator.

**

They reached the top floor and the elevator came to a slow stop. Rem held his gun as did Daniels and they waited at either side of the elevator door. The doors opened, and Rem peered around the edge of the shaft.

"Anything?" asked Daniels.

"Nothing," said Rem. "But it's pretty dark."

A blood-curdling scream billowed out into the night and they shared a quick glance before jumping out, guns raised, Rem going right and Daniels left. Rem squinted in the darkness. The light beside elevator provided little illumination, but he saw very few areas for them to take cover. He felt like a sitting duck. The faint sound of a siren traveled from below and he knew their back-up would arrive soon.

Daniels signaled he would continue left and Rem signaled right. The scream came again, coming from the opposite side of the building but it was hard to tell with the wind and lack of light. He began to move, trying to see, when shots rang out. He dropped low and he heard Daniels cry out. Looking over, he saw Daniels go down.

Rem jumped to his feet as a bullet whizzed by his head, grabbed his partner by his arm, and dragged him to the only cover he saw – a pile of bricks beside the elevator. Another bullet pinged against the wall and the light beside the elevator shattered, shards of glass spraying outward.

Rem got Daniels behind the bricks. Daniels moaned and Rem checked him. Pulling open his jacket, he saw a dark circle of blood begin to spread.

Daniels sucked in a breath. "My shoulder. I think it went through. Not fatal."

"Tell that to blood running down your shirt," said Rem.

"I'll be okay."

"You need a doctor."

Another terrorized scream reached them. Rem considered his options. Back-up would be here soon, but based on the screams, he didn't think Danni and Jace had much time.

"You stay put. Call back-up. Tell them where we are and that he's got a gun."

Daniels, his face pale, held his injured arm. "What the hell do you think you're doing?"

"I'm going after him."

"He'll shoot your ass the minute you show your face."

Rem shot a quick glance over the bricks and saw no movement. He ducked back down. "I'll stick to the perimeter. He shot out the light. He won't be able to see me."

"Rem. You don't know that."

Despite the chilly breeze, Rem wiped the sweat from his forehead. "Well, I sure as hell can't see him. It can't any easier for him to see me."

"I'll go with you." Daniels attempted to move, but bit back a moan of pain. He put a hand against the bricks to steady himself.

"You can barely move. Stay here. I'll be back."

"Rem, don't..."

Rem shot out from beyond the bricks, hearing a muttered curse from Daniels, and plastered himself against a piece of exterior wood. He held his breath, waiting for more shots to ring out, but nothing happened. Another scream billowed and he wondered what the hell was happening. He tried not to think about Daniels. The worry would only distract him. Inching slowly along the wall, he kept an eye out for Henry, but all he saw were the crazy shadows of wooden beams and scaffolding cast by a sliver of crescent moon and the city lights.

The wood ended and he stopped. The next step would put him back out into the open, with nothing but the edge on one side, and interior on the other. His silhouette would make an easy target. Holding his breath, he shot across, making it to the other side. No shots rang out.

He dropped down, crawling toward the end of the building, staying low. His gun still in his hand, he made it to the back and stopped beside a pile of wood. The screams were much louder now, and crouching low, he peered above, and froze.

Jace was on his belly, his upper half leaning over the edge, one arm holding a pipe, and the other below. A shriek came again and he heard Jace yell.

"Just hold on, Danni. Please." His arm quivered and Rem could see the blood. *Jesus. Was Jace holding Danni?*

Jace briefly turned his head and shouted. "Help. Somebody. I need help."

Danni screamed again.

Rem didn't hesitate. He darted out of his hiding spot and raced to Jace's side. Holstering his gun, he got to his knees. His heart thumped when he looked over the edge and found Danni below. "Shit." He was not fond of heights but he swallowed and pushed past his fear. "Hold on."

Jace realized he was there. "God, please help. She's slipping." His sweaty face pleaded with him.

"I'm coming." Rem leaned over and started to lie down when something pressed against his head. He froze.

"How nice of you to come, Detective."

Everything went still, and a cold spike of fear shot through his stomach. He tried to think. "Henry. Stop." He raised his arms. "Don't do this."

Sirens wailed from below.

"I'm sorry, Detective. I don't have time to debate with you. I have to go."

The gun cocked and Rem felt the vibration against his scalp. Danni pleaded from below. Rem shut his eyes, waiting for the boom, and mentally apologizing to Daniels for his failure.

"Rem," he heard his name shouted, and he recognized Daniels voice. Instinctively, he dropped flat. Opening his eyes, Rem saw Henry swing around, the gun raised, and Daniels, his shoulder soaked in blood, leaning against a beam, aiming his weapon. Two shots rang out. Henry jerked, taking a step backwards, but still holding his gun. A third shot rang out, and Henry fired, but in the wrong direction. Stumbling back from the shots, he tripped over Rem's legs. Rem reached for him, but it was too late. Henry went over the edge, his arms and legs flailing, and Rem saw him fall and hit the cement hole below.

Danni shrieked again, and Rem, forgetting Henry, scrambled back over to Jace, lying next to him. He got on his belly, and leaned over. He quickly realized though that he wouldn't be able to reach Danni without going over himself.

Jace cursed, his arm shaking. "Rem..."

"I know," said Rem. He stretched as far as he could and almost gave up when he felt a weight on his legs and someone grip his belt.

"I got you. Go," said Daniels from above.

Feeling secured, Rem tried not to look down, but focused on Danni. Her face was etched in terror and soaked in tears, and she continued to scream.

"Please help me. Don't let me fall." Zip ties cut in to her skin where Jace held her and the blood from Jace's injury oozed between Jace's fingers where he gripped her.

Rem stretched as far as he could and wrapped his fingers around her wrist. "I got her." He gathered his courage and swung his other arm down, grabbing her with two hands. Daniels was the only thing keeping him tethered to the ground.

"Pull up," he yelled to Jace, hoping Daniels could hear. "I got her."

His added support helped Jace gain additional leverage and he groaned and pulled. Rem felt Daniels yank on his belt and pull him back.

Rem grimaced with the strain, but Danni lifted slightly. Her sobs combined with her shrieks, and she continued to plead.

"Keep going," he yelled.

Jace made a guttural sound and yanked up again. Rem pulled too. Daniels moved down his legs, but still held on to his belt, allowing Rem to scoot back enough as Jace found more leverage. With one more mighty pull and with Jace's added strength, Rem got his legs under him, and Jace yanked her up high enough to where her arms reached the edge. Rem grabbed a shoulder and pulled her the rest of the way. She rose up and into Jace's arms. Jace fell back against the pipe and Rem collapsed on his side, breathing hard, and sweating profusely. He was almost too tired to look for Daniels, but saw him sitting and leaning back against a piece of scaffolding, the front of his jacket stained a deep red.

Rem breathed heavily, and then rolled on his back, looking up at would one day be the ceiling. He held his stomach, and waited for his heart to slow. "Holy shit," he said, trying to catch his breath.

"You okay?" asked Daniels.

Rem blinked, still processing what had happened. "Just great. You?" He rolled his head to the side.

Daniels, his face worn, grimaced and held his arm. "Never felt better. Want a catch a movie after?"

"Sure." Rem groaned, rolled over and pushed up, his body aching. "What did you have in mind?"

"How about *The Towering Inferno*?"

Rem couldn't help but smile, recalling the old movie about a group of people trying to escape a burning skyscraper. "At least we don't have to worry about fire."

"Miracles do happen," said Daniels.

Rem eyed Jace, who lay back against the pipe, breathing hard, his good arm around Danni, his bad arm laying limp beside him. His chin rested on Danni's head, which was buried in his chest, her fingers coiled his shirt.

"How is she?"

He raised his head. "I think she's in shock."

"How are you?"

"I'll live, but I'll pass on the movie."

"Understandable," said Rem. He tried to sit up, but sat back down with a groan. "We need an ambulance." He caught sight of bobbing flashlights back toward the elevator. "Over here," he yelled.

Two uniformed officers jogged over, directing their light over the group. Rem recognized one of them. "Hey, Pickens."

"Rem. Daniels. What the hell happened? You all right?"

More flashlights appeared.

"We're okay. We need an ambulance," said Rem. "And there's a nasty addition to the structure below that you might want to remove. I don't think they'll want it in their pool on opening day."

"Fountain," said Daniels, exhausted.

"Whatever," said Rem. Moaning, he got to his feet.

CHAPTER THIRTY-FOUR

Jace sat at his table, drinking coffee and wishing it was alcohol. His injured arm hung in a sling and it ached slightly. The doctor had given him pain pills, but he hadn't taken them. He wanted to stay clear-headed.

He'd brought Danni home from the hospital two days ago. Jace luckily had not needed surgery on his arm, but he would need to check in with the doctor next week to get examined and ensure he was healing properly.

He took the last sip of his coffee and went to get more. He hadn't slept well since coming home. Nightmares had plagued him. He'd dreamed of Danni hanging from the edge, screaming, and him letting go and seeing her drop, and he'd dreamed of the two women who were maybe his siblings in the same predicament, falling from his grasp. Even now, a cold sweat popped out on his skin when he recalled Danni hanging, her only lifeline his hand, her face twisted in terror, his arm in agony and his grip slipping. It made him want to throw up. His hands shaking, he refilled his mug, still considering a sip of tequila.

Danni hadn't slept well either. Once they'd gotten her to the emergency room, she'd vomited. Her skin was cold and clammy and her pulse raced. They'd taken her back and managed to stabilize her. They determined she had a mild concussion and they had kept her overnight for observation. They'd given her some sedatives when they'd released her and he'd brought her back to his place to recuperate. He thought of her now, sleeping in his bed. She'd awakened last night, screaming, thinking she was about to fall. Jace had held her until she calmed, given her another pill, and she'd drifted off. He'd checked on her an hour ago, but she still slept.

She'd been sullen and quiet since her return, not wanting to talk about what had happened. Not that he could blame her. The thought of how close he'd come to losing her terrified him as well. Before going to bed the previous night, he had taken that shot of tequila and he suspected he'd take another tonight.

Adding more cream and sugar to his coffee, he leaned against the counter, wondering what to do next. He and Danni had been through hell and they needed time to recover. But what concerned him was Danni. Would she want to stay with him? Would she blame him for what happened? He couldn't help but wonder.

He heard a door open and turned to see her standing outside his bedroom, a blanket wrapped around her shoulders. Her puffy eyes looked haunted; dark shadows hung in half circles below them, and his heart dropped. He could only imagine how she felt. His own anxiety increased.

"Good morning," he said. He eyed the clock on his microwave. "Or should I say afternoon."

She stepped out timidly. "What time is it?"

"Noon."

Nodding, she entered the kitchen, seeing his coffee. "You have any more of that?"

"I'll get you some. Go have a seat."

Adjusting her blanket, she left the kitchen. "Thanks."

Jace eyed her. She'd eaten little since leaving the hospital. "Hungry?"

"No," she said, and sat at the table.

He poured her some coffee and brought it over to her. "I added some cream."

She held it, and took a sip. "How's your arm?"

"It's fine. Better."

"Good."

He held his coffee and sat across from her. "How are you doing?" He had to try and get her to talk to him.

She sipped her drink. "Fine," she said.

"How'd you sleep, after the nightmare?"

"Fine."

He nodded again, gauging how far to push. "You want to talk about it?"

She stood quickly, holding her coffee. After tossing her blanket into the chair, she walked over to the couch. She wore a long t-shirt that Jace had given her to wear and it almost stretched to her knees. Her bandaged wrists reminded Jace again of how close Henry had come to taking her away from him. "No, I don't." Looking out the window, she asked a question. "How are Daniels and Remalla?"

Jace put his coffee down. "They're okay. Daniels had surgery on his shoulder, but he's recovering. I talked to Remalla and gave him my statement. He wants to talk to you, too."

She started to pace in front of his sofa. "I should go home." Her eyes widened. "Seymore. My cat. Is anyone checking on him?"

"I talked to your neighbor yesterday. Seymore's in good hands."

She sighed, her shoulders relaxing. "I'll get out of your hair today. Go back to my place."

"I don't want you out of my hair, Danni. I want you to stay."

She stopped. "Why?"

"Why?" he asked, sitting forward. "We've been through a hell of a trauma. We need time to recover, and it's easier to do that with someone by your side, and not alone where you can lock it all away and pretend it didn't happen."

She ran a shaky hand through her hair. "I...I'm not..." Her face paled. "I'm not pretending."

"Then what are you doing?"

She put her coffee down on the side table beside the couch and hugged herself. "I'm coping." She spoke in a whisper.

He stood, wanting to go to her, but he stayed near the table. "I want to help, but I don't know how."

She made a nervous chuckle. "I don't know, either." She bit her lip. "Those pills are sure nice, though."

"Those pills can't fix this. It's not going away if you don't deal with it."

She moved her hands to her shoulders, her fingers rigid. "I don't know if I can."

He walked closer, aching to take away her pain. "Danni..." He reached for her, but she stepped away.

"Don't," she said, holding out a palm.

He backed off. Forcing himself, he asked the question he most feared the answer to. "Do you blame me?"

She stopped; her brows furrowed. "Of course not. This is not your fault."

"Maybe it is. If it hadn't been for me, you wouldn't have gone through any of it."

Tears welled up in her eyes. "You idiot. It's not your fault. It's mine." She wiped away a tear. "I opened that stupid door. I let him in. I answered his stupid email. I'm such a fool. I should have fought back in that building, but I didn't." Tears spilled over her lashes and streamed freely down her face. "And then he grabbed me, and I...I...," she sniffed. "I didn't do anything. I froze, and...and...then I went over..." She held her stomach. "Oh, God. I was so scared." Her knees gave way and she crumpled to the ground.

Jace walked over, dropped beside her and pulled her into his arms. Holding on to his shirt, she cried into his shoulder and he let her, feeling his own tears surface. "I'm sorry." It was all he could think to say. "I'm so sorry. I tried to pull you up. I tried."

Her sobs slowed and she lifted her head, her cheeks tear-stained and her eyes red. Her fingers curled in his shirt. "You saved my life."

"I almost got you killed."

"No," she shook her head. "You stopped me from falling. If it hadn't been for you, I'd be dead. You protected me."

"I should have never left that house. I left you vulnerable."

Another tear slid down her cheek and she rested her forehead against chest. His slid his hand to the back of her neck and held her.

"This is going to take some time, isn't it?" she asked through a sniff.

He rubbed his thumb against her skin. "Yes, it is."

They remained that way, her lying against him, as he gently soothed her.

"So what do we do now?" she asked. Her crying had stopped and she shifted to lie sideways against him, her head in the crook of his shoulder. He curled his good arm around her and lay back against the couch. "Where's Rutger? Do we have another madman to worry about?"

The question surprised him. Rutger had been the last thing on his mind. "I don't know."

"What about Sonia?"

"She's in the hospital."

She sat up. "What? What happened?"

"It's a long story, but she'll be okay. I went to talk to her, but they'd sedated her."

She lay back against him. "I'm afraid to ask."

He took a deep breath, and told her his other news. "I went to see Devyn, too, before you were released." He felt her stiffen.

"And?" she asked softly.

"We talked. I think they're releasing her today. She's going to stay with her mom while she recovers."

Danni played with his shirt. She spoke softly. "You want to go back to her?"

He almost laughed out loud. "No. Of course not. We...I just needed to talk to her. About Justin. She felt terrible. Kept apologizing, cried. I listened to it, but felt this odd detachment. Like it didn't matter. Not about Justin. I miss the hell out of him, and I'm pissed about what they did, but Devyn...she's...she's a distant thought. I'm not worried about her. Nor do I want her back." He stroked Danni's back. "Everything I want is right here." He heard her sniff and wondered if she was crying again. He pulled her close. "Are you okay?"

She nodded against his chest. "I'll get there." She sat up and wiped at his shirt. "Sorry. I think I got snot on you." Rubbing his chest, she met his gaze. "I want you too, you know."

He sighed and smiled. "What do you say we get out of here for a few days? Just get on my bike and go?"

Her face brightened. "What about your arm?"

"It's good enough to ride the motorcycle. I don't have to see the doctor till next week. And even if I don't, they have doctors in other cities. Let's just disappear for a bit. It'll be good for us. Good for the soul."

"I'd have to be sure Seymore's okay, but I'm sure the neighbor would watch him. What about the bar?"

"It's not going anywhere."

She brought her hands up to his neck and stroked his jaw. "I'd like that." She brought her face close to his. "Thank you."

"No," he said, his breath mingling with hers. "Thank you." And he met her lips in a kiss.

CHAPTER THIRTY-FIVE

Rem sat at his desk and typed on his laptop, his coffee beside him. He kept the pot full because all he seemed to do now was fill out reports. Reaching the end of a paragraph, he sat back and rubbed his eyes, groaning at the same time. He needed to get in a good run and break up some of this monotony. He could only handle so much paperwork.

"You look like you're having fun."

Rem dropped his hands and saw his partner, his arm in a sling, standing across from him.

"Daniels, what are you doing here? You're not supposed to be back until tomorrow."

Daniels pulled out his desk chair and sat. "Marjorie kicked me out of the house."

Rem stilled. "Forever?"

Daniels rolled his eyes. "No, you bonehead. For the moment. I think I'm getting on her nerves."

"What? She doesn't like you under her feet?" He smiled. "How many closets have you rearranged?"

"Three. The front coat closet, our master, and J.P.'s nursery. Plus, the pantry."

"Oh, boy," said Rem.

"I accidentally threw away two boxes of, apparently, a gourmet mac-n-cheese, and her favorite pair of sloppy jeans." He leaned back against his seat. "I mean, who eats that stuff?"

"Normal people," said Rem.

"You're not normal."

Rem shrugged.

"And those jeans had holes in them."

Rem grinned. "Never touch a woman's favorite pair of jeans. You should know better."

Daniels sighed audibly. "She's right though. I've got to get out of the house. I'm going stir crazy."

Rem picked up a paper from his desk. "Don't get too excited about coming back here. You'll be on desk duty for at least a week, and you'll only get a bunch of this." He waved the paper.

"Lozano's got you catching up on reports?"

"I feel like my fingers need a fancy sling like yours. How's your arm?"

"It's fine. Sore. Hard to sleep, but it's okay."

"Good."

Daniels eyed the coffee and pointed. "You sharing?"

"Only because I like you."

Daniels stood, found a mug and filled it. "Where's Lozano?"

"In some meeting," said Rem. He sipped from his coffee, enjoying the break in routine.

Daniels returned to his seat, sipping his drink. "What did you say in the reports?"

Rem raised a brow. "You mean about Sonia?"

Daniels nodded.

"Just that Rutger grabbed the letter opener and stabbed her before any of us could stop him. Jace rushed to help her and we took off after Rutger."

Daniels sat up. "You know we look like idiots, don't you, when it comes to Rutger? Guy keeps getting away. Lozano's going to demote us if Rutger keeps doing it."

"What do you want to do? Come clean? You think he won't demote us for being certifiably insane?"

"I know." Daniels put his coffee on his desk. "We're kind of stuck between a rock and a hard place." He adjusted his sling with a grimace. "You know, there's something I meant to ask you about once we got some distance from all this craziness."

"What's that?"

Daniels pointed with his good arm. "When we were at Maxwell's and Rutger showed. Jace attacked him and pinned him. Remember?"

Rem rested an ankle on his knee. "Hard to forget."

"Why didn't Rutger retaliate? Throw him off? Push him back? From what it looked like, if Rutger hadn't injured Sonia, Jace might have taken him."

Rem thought about it. "Interesting. I hadn't considered that. You think he didn't want to hurt his brother?"

"He killed his brother's best friend. What's to stop him from throwing him across a room?"

"You think it's something else? Like maybe he can't use his mojo against his family?"

Daniels shook his head. "I don't know. But it's something to think about. If Rutger does show his face again, it might be important."

"I wonder if Jace will see it the same way," said Rem.

"Did you talk to Jace? Get his statement?"

"Yup. Danni, too. She came in yesterday."

"Really. How's she doing?"

"Hanging in there. They are together though. I confirmed that much. They're getting out of town for a few days. Going to Phoenix."

"Phoenix? Arizona? What's in Phoenix?"

"I don't know." Rem swiveled in his seat. "Cactus. Desert. Turquoise jewelry."

"We can get in touch if we need to?"

Rem tapped his phone which lay on his desk. "I've got his number."

"Good, although I doubt we'll need it, since Rutger's gone to ground again." His face furrowed. "Hey, did you talk to Sonia? How's she doing?"

Rem found a pencil behind his ear and tossed it in his desk drawer. "Interesting you should ask. I went to see her the other day in the hospital. Wanted to get her statement, too."

"And?"

Rem rocked back in his chair. "She's gone. Checked herself out, against doctor's orders. Nurse couldn't tell me where she went."

Daniels scowled. "Wonderful."

"I thought so."

"Rutger's disappeared and so has Sonia. Jace is taking Danni out of town, and what are we doing?"

"Left holding the bag. At least Justin's murder is still considered unsolved, based on what Danni told us. Rutger's APB is still active."

"A lot of good that will do."

Rem saved his work and closed his laptop. "You win some, you lose some. Want to grab some lunch?"

Daniels sat forward like an eager child waiting for chocolate. "Does Detective Remalla like to watch scary movies at night and drive his partner nuts the next day because he didn't get enough sleep?"

"I'll take that as a yes," said Rem. He grabbed his cell.

"There's something else to discuss though, over lunch."

Rem stood. "What's that?"

"Jill and Madison." Daniels stood, too, holding his arm. "What do we tell them?"

Rem picked up his jacket from the back of the chair. "I've been thinking about that and I've finally decided. Nothing."

Daniels paused. "Nothing? You don't want to tell them what's going on here?"

Rem slid on his jacket. "Think about it. Nothing's really changed. What's to tell? Rutger is a ghost. We have no solid proof of anything other than Rutger himself. Sonia's disappeared. Jace has left town. Why throw them into something when we literally have nothing solid to give? What are we going to say? You might have a long-lost brother? You might be siblings? They both have parents. How are we going to answer those questions?"

Daniels hesitated. "You sure that's the best way?"

"I'm not sure about anything anymore. Lozano was right. We need more to go on. It's not worth charging in and disrupting their lives."

"What if Rutger does it for us?"

"He already has. My hope is he's done. He's vented. Sonia may be next, but we can't help her if she doesn't want it, and Jace is moving on. I say we do, too."

Daniels followed Rem to the door. "I hope you're right, but something tells me we haven't seen the last of Rutger. He said there would be others."

"And if there are, we'll figure it out. Like we always do." Rem held the door for Daniels. "Can we talk about something else now? How about that ring you're holding on to? When are you going to pop that question?"

CHAPTER THIRTY-SIX

Jill adjusted her top in the mirror, debating whether to add the scarf. Impatient, she threw the scarf she held on her bed and left the bedroom. Checking her watch, she realized she had a few more minutes than she thought. Her father was expecting her at noon, and he hated tardiness, and Jill hated his grumpiness, so she tried her best to avoid it.

They'd been down a long hard road over the last six months, but their relationship had survived. His declining health made her realize he wouldn't be around forever, and holding on to past grievances served none of them. Her brother Brian still needed help with that one, but she figured time would eventually heal.

She grabbed a mug and added some coffee to it from the pot on her kitchen counter, thinking of Rem. She always did when she drank coffee. Seeing his face in her mind, she smiled, remembering their shared coffee moments, some heated, and some humorous. Sighing, she thought about calling him, wondering what he was doing. He'd been busy with an ugly case and Daniels had been shot, but thankfully was okay. When she'd last talked to Rem, he'd told her Daniels had been on desk duty but was supposed to return to full duty the next day. Jill hoped once things settled down for him, they could take a weekend together. They hadn't seen each other since the holidays, and she missed him.

Her phone buzzed and she pulled it out of her pocket. It was a text from Neil Wilder. She closed her eyes, groaning. She'd met him two weeks ago after she and a couple friends had gone to dinner, and then drinks. Neil had danced with her, and Jill and he had talked through the night. He seemed like a nice guy, and was a private investigator. They had bonded over her police background and in a drunken state, she'd given him her number. They'd talked a couple of times since, and even had coffee the other day. Jill kept telling herself they were friends, but then he'd kissed her after coffee, and she'd almost spilled her drink on him.

She read the text.

Dinner tonight?

Jill swallowed. Why hadn't she told him about Rem? She mentally warred with herself.

Because we're just friends, that's why.
No, you're not.
He kissed you.
But I pulled away, so it didn't count.
Didn't it?

Confused, and not wanting to deal with it, Jill put the phone down, deciding to answer later. She'd have to get going so she wouldn't be late. She looked for a thermos for her coffee when the doorbell rang.

"Crap," she said. "Who's that?"

Leaving the coffee, she went to her door, old anxieties making her heart thump. The damage the Artist had done to her would never fully be healed. She looked out the peephole.

Seeing who it was, Jill held her breath. "What in the…" She opened the door.

The woman at her door smiled, her cherub cheeks rising. "Hello, dear," she said.

"Sonia Vandermere?" Jill asked.

"You remember me?" Sonia held her chest. "I'm flattered."

"How could I forget? You were a witness in the Artist case, and you gave me this necklace." She patted her neck, and pulled out a black stone.

Sonia blushed. "I'm so glad you're still wearing it." Fanning herself, she walked in. "You don't mind if I sit dear, do you? I'm recovering from a nasty fall, and I feel a bit tired."

Jill started to object, but stopped when Sonia walked in and entered her living area. She sat on the couch.

"Sonia, I actually have to go…"

Sonia patted the seat beside her. "I suggest you reschedule. Come sit, dear. We need to talk."

A familiar warm heat flared up inside Jill, and her heart thudded. She knew this feeling of dread, and she didn't like it. Something was wrong. Closing the door, she thought of her father, deciding she'd have to be late. Anxious, she walked to the sofa and took a seat beside Sonia.

"What is it? Why are you here?"

Sonia held her gaze. "It's time you knew the truth, dear."

ABOUT THE AUTHOR

Born and raised in Dallas, TX, J. T. Bishop began writing in 2012.
Two years later, the Red-Line trilogy was complete. She's not done
though. J. T. continues to create new characters and story lines to
entertain her fans.

J. T. loves stories that explore characters' unique abilities and origins.
It's a theme she finds intriguing and provides a wealth of inspiration
for her books. Drama, angst, passion, and humor all add to the fun. A
little bit of romance doesn't hurt either.

J. T. loves to spend time with family and friends, traveling whenever
she can, and spending time in nature (despite the heat in Texas).
Getting up in the morning with a cup of coffee, ready to write is the
start of a perfect day.

ACKNOWLEDGEMENTS

Thank you to my family, friends, coworkers and fans, all of whom make this possible. I wouldn't write if it weren't for you and your continued support and encouragement. I hear it, I see it, and I thank you immensely.

And thank you to Golden Pomegranate Tarot for your help with the tarot cards and readings in this book. Your knowledge of tarot and your explanations of the cards were invaluable and I couldn't have done it without you!

Retired Judge Martin Hendrix adjusted his tie in the mirror. He'd chosen the red one with the gold golf tees because his wife of forty-eight years had given it to him on his previous birthday. Smoothing his hair in the mirror, he observed the gray sprinkled within it and the minimal wrinkles on his dark skin. "You still got it, Martin," he said to himself in the mirror. His friends had told him he didn't look a day over sixty. He chuckled.

"Are you talking to yourself again?" Martha entered the bathroom.

"Just telling myself how handsome I am." He took a last look and faced her.

She gave him a quick kiss. "You are pretty handsome."

"Not as good looking as my wife though. She's something else."

Martha grinned. "Still a charmer after all these years." She eyed his outfit. "Where are you going with a tie and all? I haven't seen you wear a tie since you left the bench."

He adjusted a sleeve. "It's been six months and I have a closet full of them. I figure I should wear at least one a year. I'm having lunch with Frank Lozano. Thought I should look respectable."

"Frank? We haven't seen him in a while. Tell him we need to have him and his wife over for dinner sometime soon. I'll make some pot roast."

"He'd love that. I'll mention it. You headed out?"

She checked her makeup in the mirror and added some lipstick. "Yes. I have my ladies group lunch today." She checked her watch. "I better get going or I'll be late."

"You tell those ladies to have a drink on me."

"Oh, Martin. It's lunch time."

"We're not getting any younger, Martha. Time to live it up a little." He reached low and squeezed her butt.

Martha jumped and swiveled. "What are you doing?"

"Just admiring my wife's fine traits."

Her eyes widened. "You are a mess today. You better behave yourself at lunch."

"I'll behave myself until you and I come home, then..." he moved closer, "...who knows what might happen."

She smiled, reached around and pinched his rear end. "We'll see if you have the strength."

"Oh, I'll have the strength. In fact, if you have the time now—" He pulled her closer.

She giggled and swatted him. "Would you stop. I have to go, and so do you." She gave him a quick kiss. "You be safe out there, my dear."

He held her hand. "You sure? Those ladies will live if you're a little late."

She giggled again. "You can still make me feel like a school girl." She gave him another kiss. "I love you, man of my dreams."

"I love you, too, light of my life."

She stepped away. "I'll see you later."

He winked. "See you."

He watched her leave and after taking a last look at himself, left the bathroom, hearing her go out the back door. Having a few minutes before he had to depart, he went into the kitchen and poured himself some milk. The paper sat on the counter from when he'd brought it in earlier and he opened it, scanning the headlines.

The door opened from the back and he heard it close. "You forget something Martha?" he asked, reading an article.

There was no response and hearing footsteps encroach, he looked up. A man walked into the kitchen.

"Hello, Judge."

Hendrix lowered the paper. "Who the hell are—"

The man pulled out a weapon and fired.

**

Detective Aaron Remalla stared into the closet. The first thing he saw was the sweater. Taking it down from the shelf, he held it, inhaling its scent. It was musty, just like any sweater would be after sitting in a closet for two years, but beneath the mustiness, he detected just a trace of what he'd been hoping for – a whiff of her perfume. Maybe he was just making it up in his mind, but it didn't matter. That one whiff brought Jennie back and he closed his eyes, thinking of her.

He'd been putting off this task for some time, but with the two-year anniversary of her death approaching next month, he decided he had to face it. Having the day off, he'd taken the morning to relax and sleep in. He and his partner, Gordon Daniels, didn't get many of those days. Daniels was taking his fiancé and son to the park and Remalla figured this would be as good a time as any to face the closet.

Not long after Jennie had died, he'd taken everything he could find of hers that was in his house and he'd put it in here. It had been too painful to see every day, and back then, any reminder would spiral him into depression, so he'd hid her things here, out of sight and out of mind.

But now, after two tears, he needed to deal with it.

He'd taken a stiff drink at lunch, and then after eating, had come upstairs. He'd brought the bottle of vodka with him, fully expecting to drink a lot while he finished the task.

He folded the sweater and put it to the side, no knowing yet if he would donate it or keep it. He wondered if her family would want it.

318 · J. T. BISHOP

Going back to the closet, he scanned it, unsure what to pull out next. There were plenty of clothes, some scarves and a couple of jackets, plus her shoes. The memories swirled, and he forced himself to not think, but just do. Sometimes, that was all he could trust.

Seeing a box on the floor, he squatted down and picked it up. He brought it out and set it on the bed in the room. Having some idea what was inside, he poured himself a shot of vodka, but didn't drink it. It would be there when he needed it.

He stared at the box and slid his hand over the top. Taking a deep breath, he opened it. The first thing he saw was her makeup. He remembered swiping it into the box not long after the funeral. There was her bottle of perfume, bottles of shampoo and conditioner, and her soap. The box smelled of lavender. He swallowed. He'd have to toss most of it.

He reached in and dug around, and seeing something small and delicate, he picked it up. Holding his breath, he pulled it out, knowing what it was.

The silver bracelet had darkened with exposure, but the inscription remained. He read it. *To my angel. From your devil. I love you.*

The memory of him giving it to her on the anniversary of their first date reared up and hit him in the gut like a gunshot, and he dropped it on the bed, grabbed the vodka, and downed it one gulp.

The liquid burned his throat, and he poured another, ready to drink it, when his cell rang. Unsure he could answer, he let it go to voicemail. Taking a few shaky breaths, he eyed the liquor, debating whether to drink it, when his cell rang again.

Cursing, he pulled it out of his pocket, and saw it was his partner, Daniels.

He inhaled and exhaled several deep breaths, trying to pull it together, and answered. "Yeah."

There was a brief pause. "Rem?"

He cleared his throat, and forced some levity into his voice. "What's up?"

"You okay?"

He shut his eyes. Sometimes their friendship could be a pain in the ass. "Yeah. I'm fine. How's the park?"

"It was nice, but I'm on my way home. Lozano called. Judge Hendrix is dead. Gunned down in his home. He wants us there."

Rem opened his eyes. "What? Judge Hendrix? Shit."

"I know. Hard to believe. So much for the day off. I'll text you the address. I'm dropping Marjorie at home and heading over."

Rem rubbed his face; glad he hadn't taken the third shot of alcohol. He'd have to get some coffee on his way. "I'll meet you there."

"Okay."

Rem hung up and turned back toward the box, seeing the bracelet on the bed. He sighed again. "You'll have to wait, Jennie. Sorry."

Sighing, he left the room, closing the door behind him.

Made in the USA
Columbia, SC
19 February 2021

33072311R00195